TRINITY

ALSO BY ZELDA LOCKHART

Mama Bear: One Black Mother's Fight for Her Child's Life and Her Own by Shirley Smith with Zelda Lockhart

Diamond Doris: The True Story of the World's Most Notorious Jewel Thief by Doris Payne with Zelda Lockhart

The Soul of the Full-Length Manuscript: Turning Life's Wounds into the Gift of Literary Fiction, Memoir, or Poetry

Cold Running Creek

Fifth Born II: The Hundredth Turtle

Fifth Born

Y ZELDA LOCKHART

ear: One Black Mother's Fight for Her Child's Life and Her Own
y Smith with Zelda Lockhart

l Doris: The True Story of the World's Most Notorious Jewel Thief
Payne with Zelda Lockhart

of the Full-Length Manuscript: Turning Life's Wounds into the
terary Fiction, Memoir, or Poetry

ning Creek

II: The Hundredth Turtle

TRINI

ALSO B

Mama B
by Shirle

Diamond
by Doris

The Soul
Gift of Li

Cold Run

Fifth Born

Fifth Born

TRINITY

A NOVEL

Zelda Lockhart

An Imprint of HarperCollins*Publishers*

This is a work of fiction. Names, characters, places, and incidents are products of the author's imagination or are used fictitiously and are not to be construed as real. Any resemblance to actual events, locales, organizations, or persons, living or dead, is entirely coincidental.

FIRST EDITION

Designed by Janet Evans-Scanlon

Library of Congress Cataloging-in-Publication Data is available upon request.

ISBN 978-0-06-316095-8

23 24 25 26 27 LBC 5 4 3 2 1

Dedicated to my daughter Alex Lockhart and my granddaughter Maddison Teylor Lockhart and to my mother's, mother's, mother's, mother who held on to and passed on the stories and the untamed untainted seeds. And to my son and grandson, may the omniscience, innocence, and joy of childhood guide you in all of your relations, break the chain of violence, and re-seed the love gene.

Prologue

When the Black bodies have let go and the spirits exist, they are able to come to folks and tell them all of the mistakes made in the flesh and lessons learned after the flesh. They are able to know life without time, without the limitations of the body, the pains of the mind. But what good is all their knowing unless someone with hands, feet, flesh, and bone can make right what has for so long been wrong? I didn't know that's what I was being called to do. But by the time I was six years old, I knew that what I was experiencing about living and what other people were experiencing were different dimensions of remembering.

I saw my great-great-grandmother's capture, as she ran across the sun-hardened earth of the Congo, having been chased out of her village by white men just after pounding the cassava and plantain flour to make fufu and swatting the morning flies. The heel bones of her feet pounded on the hardened clay. She carried in her womb two precious things: One was the stories of every villager since the first tree sprouted from the first seed. The other precious thing she carried was the untamed, untainted seeds of her children.

I knew the accessory to the perpetrator—the chief, the uncle, father, brother, son of the villagers, who aided in her capture for some false promise of his people's prosperity to match the white man's. That temptation to collude with the enemy backfired like the clogged barrel of a musket, an explosion that diasporatized my kin, scattered them like pickup jacks all over the earth. The impact inverted his wishes for prosperity into a backward cascade of beating, raping, killing the woman with the womb as he tried to find his way out of his misery.

I witnessed his first sin, to make crooked his pact with nature: to nurture, provide, and protect his women. His second sin was the compromise made to fight white men's enemies in order to restore his own honor. His third sin was also his blessing, to fertilize over and over the extended limbed chromosomes for the eyes, hands, and feet of me who he would leave, to fend for myself and everybody involved.

PART ONE

The Father

ONE

Sampson, Mississippi
1939

It was Bennie's tenth birthday. Lottie pinched him between her knees and cropped off the tower of hair that was overheating the top of his head. "Bennie, be still." A cigarette hung from her pouty lips, hand-rolled from the store but supplied by the fields around them. The dangling ember grew a balanced ash an inch long, threatening to set his black wool naps on fire.

When Bennie was born, she was only thirteen years old, so he did not know to talk to her in a string of *Yes ma'ams* and *No ma'ams*. He called his mama by her first name.

"Ouch, Lottie! Put that cigarette out befo you burn my head."

The porch was refuge from the sun. It was so hot that day, the birds panted on the low-lying maple branches. The heat did not deter Baby Lenard. He played in the bare dirt of the yard making mud of the used wash water, his skin and the earth the same tint of copper. The sky was a clear cornflower blue except for one white cloud, comfort that passed over the three of them before it grew thin and evaporated.

"Be still, boy." She snatched him in place and chuckled. "Ain't nobody gonna burn yo little pea head. Mo likely the birds gone set up shop if I don't chop this shit off."

Like an older sister and little brother, they were so close that it didn't matter that she hadn't tied a kerchief to hold her breasts in place under her loose cotton dress. She was still gonna hold him close where he could smell the warm womanhood of her body sweating in the heat. But at the same time, she would snatch at him and teasc him like he was some meddlesome little pet.

He laid his head back in her lap, and the two of them looked in each other's big round eyes. "Okay, boy. I'll put it out fo a minute. Cain't smoke my smokes for worrying about you and Lenard gone have a complaint."

He tilted his head forward for her to cut the back. His question hung in the heat of the afternoon: "What you and Old Deddy bumping around about last night?" He knew Old Deddy whipped her with the strap that was for the money satchel in the same way that Old Deddy whipped him. Her beatings were constant, where his only came when his chores were half-done. But he didn't have to be trapped in the room with Old Deddy at night. She always had welts on her smooth, creamy legs, some of them purple from a few days back, some of them red from last night. He knew the beatings were getting more frequent but didn't know why and didn't know the right thing to ask.

She grabbed a fist of hair at the back of his head and turned his face up to hers. "Benjamin Lee, let me tell you something." She pushed his head forward again. "Don't you never trap no woman in yo house like she a cow who happened by yo barn for shelter. Don't you never be that kinda man."

"Ouch!" he complained and put his hands on the back of his head. She smacked his hand back down and tilted his head onto her thigh to get the sideburns. He felt a twinge of shame for seeing her breast beneath her arm and wanting to crawl into the safety of her lap and suckle, the way she still did for Lenard who was three years old now but still in need of her food. One of her loose dark curls fell from under her head rag, and high above her, the wasps' nest that she knocked down every summer danced with the brown insects making their home.

The next morning, the wide fan of late spring tobacco leaves made the dew sweet and heavy. For a change, Old Deddy did not come in with the gray, warm light of dawn to jerk Bennie to his feet off the pallet. Instead, Old Deddy was already with the mule in the vegetable field tilling the soil for their table crops. Lenard sat next to Bennie, tying a string onto the leg of a half-dead June bug, and the house was strangely quiet. Bennie looked out the window, and there was the washtub on the old tree stump, but she was not there. He pulled the worn overalls up over his discolored underpants and went out to the open room, but she wasn't at the pump doing dishes or putting wood in the stove for breakfast. The lump beneath the chicken bone cage of his chest squeezed tight, and like remembering a dream hours after waking, he remembered Old Deddy's voice muffled in the middle of the night: "Lottie! Lottie! Where you at, woman?"

As the sun burned the dew and blackened fallen acorns, Bennie walked to the chicken coop, fetched the warm eggs, set the birds out in the yard to peck, set his brother out in the yard to play, and waited at the door of the barn, just inside its gaping mouth where shade could offer him some comfort. This spot was a vantage point for watching his little brother in the yard. He could see down the road when she returned or see off toward the fields if Old Deddy came wondering why he hadn't come to hold the mule steady.

The two cows behind him watched over the black naps of his

head where sweat crept from beneath his hairline, their massive bodies quiet except their synchronized breathing. They were content in the shade of the barn even though it was midday and he had not relieved their sore teats with milking then setting them out to graze.

In that hot space that grew hotter with none of his chores tended to, he wished above the deafening pitch of cicadas that Lottie would just come home. He made up his mind sitting there in the opening of the leaning barn that he was going to help her with the laundry, the canning, help her keep up with whatever work she fell so behind on that Old Deddy saw fit to beat her every day.

Bennie pinched his eyes shut against the sting of sweat and wished that she was not where he knew she was, off getting what made her happy. She told him one day while she scrubbed up and down on the washboard, "I got me a secret place I go and makes me more money than Old Deddy ever gone make on this place. Gone get us money to go to St. Louis." He was captivated with her fantasy and churned the butter, glad to be in that best place he loved to be, rapt in her attention. "I slips my money off for Mr. Genorette to save it for me, and I slips a little money in Old Deddy satchel sometimes after he been gamblin too." Mr. Genorette was a tall cocoa-skinned man who was wide as the barn door. He looked like the young happy version of Old Deddy. Nobody knew by what means, but he owned the swamp-bottom tavern outright. Lottie bent down to the basket for the next piece of clothing. Her loose curls made a veil between the two of them.

"Did you hear me, Bennie? I don't want my boys goin' hungry on account of they Old Deddy cain't catch up on thangs." He didn't know anything about St. Louis, but he knew St. Louis was where his oldest brother, James, had gone, and Bennie imagined cars and men in fancy hats, tall buildings, and women strolling down the avenue like in the Easter parade. She snapped the water from a sheet before pinching it between the wooden pins and seemed to be talking to herself. "Yep, I think he been figurin me out though."

Bennie knew how to put two and two together by the time he was ten. The oldest boy at school, Jasper Jackson, said the fast women went to make them some money down at the tavern. Bennie figured his mother must have been very fast at doing something that people liked to pay good money for. He also knew from the way she looked around before confiding in him that if Old Deddy found out, it would be the last thing done wrong.

Bennie imagined her at the money place of Mr. Genorette's tavern. A man pounded out the blues on the piano. The fellow on the guitar slid his plow-worn fingers up and down the rusty strings. Grown-ups touched each other and giggled and seemed happy in the midst of what people called the Depression. He danced to jiggedy blues with her, was happy too, laughing out loud with her, until he heard Old Deddy coming out of the swamp like an angry bear. He tore down the salty, weathered boards of the joint. Bennie's imagination had slipped into dream where he slept just inside the barn door, waiting for her to come home.

The sun pushed the shade of the barn back and left him sitting in the sun, visible for Old Deddy when he came to scold Bennie about the chores. Deep in his sleep, he heard Old Deddy's footsteps enter the barn. He heard the thunk of something, maybe a board against his head. He could hear Old Deddy's voice as if it was the song sung with the piano tune: "Get yo lazy ass up. You hear me, boy?!" Bennie's small heart beat slow while he danced in the safety of the dream, smell of gin and cigarettes on her breath, ribs poking through her cotton dress when she hugged him. The sound of gospel melodies with naughty words faded into scuffling feet on the dirt floor of the barn.

Bennie came conscious when he felt the braided leather of Old Deddy's cowhide across his back and saw his gangly shadow cast against the walls when Old Deddy's whip connected with the dry, unmothered skin on Bennie's legs and arms. He tumbled and turned unnaturally, and the cows bowed their heads while they prayed and wept thick tears as he yelled for his mother, "Lottie!"

In the distance, Lottie paused between sips of corn whiskey. The rose flesh bloomed in her womb and knotted in the place where Bennie and Lenard once etched on fetal walls just before each of them followed the deceptive light out of her womb into the trap set to ensnare them. The gut-wrenching feeling almost made her put one foot down on the splintered floor of Genorette's, the next foot on the muddy floor of the swamp to rescue her sons. But before she could succumb to the spell of a mother sensing the distant cry of a child, she turned to the guitar man leaning back in his cane-bottomed chair: "I woke up this mo'nin, find my, my little baby gone." And she turned up the mason jar of corn whiskey and sang with him.

Before everything that had been done to her, Lottie was considered a rare white dove among the crows of Sampson, Mississippi. Her parents were sharecroppers for J. W. Pritchard, who also owned the land where Old Deddy sharecropped. Among her two dark-skinned brothers, she was the mulatto child born of the landlord's rape—something everybody knew, but nobody spoke about. Her parents dreamed she would become a schoolteacher and bring pride to their family. When both of her parents died in the fire of 1928 that scorched flesh and fields, J. W. Pritchard sold the children to pay the family's unpaid debt—sold them, as if the proclamation of Negro freedom had never been issued.

He sent her two brothers to work on a farm north of Jackson for his cousin, who would send back their earnings, and she was not sold but tagged with Pritchard's last name and put in will-call as wife to one of Pritchard's Negro sharecroppers, a man more than five times her age whose wife had died of tuberculosis four seasons before. Leander Lee was born just in time to escape the sweaty back lashings of slavery. The other, unscorched Pritchard farm, where he sharecropped, still benefited from the demand for tobacco, the demand for enough corn to supply a healthy underground whiskey industry. Old Deddy is what Lottie called him, since on the day J. W. Pritchard spoke the deal to this Negro sharecropper he was sixty-two and she was twelve.

All Old Deddy heard was, "the land is yours for half the debt." All young Lottie heard was "keep her," like she was some prized pig washed down in buttermilk to look white and clean before being parceled off for somebody else to feed, fatten up, and breed. Old Deddy's sloppy "X" on folded sheets of paper and he would *keep* her. She was twelve, and her new stepson James was also twelve.

Beautiful, kept, but at a price to Leander Lee of a smart mouth to feed. She walked around acting like she understood more about count and yield than him and wasn't giving birth to field hand children fast enough for his taste. In ten years, all he had to show for all she ate was Bennie and Lenard, two bodies for the two bodies lost in the fire.

"Lottie!" Bennie yelled for his mother again, and his own yelling voice brought him clearer into the moment. Old Deddy's dusty skin, hair flecked with yellow naps, a six-foot shadow on the barn floor. He flung the whip and caught Bennie in its relentless maneuvers. The boy saw his own blood like the spray of scuppernong wine caught in the shaft of sunlight.

Lenard sat in the dirt of the yard like the chickens waiting for Old Deddy to be done, waiting for Bennie to come and pitch the goat bladder ball to him.

Bennie didn't think about Lottie every day anymore. It had been near three years since she left, and his days were the rhythm of holding the mule, or tying the tobacco, or splitting wood and teaching his baby brother, Lenard, to do the same. Most days were so hot, Bennie could make skillet bread on the blade of the broken hoe, and once Old Deddy took a nap or went to town, Bennie could go to his hiding place with Lenard, and they would be free and easy in making each other laugh, which they did in quiet snickers as they splashed each other with murky pond water and watched the bats appear in the peach sky. Bennie watched the stars light up a few at a time until they expanded above him as tiny white seeds speckled on a black firmament. He'd look off at the line of woods toward Mr. Genorette's tavern and imagine himself cutting through the back end of the swamp and peering through the window until he caught her eye. He let it go, remembering Old Deddy's words, "Go up there look'n for her whore ass and I'll whip the skin off ya, boy." When Bennie relaxed like this, he knew the treatment from Old Deddy was wrong, but he was about to turn thirteen and still didn't have anything right to compare it to.

Now and then, he'd catch sight of something, like his own toes on the bank of the pond, and see Lottie's feet while she held him between her knees cutting his hair, and he would wonder if she was ever gonna save enough and get him and Lenard away from there.

On Bennie's thirteenth birthday, Old Deddy looked at him through the clear corner of his glaucoma vision and hollered, "Come on, boy. Let's go to the fights."

"Woo wee!" Bennie screamed and went to get his cleaner pair of overalls, the hand-me-downs left behind by his older brother, James. Lenard came and stood next to him while he buckled: "I'm goin' too, Beebee." He never learned to say Benjamin or Bennie, and at six years old Bennie felt like Lenard was getting too old to be calling him "Beebee."

Old Deddy honked the truck horn, which was so half-rusted it sounded like a goose getting its neck wrung for Christmas dinner. Bennie stood on the porch and yelled out to him, "Old Deddy! What 'bout Lenard?" but Old Deddy did not answer him. Bennie touched his little brother's shoulder. "Stay here and watch the cows feed." He stooped down to look Lenard in the eyes. "They behind the house now, and time we get back, they been done circled round back to the barn. Okay?" He didn't want Lenard to experience what he experienced, but it was his turn to do like his brother James had done, turn into a man and go to the dogfights with Old Deddy. It was Lenard's turn to stay behind and watch the land. Bennie and Old Deddy pulled off in the truck, making a cloud that blotted out the view of Lenard sitting on the porch steps.

The dogfights—corn whiskey, cigar smoke, fists full of bills, Old Deddy's bullfrog voice, "We gonna win. I feel it!" Bennie perked up and laughed with him, "Yes, sir. Yes, sir. We gonna win!" Men hollered and slapped each other on the shoulder. Old

Deddy and Bennie were on one side of town standing over the pit yelling and hollering in anticipation of the sweat of the angry dogs. On the dead-end side of town, Lottie was dancing and collecting the dollars from the drunk men. One of them copped a pinch for free, and Mr. Genorette took a wide stance, aimed his pistol at the misbehaving man, and tossed the body into the dark sulfur water of the swamp, where the bullet hole leaked all the blood down through the mud, a sight that caused Lottie to call on God: "Lord, Jesus, God in heaven, help me!"

Bennie's little-boy ears that once tweaked at the sound of his mother's distress turned toward the sounds of the pen. He looked up at Old Deddy's gray naps and felt a new solidarity as strong as the plow strap between man and the mule who both earned their rest through shared backbreaking labor. He knew something he hadn't been mature enough to reckon with until then. Surely, Old Deddy knew where his young wife was spending her time. "Quit goin' up to let them mens pinch on yo ass!" His little-boy ears almost awakened at the memory of Old Deddy yelling as the sound of her body struck the wall, but he didn't want any of those memories invading his place by Old Deddy's side.

The two of them stood next to the thigh-high wooden structure. "Good placement," Old Deddy kept saying with his hand on Bennie's shoulder and his head turned sideways. The corner of his right eye tipped down toward the pen to see around the glaucoma blockage. At an angle, he could see just fine down to where the action would happen.

Bennie didn't know he was grinning until he tasted the stagnant thick air of sweat in the fur of the chained dogs. The other men pushed at his back to see over in the pit, and he was glad he was up close because he was only shoulder height. All of them leaned over the pen like trees over a pond.

They got to hooting and hollering when the men came from either side through the little path with the dogs on chains, muzzles strapped around their faces. The dogs were docile, looking not at each other but around at the crowd, obeying the occasional jerking motion of the handlers. *Nice dogs,* Bennie thought and imagined himself running through the woods at dusk on a coon hunt with them at his side. He reached to pet them, but at the sight of each other across the pen they growled.

Off came the muzzles, and the sound stirred the organs in his stomach, a tangle of guttural gnarling, anger, and madness. Bennie turned his head toward Old Deddy, who grabbed a fist of his wool naps and turned him back. The thick red of blood on the dogs' necks and Bennie was inhaling, but not exhaling. His eyes measured the tightness of the pen, the density of the crowd, and the sun that beamed in from the edge of the enclosure. He told himself to stand still like a man, to earn his place by Old Deddy's side.

In his peripheral vision, one dog was on top of the other piercing its neck in a tangle of slick black fur. Bennie's stomach churned and sent projectile vomit into the pit. None of the men turned away from yelling and rooting for the right death that could make them rich for a day.

He covered his nose with his shirt collar, closed his eyes, and acquiesced to the peaceful memory of Lottie's hands on the washboard, singing and hanging clothes beneath the blue sky, bare feet on orange dirt, the stark frame of her slender body, black hair in a bun. He reached into his overall pocket and held tight to the little chip of lye and lavender soap that no one knew he carried around.

And it was over. He felt shame for needing Lottie's coddling over the hunger for men's games. It was a defeat that brought the slow brewing of anger over her absence. The men laughed in jubilation, and some men cussed as money was counted and passed between brown calloused hands.

When he and Old Deddy left for the dogfights, there was only half the money for the landlord, and now there was none. Old Deddy ground his back teeth beneath the thick-aired hum of the truck. He cussed, banging the steering wheel, "Shit! Shit! Shit!" Bennie could tell that the pounding was not enough to satisfy his rage.

Old Deddy punched him, and before the boy could gain composure, Old Deddy punched him again. The next three swings did not connect, because Bennie maneuvered forward on the seat or toward the door or used the empty leather satchel, to block Old Deddy's fist. "Little shit bastard! You messed up my winning!"

He told himself to use his right fist to punch Old Deddy in the blind spot of his eye. In that moment, he caught sight of Old Deddy's handgun strapped down at his calf; the tip of it poked out from his crumpled pants leg. Bennie reached down, but his eye caught Old Deddy's wayward punch. That did not deter Bennie as he held his breath to keep Old Deddy from sensing where he was, and he reached again and caught hold of the gun handle this time. At the same time, Old Deddy turned his attention away from the boy to swerve back on to the road, never noticing that he had taken the gun.

Old Deddy leaned forward to steady his sight, still blaming Bennie for his poor judgment: "Little shit!" Dusk fell over Old Deddy's vision.

Aiming the way he aimed his pellet gun at crows in the corn field, Bennie breathed in a heavy rhythm. He wanted Old Deddy to see his advantage but grew angry that his father's waxing vision could not acknowledge that he, Bennie, was in charge. Angry at himself for hoping the dogfights would mark some rite of passage to end the beatings of his boyhood and begin the benefits of manhood. Angry at Lottie for leaving him and Lenard to let men slide their hands up under her dress.

When they pulled into the yard, Bennie flung open the truck door and ran toward his little brother, reached for his hand in the cloud of orange dust, and fled as fast as his worn-out boots could carry him. He heard Old Deddy's boots pounding on the earth behind him and then it was just his heart beating in his ears and Lenard's bare heels.

When the two of them reached their hiding spot, Bennie gave Lenard the piece of bamboo he cut from the grove near the woods. Gave him his carving knife. "Work on this until I get back. You hear me? Just cut on it to make your pole and when I get back, we'll fish for dinner. You hear me?"

"Yeah, Beebee."

He scruffed his little brother's hair of naps and went off through the line of trees toward town.

Bennie snuck in to Genorette's to see if Lottie was still working there. He walked out of the light of the day and into the darkness and stood among the musk of cigarettes, sweet corn whiskey, and body odors before his eyes adjusted to the lamplight. He caught a glimpse of her hips in tight red satin; her wavy, black hair flowed from her face. No bruises around her eyes. She looked sturdy and put together and distant from him in a way that made him feel like she was better off without him. "Lottie! Hey Lottie! It's me."

She didn't hear her child; she heard some young fella hollering for her to come out from this darker, better world and back into the unforgiving light of the fields.

The *country* Lottie, the one Bennie knew, hid behind a minstrel smile that she cast at him to make him hush, then beamed at the laughing men with crooked teeth, and she took their dollars, tucked the money between her breasts. *Those men matter more than me,* he thought where he stood shrinking, disappearing as the blues piano, washtub bass, and harmonica sounds warped grotesque around him. That's when he yelled above them like yelling to awaken her from a trance, yelling to remind her of the cotton-dress washtub promise she made in the sun that day. He yelled to give her up so those men would see the country woman she was: "Lottie Lee! Old Deddy said come home right now!" The music stopped. The men in crumpled hats with half-had jars of moonshine turned to him, and in perfect pitch and on perfect cue they belted forward with laughter. The piano started up again, and she turned away from the boy she recognized as her own.

Mr. Genorette turned toward him and held the boy by the back of his overall straps. Bennie wished he was strong enough to break free of Mr. Genorette and turn and shoot him between the eyes. But Mr. Genorette's giant fist pushed between the boy's shoulder blades, forcing tears up from the well of his chest. The light of day burned Mr. Genorette's eyes as he tossed Bennie out into the swamp. "Stay out of here, boy. You hear me?" He intended threat, but seeing the gangly boy clod on the boards of the deck to get his footing, some note of sympathy said, *Look, this is a business. I cain't help that you ain't got no mama.*

That's what the kids chanted at the school that Old Deddy let

Bennie walk to a couple times a week: "You ain't got no mama." Going to school to get his teasing was the lesser evil compared to having Old Deddy wipe the sweat from his brow with one hand and swing at Bennie for not being strong enough to hold the mule steady. He toughened, and for those three years he had told himself, Lenard, and the kids at school that his mama was dead.

That evening, Bennie walked back to where he left Lenard at the pond, mumbling at Lottie in Old Deddy's voice, "Bitch. Lying bitch."

He sat beside Lenard, fished for pond trout, and made the little fire that they put out before Old Deddy could smell the food. Bennie took the lye soap from his pocket. He and Lenard stripped down naked as the sun set in blue and pink stripes over the pond. He could not relax the way he usually did. Agitation and sadness from the deaths and disappointments of the day stirred inside of him. He fought resentment for his mothering duties—scrub Lenard, himself, make a bed in the trunk of the oldest maple tree. He tucked the gun on a termite-moistened spot inside the tree, folded his overalls on top, and slept in underwear and T-shirt next to his little kin past twilight.

He dreamed the smell of the soil in the tree that was damp from his sweat, the chalk smell of earth receiving moisture. "Sshh," he heard somebody whisper, pitch-black in a void of his own dreams, "Sshh." He felt the sensation of opening his eyes, but all he heard was "Sshh."

Bennie woke to the sound of mourning doves cooing and her voice: "Bennie, Bennie?" There was a white duck of some sort floating on the pond. He shook the thought of it calling his name. She whispered again, "Bennie." He and Lenard's legs were exposed out of the trunk, and he pushed himself up to sitting to see her.

"Lottie!?" Her eyes were bulging like a fiendish bugaboo was chasing her. Scooching on his bottom, he sat outside the trunk to get closer to her.

"I need you to listen."

"Lottie?" She put her finger upright over her cracked lips and shushed him.

She wore a wide-brimmed hat to protect her from the sun that would soon rise. It was so brand-new he could smell the sweetness of the straw. The edges of her hair were not covered by the hat she wore, edges smooth like crows' wings.

"Sshh. I got to go. I don't want you actin like a baby about it. You know I care about you, and I care about Lenard." He watched her eyes for better understanding, but the round black marbles looked away from his questioning face that said, *How come you acted like you didn't know me?* Lottie looked off nervously in the direction of their home. "I just got to go. You ain't old enough to understand, but I wanted to come to you and Lenard and tell you yo mama care about you." He wanted to shut her up and tell her he was a man. Tell her that he didn't want to hear anything out of her mouth after she let Mr. Genorette treat him that way and let them men laugh at him like he was ignorant.

"I'm gonna make good in St. Louis, then come back for you." She put both hands on her belly, to hold herself and the new life inside her in place. Her eyes let loose two streams of tears for the grief that discounted the whippings he bore in her absence. "You listen now." She pulled his chin to get him to look at her, "I cain't make do down here no mo. And Lord knows, I cain't stand all the killing the men be doing for a piece of earth or a piece of ass. Things is fix'n to be better for all of me and mine." And then the thing that resonated like a nail hammered in a coffin to keep his mangled spirit from escaping: "I love you."

Before the air of the morning went from syrupy and cool to syrupy and hot, a trail of questions tumbled out of Bennie's chapped lips, "What you do with them men, Lottie, that you cain't be here? Why you leave us? Why cain't we come?" And then the proclamation that came in Old Deddy's voice, "You just a two-bit whore!"

Some fledgling part of him knew what he had said, knew the power of his words. She stared at him until the sounds of the cicadas came back into her hearing. Tears quit streaming. She tilted her head sideways as if she had just realized that she mistook him for someone she knew. He resisted calling her spirit back to him. He let her liken him to being as dangerous as any other man. She went to stand up, and he grabbed her arm and let the rage have its way: "You lying whore! You wasn't never gonna take us nowhere!"

She snatched away, was up off the ground, still with her eyes on him. He saw her eyes justify leaving him and his sleeping brother there in the muck of Mississippi. She turned on her heels, her new blue-and-white cotton dress and new hat mocking his hand-me-down rags. His hand slipped past the roughness of the stiff cotton of his overalls, weighted down by Lenard's sleeping head, and he grabbed the handgun.

One shot pitched into the thick air, waking the little boy in him, who hoped he had shot an aimless warning; but her body went limp and fell to the ground. His head jerked up and down as the nerves in his body tried to erase the moment like the rag on the schoolhouse chalkboard erasing his mistaken calculations.

Bennie lost time; the sun had made its way to peeking up over the land while he sat staring at the pond. Lenard's legs turned over toward him. "Beebee?" Bennie held on to Lenard's small leg, looked down at him trying to ground himself in the reality of his brother's eyes.

He walked to the pond where the rising sun duplicated itself in the reflection of the water and hurled Old Deddy's gun and the memory of Lottie far from where he stood. The seraphim fog glided over the black glassy surface of the pond, and two wispy white spirits ascended, one tall, the tip of its head reaching, the other the same but little, faint, and weak.

TWO

Sampson, Mississippi
1942

If she could, she would go back and kill the collision of the whip on her own back as Old Deddy's child-wife whose spirit bloomed from the dust of the Mississippi road on the heels of her son's shoeless feet. "Dear heart," she whispered to Bennie as her spirit caressed the welted flesh of his raw ankles.

Crows flew overhead to escape the coming cold. She would have called him home then, but he stood at the hope-fork in the road where he might still turn back to his innocence. She could feel the light inside his heart that was the light she put there with the blood and milk of her own body, and she did not ask him which way he was going. She trusted that being hers was enough for him to go the right way at the crossroads.

Bennie went to the barn to do his chores, which he did every morning that fall before dawn without complaint, and if it brought the whip, he bore it without complaint, like a man. Jasper Jackson, his schoolmate, was sleeping on the hay pile. His felt hat was pulled down so far it was round on top. Bennie woke him up with the handle end of the pitchfork. "Get up, fool! And get out of here!" His voice wavered from boyhood tenor to manhood baritone.

Jasper turned over as if Bennie's pitchfork had tickled him, grabbed his hat, and dusted the hay off his pants. "You damned fool. I'm headed to sign up for the Army, boy. Gonna kill me some Japs. Too bad yo baby ass cain't come."

The Japanese had bombed Pearl Harbor the previous winter. *Hawaii, Japan*, words and news that didn't mean anything to Bennie out on the farm where Old Deddy didn't allow him no radio, no newspaper, and school only twice a week as his chance to rest. Jasper asked him if Old Deddy was still asleep and told Bennie all of his fantasies about the women he was going to see in every little town.

Jasper's deddy was like Old Deddy, but younger and meaner with the whip. "Oh, Lord, when I get me some of them yellow women. Ooo wee." Bennie glared at him, not going along with his celebration, and Jasper rubbed on the bulge in his overalls.

"You gone get the whip. Now, get the hell outta here!" At fourteen, Bennie had arms like fence posts from plowing, pulling, cutting, hauling, and what he said and how he said it made other boys think twice.

Jasper had known Bennie since he was a wide-eyed little scrawny boy and called his bluff with laughter. "Quit being a sissy. You the oldest boy at the school now. A little talk about pussy ain't gonna get you beat." Jasper pinched his hat and leaned out the front of the slanted barn to check in the low-lying fog for signs of life. "I'm gonna show you what I did for Sara and her sister Ethergene. Leave you with my legacy of how to please a woman befo I go off to war."

Bennie remembered finding a book when he was six years old. "Human genitals," the book called them. He stole it from under James's floor mattress, which had the most hay and cotton stuffed into it. Old Deddy said James got the good mattress because he was a man and had earned a better night's sleep. Old Deddy told Bennie the lie that suffering and figuring a way out of that suffering would make him a man too. Old Deddy didn't even know that James was in the midst of figuring his way out of Sampson, Mississippi. In the middle of the night, James scuffled around on hands and knees, quietly gathering his things into a little clothes bundle tied by his long shirtsleeves. He glanced at Bennie's peaheaded silhouette squinting at the yellowing pages and climbed out the window. If Bennie knew that was the last time he would see his brother on this side of manhood, he would have hollered out for Old Deddy, but James was just gone, leaving his little brothers in the tomb of Mississippi.

Jasper Jackson told him to pull it out of his pants. Bennie said, "You crazy. Get the hell out of here."

Jasper laughed, "Who gonna teach you how to do the girls when I'm gone?"

Bennie knew Jasper was right as sure as he knew a man couldn't learn the rhythm of topping and suckering a tobacco plant without the guide of an experienced farmer. He looked toward the house to make sure Old Deddy or Lenard wasn't awake, and he took it out. Jasper laughed at how small it was. "Rub it," he said, looking behind him and rocking side to side. "It's like a genie. You rub it, and you get what you want, get what you need." He told Bennie what he already knew, that it gets big because you pull it with your hand till the milk comes out.

Jasper laughed so hard that Bennie could see that he was missing back teeth. "The milk?!" His guttural laughter was absorbed by the morning fog that lay over the fields, and Bennie wondered if he could taste the sweet cow manure of the barn on his tongue.

He looked out to the house again, and Jasper fussed, "His old ass is sleep. Quit acting like a scared girl. You ever done a girl before?"

Jasper told him that the kingdom of the world is man's, that he could put "that thing" anywhere he wanted and make "the milk" come out, and the girls would all like it and fall at his feet. Bennie told him about the swamp-decaying bones of the men Mr. Genorette killed, and he knew different.

Jasper Jackson said, "Naw, man, that's just myth. You just got to say the right thing, look at them the right way and make them as hungry to have *the milk* as you are to have *the honey*. Then you got to tell them to keep their mouth shut so some crazy nigger don't come after you."

He pulled Bennie through the cow shit with him, took the salve for the mule off the shelf, and got behind the youngest heifer. Jasper put the salve in her gentle and said, "Look at her knees shake, she likes it. Put it in there, boy." He cackled again, "Put it in there till *the milk* comes out," and Bennie looked down at her shaking knees, his brown penis exposed to Jasper Jackson, the heifer, and the chill of the fall air. He did what Jasper said. For a while, he was alone in the barn. He was not stressed; he was free. But when the milk came, he slipped into a dream that was not the fantasy he hoped for. There were green snakes in the air above the green leaves of the trees. The girls from the schoolhouse, women from town, and all color of women like the yellow ones Jasper talked about were running around trying to get away. Lottie was the one with the iron rake, combing it through the sky to catch the green ribbons before they could fall onto the heads of anyone.

Jasper Jackson laughed loud, grabbed Bennie's jacket, which had fallen around his ankles—"Thanks for the jacket, man!"—

and ran off into the morning fog, with his laugh trailing out past the house where Bennie was sure Old Deddy was stirring in waking.

Bennie dreamed about Lottie that night, sitting by her side, a river flowing behind them that he could hear and not see, and she grabbed the naps at the back of his head. He could feel the knuckles of her fist, and she snatched him backward into the water. A baptism and a drowning that woke him in a fit of sweat and tears and his own voice hollering, "Lottie!"

The next fall, in the dusty mildew of the three-room house, with James nine years gone out in the night never to return and Lenard sleeping into his deep, sweaty sleep, Bennie went to the yellowed pages of what James had left behind, the dark ink drawings of human genitals. The moon was full enough to offer silver light. He asked himself if it was human genitals that felt like satisfied hunger when he pressed his front side into the mattress and rubbed up and down. *Were human genitals like bull genitals?* When the bull got sold for leather because his genitals wouldn't come out anymore, Bennie asked Old Deddy why he couldn't get the bull some new genitals and put them on. Old Deddy didn't look down from the solid tower of his body but said, "You cain't replace them." That and Jasper Jackson's lesson were all the talk he had been given about sex.

The next morning, Old Deddy called Bennie halfway up the road, caught him with his whip around the place where the overalls didn't cover his rusty ankles, and said, "Get back and do the chores right, nigga."

By the time he did the chores again and ran up the road, clouds threatened cold rain and he didn't have so much as a jacket to keep him warm. He was late for one of the two days he was allowed to trade with Lenard and go to school. Lenard's school day always ended with a report to Bennie and Old Deddy about winning the recitation of lines from Homer or winning a bushel of apples for taking first place in the calculation tournament. He was the youngest at the school but ten times smarter than the brother who protected him.

Bennie's face was hot with anger, until he saw Ethergene Turner. She wore that red scarf her mother had knitted long enough for her head and shoulders, since she didn't have a coat. She was late too. The suppressed upset from Old Deddy's beatings crested behind Bennie's eyes.

He started out nice, asked her if he could carry her books, and when she said no, he pushed her. When she pushed back, he pushed her into the woods beside the road, took out his hard penis and told her he would put his fingers in first, and she would like it. She didn't refuse, just laid there staring up to the sky like a body before death. Then he told her she was his girlfriend and she said okay, but her eyes were looking up at the gray sky, silent. He pushed himself into her until he felt calm and came and told her she was sweet. She didn't look at him, and the tears made streams down her dry face.

Bennie helped her straighten her dress, helped her fix the red scarf and held her hand on the way to school, and she didn't tell about the pain and blood and semen between her legs, but she did say to the schoolteacher that the back of her dress was dirty because Bennie pushed her down and touched her. The rest of the reason for his expulsion was conjured in the grown-man mind of the teacher.

There was a note written that Old Deddy couldn't read.

"What it say, boy?"

Bennie felt Lottie's knuckles holding the fist of naps in her grip—"Don't you never trap no woman in yo house like she a cow who happened by yo barn for shelter. Don't you never be that kinda man"—and he yanked his head away from her grip. He did not tell Old Deddy that the note said, "Benjamin Lee may not return to school for being rude and not God-like with girls." He told Old Deddy, "It say, Benjamin Lee isn't learning enough. Lenard Lee should come every day. Benjamin Lee is better suited for farm learning." He turned his head away from Old Deddy, hiding the shame. Old Deddy looked off the porch, sharpening the hatchet for the chicken's neck, and agreed, "That probly is best. You needed here for most all the work," and Bennie felt some invisible shackle tighten around his neck, cutting off his air there on the porch where he was now tall as Old Deddy.

The window on leaving had shut with the singe of gunpowder in his nose after he fired the shot, after the violation of Ethergene that took away his weekly rest at the schoolhouse. He was still young enough to believe that a child's only escape is through his mother's movements but grew old enough to negotiate terms with himself for how to survive the inescapable.

For Bennie's eighteenth birthday, James sent him a package from St. Louis—his old suits, his old shoes. Bennie held the clothes up by the shoulders and got a sense of his brother's height and width to go with the faded memories he had of James as a younger, light-skinned version of Old Deddy.

The fine outfits covered the scars from the whip and the mule and made Bennie look like a man.

Old Deddy reminded him of his place. "That's fine duds,

fine, but don't let that make you think you too good for overalls." Old Deddy did less and less of the work now, and Bennie and Lenard became sole farmhands. Old Deddy was like the foreman. He sharpened tools and reminded himself that he was the man by commanding the two brothers with the threat of his whip.

"Yep," Bennie said back to Old Deddy, never *Yes, sir*—an almost undetectable rebellion beneath Old Deddy's grip.

There was a note enclosed in the package from James, a note written for the innocent eyes James left alone in the dark that morning twelve years ago.

Hey Little Brother,

Bennie frowned at that endearment, though he was glad for the package, and kept reading.

> You should suit up and enlist for the Marines. They will send you to the ocean in South Carolina. They want Negro men as much as white men. Here are some fine suits for your travels.
>
> Sincerely, James

Bennie looked through the package for bus fare or a train ticket, but there was nothing but the cool industrial smell of St. Louis wafting out into the heat like old promises from childhood.

By the time Bennie was twenty, the suits fit him just fine as he sang in the moonlight up the Mississippi road toward town, "It's a new life, woooo, baby, gonna ride that train straight to da ocean!" and there was nobody to sing back to him but the spirits, who heard his singing and turned half-awake deep in the hibernating mud cavities of the dark pond.

With his first drink, he was a buttoned-up respectable looking young Negro man in a fine suit. By his tenth drink, he was cussing at Mr. Genorette, "Where the hell is a nigga s'posed to find a woman round here?"

Mr. Genorette shook his head with his arms folded and gave him that stern look: "Drinks are all you can get here, boy."

Bennie danced and sang to the moon and reached out to the woman who was growing weary of dancing with him each time he yelled, "Play that shit again." He went hard in his pants and turned her backside to him as if she was the heifer, but she was a woman he had not paid for.

Mr. Genorette's fist came down on the back of his neck, "Go home, boy, or get what ya got comin!" Bennie stumbled and stepped out into the night giggling like Jasper, who had long since died at the hands of white soldiers before he ever got to fight any Japs.

The dome of stardust swayed over Bennie's head, and he remembered those nights when Lottie came home, a breast full of cash that got deposited in the satchel before Old Deddy rolled over in the bed. Bennie steadied himself and shook the memories from his mind.

At night, the Mississippi road didn't look like the daytime road with the orange dirt, just looked like a silver road in the moonlight, and he sang his song again, "Gonna ride that train straight to da ocean!" and, like frogs waking at the first hint of spring air, he woke the memory of her voice from behind the white sheets on the clothesline. The wood-on-wood slip-sound of the butter churn in rhythm with her: "I'm gonna earn enough money to put us all on the train to St. Louis. Watch me, Bennie, just watch." The thick nighttime breeze was liquid hot around him, and then there was the smell of the green algae and frog's eggs in the pond wafting up from a half mile east off the road, carrying the whisper of her voice that morning: "Bennie, Bennie."

"Lord," he slumped to the ground under the weight of the unfetched memory of his mother's body falling limp. The drunkenness turned to depression as his mind rushed to stuff the memory back into the pockets of his soul. A muted voice woke with his song. She sang back to him the command of his death, "Keefaah, keefaah, kifo." A child's eyes he didn't recognize formed themselves in the stars and came down over his head as if they were going to swallow his soul. He tried to make his way off the dirt road where he had been sung to by the force that told him to die. He didn't see the lights of the deputy's car when it pulled up behind him, but he noticed that the stars were gone, and the silver road was orange again. He recognized his name: "Nigger! Hey, nigger!"

Hairy wet knuckles connected with the bones in his face in the slow rhythm of the blues. He was too drunk to defend himself. Some part of him wanted to feel the pain absolve him of his sins, the deputy's fists like a baptism in his own blood that kept Bennie from whatever inverted savior called for his death.

When he got home that night, he had a dislocated jaw that might have come from the deputy, might have come from the punitive spirit. Old Deddy reset the jaw, the way he reset the joint on the plow, and offered his condolences: "Quit being a damned fool. Stay off the roads at night, nigga."

Bennie couldn't talk for two weeks, just mumbled "Um-hm" and "Mm-um" to say how he felt about all the work on the land that Lenard didn't do right. Two weeks was long enough to figure out how to live, how to die. He couldn't bear to tell his brother what happened on the road that night and have Lenard think of him as less of a man. Lenard was just turning thirteen, the age he'd find out that there wasn't no grits and gravy waiting on the manhood side of things. Bennie was twenty now, with enough permanent scars to count for every year. He didn't tell Lenard that he was planning to run toward an honorable death and away from whatever womanish child-as-God intended to snuff his soul out on the southern nighttime road.

The bus took Bennie to Hattiesburg, Mississippi, where he and other Negro boys who looked beaten by the plow grinned happily. They shed the overalls of who they were, showered, dressed in the same white T-shirts, white shorts, and light-brown uniforms that gave them a new start, birthday suits for their manhood.

On the train to South Carolina, Bennie waved his hat, head stuck out the window of the train. The wind cooled the heat under his newly cut wool naps. He didn't know about breathing deeply until he could. Every time the train stopped, brown hands on the platform waved at the new enlisted men. They all waved back in the sun as though they were headed to the Promised Land.

The Black USO in a little South Carolina cotton-picking town hosted a dance with lemonade and cakes baked by the local gals who came out in droves. Bennie got to rockin' away the blues with the other men, and every minute of the fun, he knew he had done the right thing, gotten the hell out of Mississippi. No more hoeing the row and feeling the blunt impact of his manhood colliding with the soil that refused to acquiesce to force. It wasn't spoken among them, but every Black boy at that dance was rocking to the harmonica blues and thinking, *Mississippi be damned.*

All he needed now was a good woman who yielded to his touch. And for half of his pay, he had himself more than a few for the year and a half of training of homeland duty, of repair and upkeep of jeeps, trucks, and all ground vehicles. He hooped and hollered with all the other Black marines the day he was called into their commanding officer's trailer and given orders to deploy away from the American South, first to California, then to Seoul, Korea.

THREE

Seoul, South Korea
1950

She wanted her child to go to sleep. To put a spell on him to anesthetize his body from doing the deeds that make bodies break. Her soul tilted to one side the way a mother closes her eyes and sings over the globe of her child's skull. Go to sleep, don't hurt yoself, don't turn yoself into the old man that was once a boy like you are. She rose like the sun that morning and called him, but he didn't answer, just kept his eyes pointed in the direction of the long way around the globe, when home, rest, peace was right at his back.

Bennie was one of a fifty-four-man Negro Marine Reserve unit that joined the Seventh Marines of the First Division in early November 1950; their task, to push back the North Koreans through the mountains across the Yalu River into China. The rest stop for his division would be Chosin Reservoir, high in the frozen mountains of Korea. Cold, not fit for brown southern boys who were presumed to be able-bodied fighting men. General MacArthur had issued the master plan but had not counted on the streamlined loyalty of thousands of determined Chinese soldiers prepared to use their bodies to meet and crush the discordant hodgepodge of Western democracy. MacArthur did not know that the commingling of white boys who pushed the plow by day and hid beneath hoods at night with Black boys who shouldered the plow by day and stood guard against hooded demons by night would expose to the Chinese a cracked foundation of loyalty—American boys who pledged the lie of "one nation, under God, indivisible, with liberty and justice for all," though individual survival was bred into their southern blood as war motive.

Bennie's unit joined one hundred other men who disembarked from the trucks with the mindset that they were finally getting a chance to prove their fighting abilities as marines. The last warmth that was breathed by his regiment was breathed inside the truck beds, where their bodies sat knee to knee, not yet fatigued and frostbitten.

He took position in the line that climbed the winding mountain road. He and the other men wore coats like thick sleeping bags around their bodies, helmets under hoods. Sun on snow. He had seen snow only once and grinned with his mates, trying to tell stories between moments of covering his face against the bite. The mood was positive, as if they were going off to explore ice on a frozen pond.

They were told their regiment would simply fortify the already successful troops and secure the supply road. Better than nothing, they thought.

In the valley that evening, Bennie lay his head in a foxhole. Yudam-ni Mountain loomed at his back like a mother holding her boy's shoulders still with her knees. She held fear in her core for what she saw stalking below in the valley.

"Bennie? Bennie?" She whispered a warning of the pending morning down between her knees into the foxhole where he lay, but her voice was blotted out by the steady hum of the unborn and the deceased who knew that sometimes you save the crop by burning out the blight.

When night fell, he fell into a deep sleep lying helmet to helmet with his new white Mississippi buddy.

Before dawn, he heard a boom like thunder, a bugle blew, and a great roaring of voices twisted his gut like the gnarling sound of the dogs in the pen. "Stand your ground!" "Fire at will!" "Hold your position!" The commands came faster than his brain could register.

His body knew to roll over, stay low in the foxhole, and fire in the direction of the advancing sparks. The night was without time, just breath, alertness to commands, reload, reload.

Just before light rose in the sky, the bugle sounded again, and the sparks of the advancing Chinese ceased. Into the lower valley the Chinese soldiers vanished. In the light of day, the mocking brightness of the snow revealed familiar faces bloodied and upturned to the light.

"Retrieve the bodies, retrieve the bodies." There wasn't enough time for him and his mates to lift the shoulders and feet of all the bodies of their fellow marines, to feel the weight of their lives beyond the tasks and commands, before they were ordered again, "Take formation" against the swarm of Chinese foot soldiers who advanced in their dark-green coats and hats like jackrabbits across the bright snow.

A piercing subzero wind cut through Bennie's coat and shirt down through the Marine-issued long johns, like the ones he wore on Mississippi winter nights. *This*, he thought, *is how I will die*, and above his head, there was the droning sound of an enduring hum that dispersed his suicidal wish into the mist of gun smoke that hung over the snow. He watched what seemed impossible unfold in front of him. The jackrabbits halted and took position, and through a megaphone their superior shouted a phrase that echoed off the frozen rocks: "Today Americans die!"

The bullets of machine-gun fire rushed past his ears. It would be only a matter of time before one clipped through the sharp frozen air and caught him in the eye, the shoulder, or the muscle flesh of his heart. He saw his funeral in the Negro graveyard just below the town of Sampson, Mississippi.

"Cover the left flank!" his colonel yelled. A cloud of breath formed in the air where Bennie's superior motioned left with his arm. With his M1 semiautomatic in hand and grenades tucked in his pockets like pine cones, Bennie and his white Mississippi buddy plodded over frozen ground to cover the falling men on the left flank of the advance. A cloud of subzero death hung over Yudam-ni Mountain. Beneath it, men were reduced to ants, quick-frozen and scattered across the snow.

"Hold the line!" The order came when Bennie and his buddy were in midroute, and he heard the rhythm of the machine-gun fire from below cease and then commence again. For each crack, there was a two-second delay, and a marine went from shooting stance to crumpled in the snow. The hum became a high-pitched screech that muted everything except the sound of Bennie's own breath and the muffled sound of his boots in the snow tunneling up through the warmth of his body. Bennie saw the two crows in the tobacco field of his childhood fall with the delayed rhythm of his pellet gun. He saw his body fall with the others; he wanted his body to fall with the others, but the roof of heaven did not open for him and pinch the spirit out.

Let me die here, he prayed, and he heard a child's faint voice comply, "Keefaah, keefaah, kifo," and then he heard a deeper, familiar voice with an elusive smell of gin on her breath pull him away from harm: "Run!"

Up the frozen hill he and his buddy ran, though they were told to hold the line. In his peripheral vision, he saw the dark shadows of a few other runners of his unit climbing up Yudam-ni Mountain, making themselves easy targets against the snow. Behind them, the locust cloud of Chinese soldiers advanced on his unit. And there was the sound and sight of single-engine planes as low as crop dusters buzzing over the naked treetops. Bennie and his buddy and the shadows of the surviving runners tucked themselves into the rock face to shield against the inevitable spray of fire meant to exterminate.

The napalm was not for them. It exploded at the bottom of the hill, burning the cloud of foot soldiers behind them. Bennie could taste rust in his saliva that matched the sight of something he had never seen in the Korean sky, a rust-colored sunset illuminated by fire that sent him and his Mississippi buddy charging away from the enemy line up the hill until near darkness. When they finally reached the summit, gravity pulled them down the other side into the shadow of the frozen rock face, where spirit and man could not find them.

Separated from their unit, the two of them clung to their M1s as if clinging to those frozen walnut branches carved and smoothed in Ohio factories could soothe the terror of the advancing darkness. The absence of light made the cold freeze the flesh of Bennie's hands and feet and nose.

He didn't know how to pray, but he heard his buddy whimper in pain, and inside his head, he asked God to please take the two of them. To die an honorable death after having survived

Old Deddy beating him and Lottie turning her back on him. *Let me die here*, he prayed. Then he heard a sound that silenced his prayers for death. The squealing grew louder as he instinctively followed the sound of food. The snared pig came into his dilated vision squirming where it was caught in barbed wire. To satisfy his hunger and end its suffering, he plunged his knife into its neck. He and his buddy were walked backward from visions of death by the flesh of the livestock, by the flint and kindling and warmth inside of the hut that they did not recall emptying of its inhabitants—their knives plunged into a frail man, the wailing of the two women who stood over the man's body curdling the air with their high-pitched grieving until more plunging of the knives silenced them. A pain-coma fell over Bennie and his white mate, both of them soothed by the sounds of their slowing heartbeats.

Her spirit rested in the coals of the fire, laid herself there without true breath. With nothing but her soul to save the life of her son, she shuddered. She was the energy that pushed him into this life—the energy that forced him from a safe place out into the world where she would forever regret the trick of birthing him and leaving him. Her spirit stoked the coals and whispered between breaths an inaudible plea for him to turn his eyes back to the deeds left undone by his mother and to promise to save more than his own life. To agree to tell the truth, the shameful truth, the fatal truth, the truth that would help him be the vessel to bring forth the girl-child he did not know he'd snubbed out, though she was the one fated to save them all.

It took a whole day for the fire in the hut to die out, two days before the two marines were found curled into each other. The white and Black rescue unit that found them assumed they were among the count of the frozen dead in the hut—but no.

They were flown to a Navy hospital in Japan. Bennie was prepped for surgery to remove the unsalvageable frostbitten skin and the unsalvageable pinkie toe. Iodine on the skin and anesthesia in the veins that sent his lungs to grow gills deep beneath memories. He was sitting under the tree where he and Lenard spent so much time hiding from Old Deddy. The smell of Lottie's perfume of rose water stolen from some store he was never allowed to enter. Then the surprise of night falling over a pond of dragonflies, their green-and-turquoise wings so humid that they fluttered slow. He caught sight of movement shifting in the line of trees. He and Lenard scaled and gutted their dinner, spilled heart, lungs, stomach sack, and roe into the pond.

He struggled for breath beneath the diluted anesthesia that barely kept him under. "Don't wake up." He heard her voice tempt him toward the depths of the memories.

When the surgeon cut the necrotized flesh from Bennie's ears, he plummeted from the banks of the pond where his feet and Lenard's feet were planted in the weeds. He yelled for Lottie and saw her come into view deep in the green darkness of the pond, where mud plugged her nose and mouth like a newborn woman not yet having come alive with breath. Her face and mouth reached up to pull him toward something that felt like relief from homesickness.

With the anesthesia wearing off, the surgeon sliced the pinkie toe with the scalpel and severed it at the distal phalanx joint, as Bennie had learned to sever the wing of a chicken bone from the bird. With what was left of his will, he shut his mind off to the wailing Korean women inside the missing day of how he and his Mississippi buddy survived Yudam-ni and the missing morning of how he survived his mother's disappearance.

The survivors were lined up in the sun, all spotless in dress blues that did not show the cut-down men inside the uniforms. His fellow white marines held their faces with a little more confidence in the knowledge that they could go back to the southern soil as survivors deemed heroes. He, who would be a survivor deemed nigger, boarded the gray metal bird that would take him stateside.

FOUR

Seoul, South Korea, to Sampson, Mississippi
1953

Her sons were an almost-lost species. Hunting and hunted, the sound of calabash clashing and boars' hair plucking warned even mourners and spirits on the wind to fly, to run away from the untended children who were likely too famished to be saved. But she knew better, knew that holding out for the residue shavings of partly fulfilled promises could be sustenance for the next crop, and the next crop, until "almost extinct" sat in the shadow of the new spirit-child swaying in the breeze of morning.

Flying into Jackson, the terrain beneath Bennie changed from Midwest barren, flat crop circles of green, brown, beige, to the southern thickness of nappy green trees. The sweet wine smell of home brought him back. The high-pitched scream of the landing plane connected sky to ground, making Private Benjamin Lee one of the crops again, tobacco, cotton, sugarcane, nigger.

Bennie would offer his teenage brother, Lenard, a promise that he did not know was a whisper from his almost-dead night. He would tell Lenard that he could come along to St. Louis, escape the tangle of Mississippi wisteria and honeysuckle, move to the flat Midwest and stay with brother James until Bennie could make good on the GI Bill promises and the auto plants and

Black-owned businesses in the city of jazz, barbecue, preachers, department stores. The subconscious keeping of the promise to save someone else's life, not just his own. His promise to never lose anyone to the collateral damage of his ingested untold pain. His unbeknownst preparation to clear the brush from the terrain of his lineage for the soft-soled feet of the girl-spirit who'd carry the deed from there.

But the day Bennie arrived home was the day Old Deddy finally paid the last remaining debt on the fields he had bartered for with Lottie's body. That day held the inertia that slowed the course of Bennie's promises. Old Deddy became dangerous to more than his Black sons and their mother; he became a Black man who owned his land.

Earlier that afternoon, Lenard held the plow steady on his own, having grown tall, his muscles strong enough to guide the plow and the new mule, his head of wool hair cropped off by his own hands. The son of a man who whipped until he was too half-blind to see if the whip was landing. Lenard had calculated and watched the timeline, a different strategy of escape from his brothers James and Bennie. Lenard was going to read, continue his learning, pull the plow, be both forthright and docile in his agreement with himself to never make a mistake that would bring the whip from Old Deddy or the white men in town who had written them off as poor niggers on land gone sallow. His strategy had paid off; the land was theirs.

The sun played its summer heat on Lenard's neck and broad shoulders, where he wore nothing but the raggedy overalls that held years of sweat and the smell of burned brush, the smell of soil composed of years of tobacco leaves chewed and excreted by grasshoppers. The distant sound of a 1953 black Packard was heard before the cloud of orange dirt was seen looming up in the distance turning off the Dixie Overland Highway onto the mile of dirt road. Its motor purred to let Old Deddy know somebody was coming. He sat on the porch listening while that somebody headed up the road.

White men of Mississippi, like Black men of the Congo, carry the news of property changing hands by beating their chests and listening deep for the opportunity to hunt on new ground. Two clauses Old Deddy couldn't read were reported to J. W. Pritchard by the clerk of court who frequented the swamp bottom of Genorette's tavern and had himself a Black woman or two. Clause one: "She must be kept," an unread clause some twenty-four years after the "X" branded Lottie.

From out in the fields, Lenard saw Old Deddy stand, saw an old white man in white shirt with white hair accompanied by a younger white man in white shirt and suspenders. Lenard stopped the mule so that he could hear: "Woah, woah, woah!" The strap tightened against the place where he'd grown dry, rough callouses over his caramel-brown back. He had taught himself not to feel anything for or against Old Deddy, but the sight of Old Deddy standing and nodding in a way Lenard had never seen put him between worlds. There was the young man standing in the hot sun of a field beneath the broad expanse of blue sky with the few wispy clouds, something in that moment reminding him of a day, of a woman, of the scent of cigarettes, of the smell of flowery water and softness on lips, of a veil of thick black hair. He saw Old Deddy fall to his knees as if he was about to pray, and then he heard what the young white man held in his hand. The explosion of a pistol.

Lenard didn't remember removing the plow straps but was running against the rows of earth, like swimming against the current. The black Packard disappearing in a cloud of orange. Old Deddy's body, a massive pile of flesh and overalls and death, hit the porch by the time Lenard traversed the space. He undid Old Deddy's overall buckle, put his ear there in the mud of blood and dirt and coarse gray hairs on his father's chest, and there was nothing. Old Deddy's body beneath Lenard's head like the rock roots of the stump in the tree trunk where Lenard slept that morning and heard the explosion and woke to the empty feeling of Bennie with the gun.

J. W. Pritchard had spent ten years in Alabama expanding on his land profits, buying up property on the Tombigbee River that he did not know became cheaper and cheaper because the construction of the Demopolis Lock and Dam was soon to stop up the river. Try as he might, he would never hold the same insider knowledge of trading as white men whose fathers and grandfathers traded slaves. Pritchard returned to Mississippi to chase down old investments on a day that he believed was fateful. He went first to the courthouse to find out he was two hours behind Old Deddy, who fetched the deed the minute the clerk's office opened. Figuring he'd at least get the mulatto back, Pritchard went trailing off after one lead and another.

He heard that his will-call property had been earning money for a nigger who was selling her body, and she had taken the money one morning and fled. The sheriff told old Pritchard, "A near-white bitch with that kind of cash could be anywhere so I didn't go look'n. But, yep, she was last seen working at Genorette's." He and his deputies knew, because they each remembered the feel of the roll of bills in their fingers the last time they tucked them between her breasts.

Pritchard went with the sheriff and deputies to Genorette's tavern and had the man arrested. Had the place boarded up by the deputies, but they only hammered each nail twice to appease Pritchard until Genorette's could be reopened as the asset it was to Sampson's men.

Empty-handed and unsatisfied, Pritchard and his son left the law and Genorette and the jailhouse. He claimed Old Deddy had not upheld his end of the bargain. The sheriff scratched his head, claiming different, and went on with other plans for the day, like getting Pritchard to get the hell away from the jail long enough for the sheriff to go fishing with the sheriff from the neighboring county.

The sheriff was wrong in his head-scratching, Mississippi law supported the killing of an unscrupulous man who refused to uphold the second unscrupulous clause: "If she is not kept, her keeper shall forfeit the land where the kin of the landlord was to be kept." So Pritchard and his son took matters into their own hands.

Old Deddy had not seen sight or heard a sound from his white landlord in ten years. Just let Lenard handle the money and settle the debt once a month till the deed was paid for half the price. Leander Lee tilted his head off the porch down at Pritchard and his kin: "Who the hell you think you is come 'round here look'n fo that bitch after all these years? Get the fuck off my land, muthafucka."

The punitive shot, then the Black funeral director's truck, the empty house with nobody but Lenard, who sat on the porch stopped in time. "Sshh, Sshh," he heard the teary spirit soothe him, and he mistook it for the sound of cicadas.

The wheels of Bennie's plane kissed down on the tarmac twenty-five miles away while Old Deddy's body bounced in the bed of a pickup truck over potholes to town.

FIVE

Sampson, Mississippi, to St. Louis, Missouri
1953

Once they follow your wild promise of living, your children will be your children even after their bodies are gone. They arrive with the arrogance of belonging, with the expectation that you will nurture, provide for, and protect them regardless of your powerfulness or powerlessness. And if you leave here not having nurtured, provided, or protected, he will live in partial dusk until he can find a surrogate first love, and you will circle the moon chasing his soul's migrations unless he does.

No one met Bennie in the slow-moving heat of the Jackson airport. All the heroes arrived as marines until they separated in the crowd into Blacks and whites, and his survivor-buddy melded into the barrage of beige-skinned southerners hugging, embracing home.

The bus put him off in town, past the jail where he did not know Mr. Genorette hung his head between his hands, past the place of the big gaping stable where Bennie once went to the dogfights. He filled his chest with air and did not expect to feel rooted, but he did. He picked up his pace, stepping with amnesia over his memories of home. He hoped the sight of home would melt the hard snow memories of Yudam-ni, turn them to spring water that would cascade down the mountain, down the river, and be carried far off. Bennie walked up the dirt road, surrounded by the April flowering tobacco on both sides. He stopped, closed his eyes, and admitted to himself that he missed that sweet tobacco smell that hit so high on the back of the tongue that he couldn't distinguish it from sugarcane.

His eyes scanned for Lenard and imagined an embrace, the way the men at the airport embraced their male farming kin, rib cages slammed together, hands striking each other's backs like striking the drumhead. He expected to give Old Deddy a nod, to shake his hand in a shoulder hug, to show him the man he'd become. But there was silence, that way grace stops everything—the birds, the movement of clouds, the swaying of tobacco leaves—so still that he did not notice Lenard sitting, a tall, brown-skinned version of his childhood self in tattered overalls camouflaged against the weatherworn boards of the porch and walls of their home. And for just an instant, he saw Lottie with her body slumped over Lenard's head as if fingering the boy's naps for lice. She looked up, and the off-whites of her eyes, the milk-white gingham of her blue-and-white dress, faded, leaving Lenard's head hung down where she had pushed it forward for him to carry out some deed that he could not.

The next day, the two of them stood in the Negro Baptist church that neither of them had ever attended. They listened to a woman neither of them knew, sing. The two brothers and the four members of that church who attended funerals as a habit were naked in the tambour of the woman's voice. Unaccompanied, she sang up to the moldy rafters and made the particles of hair, skin, and earth rain down in dust. Her guttural call was something neither of them could discern—a life before Mississippi, a life harmonized by the continuity of brown boys fishing the African coast of the ocean, hunting in the sun and growing into men without the pain of whips. Their bellies stirred as her voice called in the words "amazing grace." Her tone resonated the dormant coding in their DNA. In that moment, time was held open, a portal between the Congo and the Delta, and the two of them bowed their heads. Stimulated by the loss of their father, they cried for the loss of their mother—Lenard's loss aligned with the stories in town that the near-white bitch stole from Genorette and fled, Bennie's loss forcing the two hemispheres of his brain to float away from each other: murderous, child.

The marine and the tall young man sat solitary on the church pew, having each made a pact to remember: tobacco blunt, mule whip, grace notes whispered in the random mouths of a congregation. But promises are hard to remember when the desire to survive overrides any other intentions.

That night Bennie sleepwalked through his dreams to find Lottie. He climbed into the dark, moldy windows of Mr. Genorette's tavern, set the mason jars of corn whiskey free from spiderwebs, wrapped the jarred medicine in his uniform shirts and stuffed it into the Marine-issued duffel bag along with her spirit that wrapped itself in the shirts, stowaway determined to see the imprisoned boy she nursed through to her version of grace.

After Old Deddy's burial, Bennie boarded the bus to St. Louis with Lenard. Got them out of Mississippi, to make a better life for both of them.

"I'm gonna pay for you to go to college. You got a good head on your shoulders."

"Where you gonna get the money for that?"

"Don't worry about it. I got the GI money, and you more fit

for schooling than I am," Bennie assured, doubting the GI Bill promise.

When the bus pulled into the station in St. Louis, Bennie tried to keep his eyes normal sized, not wide and curious looking. He and Lenard walked along the crowds going against the flow, the sound of trains clacking over tracks, buses spewing fumes outside the floor-to-ceiling windows. Lenard shouted, "Hello!" His voice bounced off marble floors and walls, and Bennie glared at his grinning face the way Old Deddy might: "Fool, hush!"

When the two of them emerged into the electric lights of the place, Bennie's chest opened up; large columns, something about the way they supported the massive arched ceiling, and he smelled the dry factory air that had wafted out of the package James sent to Mississippi for Bennie's eighteenth birthday. The top of his head tingled with hopefulness in the spot that was already going slightly thin. He took the smell of the bus fumes into his lungs, and he and Lenard walked out into the rainy city, he in uniform, Lenard in a light trench coat with sleeves just short enough to show he was not yet a man, though he was Bennie's height.

There were Negroes and whites in overcoats, and Bennie wondered, as he had once wondered about James, how they could afford such things, and he did something he hadn't done since he was a little boy. He giggled, because he knew he had survived what seemed unsurvivable.

The first chunk of what Bennie saved from his military pay was spent to set the two of them up in a little apartment above Sara Lou's, the Negro-woman-owned fried-shrimp and french-fry place. Picnic tables in the backyard, where music wafted up from a hi-fi along with joyful sounds of the good life of other folks who had come up from the South, who worked the factory by day and stopped by for their meal and some good conversation with community. That day, the two of them climbed the steep wooden steps that led to their apartment, and Sara herself yelled back at their smiling, just-up-from-Mississippi faces, "Y'all come back down here for ya first meal free on ya landlord."

"Yes, ma'am," and they hurried to pack their things away in the closets with peeling wallpaper that promised to nurture them both.

Bennie tucked the stowaway spirit and the mason jars of whiskey in the chest of drawers, but first he took a sip to soothe his nerves and poured some in his flask before heading out to find James, who it seemed everybody on the west side knew. Bennie took another sip to count out the remainder of his money, tucked a roll of bills for Lenard's tuition at Stowe Teachers College. When he counted what was left, he figured with two months' rent up front he'd have enough for another month but would need a job. He took another sip that made him more at ease about the money and another to numb the emotions of going out to visit the brother who had left him behind years ago.

With the orange dust of Mississippi coating their worn leather shoes, they entered James's tavern to the disappointment that shone in his eyes—fear that his two Mississippi kin had traversed the mountains and crossed the river into the calm of his life, bringing with them the memory of his own days of being called nigger rather than sir, of the whippings he escaped from the man who he held no remorse for and had spent years undoing any resemblance to. The sight of their boyhood eyes set into the faces of men brought back memories of his own sinful hands turned praying hands.

Lottie was singing one morning. She and James, thirteen years old and rivaling like jealous siblings, both hating and wanting Old Deddy's attention. Lottie scrubbed up and down on the washboard, her song offering that part of her soul that could find happiness wherever it abided—in the smell of spring on a sunny morning because, though the trees were in bloom, it was still crisp and chilly. James watched her from the back porch door, annoyed at how loud she was.

Stitch them quilt squares in the row
Drop the whipstitch, drop the hoe
Turn 'round Suzy, don't ya know
I ain't got no chains no mo

Gonna take ya by the hand
Drop that stitch, turn back the land
When the man say round and round
I'm gone spin you out of town

James stood there with the old dirty shirt he wore every day to do the field work, his hair cut off crooked, but as black and curly as Lottie's. He spit off the porch, half-smiling, half-mean, hoping to show himself more man than boy. "What you singin. Old Deddy don't like no singin. Don't let him get back for his breakfast after his first plowin and find you ain't got no biscuits on the table and still washin on these clothes and singin."

She rolled her eyes and sang the next verse to let him know he don't tell her what to do. "I'm the woman of the house!" and she turned her back to him.

Round and round and back again
Suzy spin around the mens
When they holler dosey doe
Don't you pay no mind no mo

She shot him a look like the bull when he was sick of being prodded, and James turned back around to the house and came back with his hand in a fist. He walked up to the washtub, frost coming from his breath, and said, just like Old Deddy, "Heifer, watch yo damn mouth!" And instead of smacking her, he threw a hand full of the biscuit flour in her face and made himself laugh, because it was better than admitting that some part of himself startled at the reality of Old Deddy's ways showing up in his hands. It was the first time he wanted to run away but didn't know where to go except around and around in his own mind. He coughed in the cloud of flour, straightened himself up, and ran off to help Old Deddy in the field. "Have the damn biscuits done when we get back."

She found her own ways to set James straight. Sometimes she'd put her cigarette in the chair where he was about to sit, then apologize when he burned his ass. It stayed like that for years, until the fistfight when the two of them were just older than eighteen.

The old preacher came to talk to James while Lottie and her Boy Bennie sat on the porch. It was late on a Sunday after church, and he made the rounds to men like James, who didn't attend but clearly sought salvation. The preacher stood there with one raggedy shoe up on the porch, the other planted firmly on the ground, like a swamp egret fishing for tadpoles. With the Bible in his hand, he told James, "God say man is the ruler, but don't never hit no woman."

Lottie pretended to ignore him and touched the little bulge of her pregnant belly under her dress. She threatened to expose her breast as she snatched at Bennie with the other hand. Under her breath she mumbled, "Bible say one thing, but the men of my house got they own crooked way of dealin with women."

Then she said out loud, shooting James a sideways look, "You cain't spect people to look up to you just cause you read the Bible and don't never hit no woman." Lottie was good at having the last word, of saying only what needed to be said, but just enough to give the men something to think about for days to come.

One night, James, who was as big as a house now, decided to go to the swamp-bottom tavern that Old Deddy wouldn't never let Lottie go to.

That night, she put Bennie down after she cut his hair. She walked ten paces behind James. Every time he stopped to see if he was just hearing his own feet crunching on the ground in the dark or if somebody was following him, she stopped and hid behind a tree.

The yellow lights hung on the deck. The springtime frogs sang, and the moss hung in the trees. It was the best music Lottie had ever heard, the piano and the washtub bass, a man playing the harmonica. Dressed in a smock dress that resembled a potato sack, she followed James right into the place. Everyone looked at the country barefoot pregnant woman and let out a cackle right along with the piano man, who struck up the laughter by playing faster.

Lottie didn't care. She took the invitation of the music to be free and cut up like she hadn't done since she was a girl and her Papa would say, "May, don't let the girl dance like that, talk so much like that, runs these boys like she the boss."

Lottie stomped up the good-time blues, and James came to

the edge of the circle to see who was making such a spectacle. He grabbed hold of her arm. "What the hell you doin! Old Deddy gonna kill yo ass. Then he gonna kill my ass. Get outta here!" And he pushed her.

She yelled back, "Preacher told you don't never hit no woman!" And she knew she had the right-a-way, and she balled up her high-yellow fist and punched him. The music stopped, because damned if he didn't punch her back.

That was the first time she'd ever seen Mr. Genorette. She heard his footsteps first, and the crowd parted like Moses was coming down from the mountain with the Word. She and James stood there looking like they were children cut from the same cloth, and Mr. Genorette looking like a cleaned-up young Old Deddy. He didn't stagger his movements when he walloped James on the back, knocking him to the floor. Then Mr. Genorette kicked him in the good pants seat of his good overalls, and the whole place laughed up to the rafters like they were watching a traveling buffoonery show, and that was that.

Mr. Generotte told Lottie, "You can come around here any time, honey, and I'll make sure you treated right." He said to James, "Tell ya Deddy, and I'll kill ya ass," which was the same as saying, "I'm the man of this house and yo house."

The next morning, James packed up his Bible and shirts and overalls and was gone to St. Louis. Little Bennie looked at him as if somebody stole food right out of his mouth on his hungriest day. James looked back at Bennie, paused at the last sight of the round head of his baby brother, and put both booted feet out the window.

Lenard came into the light off Delmar Avenue with the whites of his eyes still white, seeking, and James imprinted the energies of his best efforts onto the one he saw first. Bennie stumbled in behind Lenard with his eyes yellowed, the way that the liver and kidneys stop up and hold the worst of the body's truths. Yellowed, like Old Deddy's eyes that had stayed anonymous in James's memory until Bennie, looking more like Old Deddy than Lenard, crossed into James's life like an unwelcome ghost.

Tuesday evening was James's night off. He had planned to go to prayer meeting, pray on it, and have a plan for how he was going to handle the kin who would surely cross the threshold any day now and bring with them the chaos of Mississippi.

James wiped the bar down, poured a shot of bourbon into Bennie's outstretched shot glass with the other hand, and did not allow emotions to enter in the place where he stood the owner of his life. James held the movement in the pit of his belly still at the memory of a sad-faced little brother and the thought of the hard-dead face of the father who was supposed to protect him, provide for him, but instead set him to craft survival out of a life of disciplined emotions.

"The first order of business is church." Bennie had already taken to a flask in his pocket and drained the thing as he and Lenard walked up Delmar from Union Station to catch the bus that let them out at the door of Lee's Wagon Wheel Tavern. Bennie had already turned up the one shot of bourbon offered him and filled the glass twice on his own. He smirked and then laughed out of sync with what his older brother said. His laughter sent a light spray of bourbon across the bar, and Lenard let out a stressed giggle.

"Quit being ignorant." James had little patience for such country behavior and yelled for the barmaid, "Mary, fill the ice cooler. Yeah?" Every sentence ended in "Yeah," and there was no guttural twist of a Mississippi accent in his voice. James was far removed from the fields, no dirt beneath his nails. He had slipped away from Mississippi and slipped through the eye of the needle of war.

Bennie slapped the bar in laughter that did not reflect the stress of their reunion or the maturity of his six-foot height and 180 pounds, his slender but muscular build. He was on his fourth bourbon when James took his glass from the bar and dropped it in the sudsy water.

"You're not drinking any more in here today, but you two are welcome to help out." Lenard straightened himself to follow the brother who was a stranger yet a familiar, longed-for reflection of his own emerging manhood.

The smells of the truck fumes backing up in the alley sent James, with Lenard following, beyond the dark swinging doors to the kitchen, and they emerged each carrying a box of Smirnoff bottles.

"I'm here for the women," Bennie slurred and slapped the top of the box Lenard held.

"Man, stop!" Lenard stumbled and laughed as if they were still boys tossing mud wads at each other down at the pond.

Then, like a little boy realizing he had to pee, Bennie slurred, "Let me hit the head, man."

When Bennie disappeared to the toilet, James put down the last box and pointed Lenard to a table. Lenard smiled and wiped his nose, "Can I have a drink, too?"—still in the clowning mood set by Bennie.

James looked at him stern. "Sit down, man."

He pulled two chairs away from a table; the scooting sound brought Lenard into the mood of James's urgency. "Look, man.

Stop following Bennie's lead. Where he's at, he's got to pull himself out of that hell after war, but you ain't got to go to hell with him." James repeated what the old preacher tried to teach him in the days before he left Mississippi with broken Bible quotes and front-porch wisdom: "Some men can turn themselves around when their life is shit, and some just cain't."

Lenard's eyes flattened out from smiling. James leaned over and put his hand on Lenard's shoulder to pull his brother out toward the light, though all around them was the dimness in the cave of the tavern. "Come with me to prayer meeting." This was James's solution for which one to save, and how.

That night James scolded Lenard, "Just read the words, man." He pointed his thick finger in the hymnal for Lenard. Had told him on the way there not to write himself off as ignorant but to hold his eyes toward the best ways of entrepreneurship, education, and religion, and away from his brother who was still sitting at the bar while the two of them were at James's regular Tuesday night prayer meeting. Lenard asked, "What about Bennie? Aren't we gonna wait for him?"

"No, he's at where he's at."

James had arrived in St. Louis eighteen years ahead of his brothers, in late spring 1935, after a long bus ride that took him through towns where he hoped to remain invisible on the back of the bus. It was a ride that offered a day of mountain passes where the road beneath the bus was not visible. He could see only the edge and the beautiful, deadly fall to the treetops in the valley below. Once they reached the flat expanse of Illinois, excitement and fear caused him to press his face to the smudged window. It didn't matter that there was no more orange earth, that the smell of oil and the clanking of hammering and the sight of industrial cranes took away the memory of long-legged white Mississippi swamp cranes. He didn't pay any of that any mind. He pinched his chin, thinking how he was ready to bring it, the way Bessie Smith said bring it, beg it, borrow it, steal it. When he got to Union Station, he had already listened to conversations on the back of the bus about where to get a good tripe sandwich. "Is that right, man? Can I come with y'all to get a bite and figure myself for a place to stay?"

"Sho nuf, man, but first thing you are going to have to do is get rid of that country talking from your gut and talk from the front of your mouth." They giggled and said, "Man, man, you are going to love it up here."

He ended up at the same place where the Black voices on the bus later sent Lenard and Bennie, to Sara Lou's. Sara Lou's mama, Big Sara, first owned the place. She had kicked the father out on his ass, opened up the three-family flat as a rooming house, and was cooking up a storm with little Sara Lou old enough to help fry and fetch. Her naps were braided and pinned down, stockings pulled up to keep her ten-year-old long legs from getting cold every time she climbed the back stairs, knocked, and sat a hot meal plate at a boarder's door. James was one of those boarders, and he took Big Sara's advice to go down to old Mr. Drake, who owned the best Black-folk tavern, for a job, then go down to the church on Sunday with everybody else to keep his soul straight with God and meet all the other folk who had come up from Mississippi.

"Don't be no hobo," Mr. Drake told him. "Don't be sorry to have left that place." Mr. Drake groomed young James: "Get rid of them suspenders. Hold your head up. Memphis and Sampson and all them places is good for the food we have and the music we have and the church-bell worship we have, but leave the rest where it is." Mr. Drake dropped wisdom every time he and James carted a crate of whiskey, half of it moonshine, from the wagon in the alley to the place where it stayed hidden beneath the wooden case under the counter where the shotgun was kept.

"Up here," Mr. Drake said, "up here, when somebody do wrong they take you to jail, no questions asked. So, talk to every Negro like you respect them but like you will put yo foot up they ass if they cross you. That way, you'll get folks all around you that will keep you from the prison cell." Mr. Drake said, "Go to church. Shave. You a big man, so walk like you a big man, not like some boy somebody been had the whip on. Show up every time, same time, be counted on. And most of all don't follow the lead of no man who don't earn yo respect. Only follow the lead of men who earn yo follow'n."

James did as he was taught, and Mr. Drake passed on and the tavern passed hands to the young man who never walked away, the man who held prayer meeting over Mr. Drake's deathbed the way a son would have. Mr. Drake collected the seeds of James's young life and claimed him as his son. James, the man people knew to come to, came into view. Mississippi shadows faded away until his brothers came walking through the door, reminding him of who his real father was.

The next night, while Bennie was still out asking about work by checking out all of the corner taverns and having at least one drink at each bar, James and Lenard climbed the back steps to Bennie and Lenard's West St. Louis apartment and retrieved Lenard's meager belongings.

Two weeks later, James spent their third prayer meeting together guiding Lenard into the arms of God. Bennie sat in his apartment above the restaurant alone. For those two weeks he had endured what he called shitty silence. "That's some hypocritical shit! Muthafucka's stocking a bar by day and praising the Lord at night. Fuck you! And fuck you!" He yelled out into the apartment.

That night Bennie fell into fitful dreams. James and Lenard were little boys but in their grown-men bodies stood in front of the old schoolhouse taunting, "You ain't got no mama. You ain't got no mama." Bennie woke with little-boy tears on his grown-man face.

He packed the same Marine-issued green duffel bag. "I'm paying for his fucking college and he following that highfalutin asshole?" He punched his clothes down into the bag and stashed the spirit, his hurt, and the new bottles of bourbon stolen from behind James's bar between them. "Fuck these muthafuckas."

He stood in Union Station not sure where he wanted to go.

Her spirit pulled at the liquor bottle each time he reached for a sip. She wanted to tell him that his earth is made of red clay and with it he can build home and have whatever he needs, that everybody ain't made for the land of promises. For some, it is a trap to try and get what they got, rather than to reclaim what is homespun.

She wanted to tell him that he does got a mama. That it is alright, that the grave is not cold and lonely, that his sins lie there and decompose into food for the knots at the end of the turnips he will eat with vinegar when he gets home. That murder is not the end of the story, that wickedness can be bloodlet and through testimony called back to life as freedom.

Reversing the curse of "Mississippi be damned," Bennie boarded the bus crossing back over the Mississippi River meridian eastbound, first to Louisville, Kentucky, where he was kicked out of a club by the seat of his pants in much the same way he had been kicked out of Genorette's tavern. The owner was apologetic that Bennie, like so many others, didn't fare well after the war, but he wasn't about to let his fellow Negro vets mess up what he was able to establish for himself as a Negro businessman. Bennie caught a bus to Virginia Beach, where he hoped to find employment and decent nightlife around Camp Pendleton. In a Negro-owned club along the strip, he started up about killing the gooks and fucking yellow women until a young Negro Navy ensign spoke up: "Shut up, you lying country motherfucker."

Bennie heard the voice of Old Deddy: "No good muthafucka." Heard the indecipherable words of Korean women singing chaotic cries over the bodies of their dead, sounds that only running and drinking could silence. He made a fist to punch back the pain and beat the young Negro Navy ensign within an inch of his life. With a mob of brown ensigns threatening to kill Bennie and the subconscious pleas of the spirit in his head, he took two buses against the flow of migration and went homeward, south. Not south so deep that the bones of Black bodies curdle swamp sulfur and boardwalks are built for the comfort of evening strolls. But just south enough that the familiar of fishing creeks, bamboo, and nappy green trees could soothe his soul back to some innate jungle before brown skin was hunted. He traveled the seven hours in his dress blues to earn the respect, the nods, and sometimes the sweet glances of young brown girls who hoped to marry a marine from Fort Bragg.

SIX

Fayetteville, North Carolina
1954

She wished he could hear her in the wind, the sound of her whisper in his ear calling him to speak, not just the words to put a shine on the lackluster of his pain, but the sin of his story, in order to give way to the sun. Then to Love.

His transistor radio, a one-man Styrofoam cooler with ice for the fish he would catch and for the beer. The sound of the release of cold mist from the pop-top can of a cool one. The taste of the liquid barley of some distant field on the back of his tongue. Home was inside of moments like this. Ray Charles, singing his wishes, "I got a woman, that's good to me," offering that bopping, finger-snapping, heat and sardines and sun and fishing good solitude. Ice making the cool beer go down over the tongue, like sun melting snow off the top of the mountain and sending it down into the mellow stream in the valley. Positive ions that rose up from the rushing creek to the bottom of his booted feet on the bridge. Fishing, his hand on the bamboo pole, the nylon line from the pole into the flesh of the water. This was his church. He was connected to everything, and he was calm.

His first days as an auto mechanic at a Texaco station near Fort Bragg made him feel like a man again. He rented a trailer, shaved, scrubbed himself clean every morning, and was grateful that the respect for his military service had followed him to North Carolina without his civilian arrest record. "James, Lenard, Old Deddy, Yudam-ni, fuck 'em all!" And he proceeded to start a new life, with his childhood truths along for the ride, dormant in his body.

Each day before leaving work, he changed out of his grease monkey gray jumpsuit and into the polo shirt and the slacks he neatly rolled, military style, and stuck in his locker at the beginning of the workday. The bus from the base let him off on Ramsey Street, where he proudly walked into the corner store for a pack of Kools, a pound of sliced bologna, a loaf of Wonder Bread, a few cans of sardines, and a six-pack of Michelob.

Two young women leaned off their porch, girls who had no business looking backward toward the wayward boys from the bottom. Rebecca and her sister Beverly were eighteen and nineteen, but their father treated them like twins. They were both caramel brown, Rebecca with a narrow playful smile, Beverly with a broader, more knowing smile. Bennie noticed Rebecca, not her sister. Rebecca wore a familiar cornflower-blue sleeveless cotton dress that when worn to church was worn with a shawl. "Where yo deddy at, gal?" Bennie called up to her and flicked his half-smoked Kool into the craggy weeds that grew along the cracked sidewalk of Colonial Drive.

"My deddy ain't here. Why? You wanna come up here and talk with us for a while?" She giggled, and her older sister Beverly giggled less enthusiastically. Their father, Thomas Jemison, was an independent man, spent his days digging wells and pumping septic tanks for new houses in Fayetteville and served his church by digging graves for the members laid to rest. Having been denied a veteran's loan to buy his house, he dug enough shitholes and grave holes to buy the dilapidated thing outright. His girls were destined for Fayetteville State Teachers College. He would have beat Bennie or any other grease monkey within an inch of his life if he saw one of them flirting with his daughters. A church-going military vet like himself for either of his daughters, maybe. The likes of Bennie, never.

Bennie giggled, put his hand in his pocket, and threw Rebecca something. A shell he had retrieved the day he caught the bus to Virginia Beach and walked the beach until sunset, letting the waves and the tide leach his pain away just before a night of drinking and hell-raising.

Rebecca caught it. "Man, what this supposed to be, an engagement rock?" She and Beverly giggled, and he walked on whistling, one hand in his pocket, one arm hugging the brown paper sack, telling himself he was gonna get that gal. *Let James and Lenard praise the Lord. I'm fixin to have the life cain't no Negro man have in Mississippi or St. Louis.*

Rebecca played the piano every Sunday at the Baptist church on the corner of Ramsey and Colonial. "Hold on to your girls," Reverend Boller preached, as if his round, sweaty brown face could sense the unhealed men returned from Korea to cast shadows on the faces of the young women of his congregation. "Hold on to your girls," he preached to their mothers and fathers. He wiped his face with his handkerchief, and Rebecca was not listening as she played "Walk the Streets of Glory" gently on the piano, gently behind his words as if she were playing a love song. She daydreamed of standing before the pulpit with the tall marine she saw each day. Somewhere in her heart, she knew he was a distorted version of himself, but there is a way that the dark potholes of the heart long to be filled with more darkness, black asphalt craving gravel and tar.

From that same pulpit Reverend Boller preached, "Hold on to your daughters, Brother Jemison," on the day the girls sat six and seven years old on either side of their father and cried into his lapel. Their mother's face caked in the wrong shade of brown makeup crested above the varnished pine casket that would soon be set into the hole dug deeper than the other holes dug by their father's own hands, deep to keep the tuberculosis from leaching out of the cloth of her lungs and into the community. Rebecca played that piano smiling, imagining her life as Mrs. Bennie, Mrs. Benjamin Lee.

The next day began as every workweek did on Colonial Drive. The sun rose over the creek at the bottom of the neighborhood. The kids, tiny and brown, and tall teenagers with promise or worry in their step walked the newly asphalted road to Ramsey Street, where they crossed over and banked left or right depending on their grade level. Their parents, most of them head of household, solo in rearing the children, kissed the hand of an elder being left behind or fed the scraps to the dog and headed out to their domestic or agricultural jobs. Their steps were quick because their choice was to be either broke and regretful, or hopeful and looking in the direction where prosperity is hoed one row of the earth at a time.

That Monday morning, Thomas Jemison's earth-soiled hands held the round globe of the backhoe knobs in his palms. He pushed and pulled and did not let the muscle tension in his chest act as warning or deter him. He was independent, had two teenage girls to send to college. If he didn't do it, it didn't get done. But the cycle of the rising and setting sun and the twenty-eight days of the moon don't know any better than to give life and drag it back with the next tide. His heart arrested, and he fell headfirst into the shallow hole he'd dug to put in a new septic system for their neighbor.

Two months after Thomas Jemison's funeral, Rebecca and Beverly, who were two weeks from going to Fayetteville State Teachers College, sat with pad and pencil on the porch shielded by the neighbor's high tobacco leaves. Beverly wore her sister's bright-yellow dress, which made her stand out more than she liked. Neither of them had time to do laundry with all of the grieving and worrying that needed to be done. Beverly did the figures to see if her and her sister as the heirs to the property had enough workforce between the two of them to pay the taxes on the place. Rebecca did the figures to see if she could catch the half-drunk marine as he passed by, sweat drenched, fingers still with blackness from changing oil. Both were desperate to rescue their home from auction for unpaid taxes.

Sometimes survivors of war work hard not to provoke the devil. Thomas Jemison spent his whole adult life perfecting the strategy of "do not provoke," but his death awakened red-faced devils who had long since convinced themselves that it was honorable to their ancestors if they stole back the land their fathers once stole. The death of a Black landowner was the same as the megaphone the Chinese major used to shout over the fields demanding that his soldiers rise out of their camouflaged foxholes.

That day, a dry wind blew through the streets of Fayetteville. It was in the diesel exhaust of the bus that kissed the hairs on Bennie's arm. It was in the life that danced in the crumpled tiny oak leaves that swirled as he passed them on the sidewalk. "Go home," it warned, but he did not hurry home past Rebecca and

Beverly's porch and to his rusted trailer down near the tangled vines of the creek bottom. Instead, he tried to silence the voice by walking into a backdoor bar that opened in the alleyway behind the corner store. "Go home!" he heard the voice again and forced himself to focus where he stood, in the dank back room of the bar where he purchased the new white dusty drug, laced onto the marijuana cigarettes they rolled especially for marines.

He leaned away from the looming voice and into a relief of colors, the turquoise of the lights in the sky above the pond just before dawn. As his high lifted, he saw blue and black like dragonflies' wings and the black tendrils of his mother's hair. All the while, the sisters sat figuring on their fate.

At the top of Colonial Drive, where Ramsey Street rushed with cars that veiled the inhabitants at the bottom from being witnessed, sat three white men, who had already purchased and begun to develop everything on the other side of Ramsey Street. Their pillowcase heads were framed by the windows of the cream-and-red two-toned Chevy whose oil and tires Bennie had changed the day before. A deep chord, the same one that resounded from the hammered half-rusted strings inside the chest of the piano to their right resounded in the new red-brick white Southern Baptist church at their backs. In the stained glass reflection of Reverend Boller's misplaced omen for holding on to daughters, the hooded-driver let out the clutch.

Earlier that day, they had sat in the white barbershop perking their ears at the talk of the Jemison property going into probate. With Ramsey Street rushing at their backs, they leaned forward, their breath audible inside the off-white pillowcases as they rolled down Colonial Drive. They approached the clapboard house with the two brown women, one in yellow, one in black. They leaned out, shouted, "Nigger bitches!" and shot twice. Porches cleared behind slamming screen doors. Their tires screeched and turned at the bottom. The bullets spun side by side, chasing toward the sisters. The force that was the spirit stood at a fork in the road and wailed as she chose the host for the girl-spirit, the host for the new baby of the family. One bullet went directly into Beverly's heart—her yellow dress the easiest to sight for a moving assailant. From yellow to red, color burst out onto her chest. The other bullet changed course on the force of a spirit-driven wind, shattered the glass and entered the living room.

Rebecca rocked her sister's limp body and hollered, "Deddy!?," as the growling motor of the Chevy stopped, spewing smoke from Bennie's botched oil change. The driver, the bystander, and the shooter who plucked the life from one heir, missing the other, then sped across Ramsey. Like their ancestors, they set in motion the reversal of morning and midnight in the hearts and minds of children twisting in the energy inside the cracked gourd of their home.

Bennie proceeded down Colonial Drive in time to find Beverly lifeless, in time for his high to dissolve just enough for him to hold her in his arms, and yell out, "Medic, medic!" as if he was holding a marine buddy on the frozen mountain, half out of his mind, holding on to her like a comrade who would bleed out long before they were found.

That summer, he and Rebecca held hands before Reverend Boller, whose eyes held sorrow for his flock, for whom doors never opened. He sucked in his lips and read the words to unite the two wounded halves.

Three days before the Fourth of July, one day before the house went into probate, with nothing in their pockets but dried tobacco-leaf crumbs and the crumpled handwritten coordinates of Thomas Jemison's grave, they caught the bus to the courthouse and paid the taxes using Texaco wages and the church's collection plate.

The dreams of rock shards from the frostbitten mountain slicing into his foot ceased. The tactile dream of something pressing on his chest until he couldn't breathe, and then realizing he was being buried alive, ceased. The lights came on in his heart, and he emerged from the underground. Neither of them knew that their love was remission from grief.

For a while, out of habit, he went to the PCP-laced marijuana, thinking, *Don't I need that?* Then he just forgot about the drug, smoked his Kools, had a beer or two like any man. His eyes cleared, his beard came in just so, and he cut it and kept it neat, and in those days, he could feel the muscles around the tall skeletal frame of his body, could feel himself carrying himself, felt proud and whole like somebody resurrected.

In the gestation time of the new life that grew in Rebecca's womb, he assumed the past could not reach him where he was tucked in the Atlantic coast elbow of the South with his new wife. Head of a house with taxes paid and a child on the way. The serpents that floated above his head like electric currents interfering with his brain signals dissipated.

Love was when Rebecca held him, and his body remembered something, then his mind remembered, then his heart remembered—the touch of his mother's knees on his shoulders, the comfort that was interrupted by the cowhide whip that had torn the flesh of both of them.

Love was when Rebecca held him. With his touch she came back from the edge of grief, that point where grief can take you dizzy to the edge of water, can make you forget the sensations of the living and not feel the cold or the sting of water in your lungs. When she held him, she knew that she would not walk off, following her father into death. Without her father there, Bennie's smell of musk and the just-enough roughness of his calloused hands that tried hard to pull himself forward by the roots comforted her.

Comforted, unless they were getting on each other's nerves with their askew longings for the ones who left them.

"Why can't you just remember to put out the damned trash?"

"Why can't you quit nagging me long enough for me to have just a minute to myself?"

"Nigga, ain't nobody nagging you. What do you have to think about when all you do is change the oil on cars?"

"What you have to think about that make you think you better than me? Don't no nigga out there want your scrawny ass besides me."

Then the silence between them that neither of them could endure. Then the promises that neither of them was designed to keep: I am the intelligent, learned Black man that you want; I am the Black, devoted housewife that you want. Then the shattering of their intense longing by holding and suspending their lives in orgasm until the first seed was fertilized.

The spirit lay down in the sun inside the raindrops that fell outside their window when they made love. She exhaled in satisfaction the way a mother who thinks maybe her tears can cease exhales, believing that maybe her waiting has borne fruit.

And then, the feisty dark-skinned delivery nurse at the county hospital wiped the blood and mucus from the baby's body and cussed over the baby's head, "Lord God Jesus in heaven. This town don't need no more Black boys." When Rebecca and Bennie returned home with the little soul, the walls leaned in to behold the child, as if the walls were all of the grandmothers who ever leaned over the crib to behold who might carry forward their work and their Word.

Two months after Benjamin Junior was born, Bennie donned his black hat on Sunday morning: "Told ya it was gonna be a boy." He bragged, "This my li'l nigga." And Rebecca didn't go against him, even though in her head she sassed, *Nigga, you didn't know shit.*

Bennie and Rebecca took their newborn B.J. in knitted blue hat and knitted blue sweater and booties to do like the Catholics. Rebecca asked Reverend Boller not to wait for the child to consent but to splash him in the baptismal waters of the holy soon after his soul entered this world.

Bennie saw himself in the reflected mirror above the pulpit—hat off, blue suit, white shirt. Rebecca in her pink dress and white jacket and small white hat with mesh. He saw his baby boy, a delicate bundle of blue flowers in her arms. The reverend hunched over them in a black robe, his body round and stout. Bennie felt. He felt the Yudam-ni Mountain thaw, felt Old Deddy's whip welts on his chest that crossed over his heart like barbed wire, flattened out from their raised scarring. "In the name of the Father, the Son, and the Holy Spirit"—a chant that called forward a spirit that could hold their son in this life.

Spring outside the church that morning was as it was most spring mornings, sun and rain showers and the bright-green, new leaves and fuchsia dogwood blooms. Bennie smelled the dampness of rain on the concrete that hissed under the tires of the cars on Ramsey Street. He filled his chest with the full expanse of loblolly pine pollen that gently scrubbed away the rust of napalm in his lungs. He felt love, and it was strange for him, but he was happy.

And the spirit rested, because she remembered that freedom is best sought with companionship, but forgot that if freedom is disguised, both are headed toward hell. She forgot that if she rested, not remembering that Black mothers must remain vigilant to the shape-shifting of the evil inside their children, the evil born out of a belief that escape and freedom are not options, then the lacerations, bullet wounds, and rope burns that she hopes to save them from, float like omens in the arch of their happiness.

PART TWO

The Son

SEVEN

Fayetteville, North Carolina
1960

Before divinity can be born, there must first be the birth of the protector of that divinity. "Will you harbor me? All that I am, all that I came to do?" And when the answer is yes, it is a whole life, a holy, divine pact.

On B.J.'s sixth birthday, Rebecca paced around in the kitchen before dawn making sandwiches. Her house shoes hushed on the linoleum that could use a good sweeping. B.J. followed her whispering, because she told him to whisper and let Bennie sleep. "Mama, how far to the beach? Is it like a big ole fishing hole?"

"Shh, hush now."

"Is Dad gonna fish?"

"Boy, I said hush."

In the next room, Bennie's long, dark legs turned and turned in the covers like black chopsticks twisting noodles. By the time the sun heated up the kitchen, B.J. knew it was too late to make it to the beach. He sat on the back steps listening to the neighbor girl, Mr. Tunnelson's daughter, Sheila, who visited her father only in the summer. She sang with her voice free—about what, he didn't know—but the summer wind blew through the leaves bringing the heat and boredom, and he wanted to play with her.

Rebecca said, "No going up in neighbor's houses," so he had to wait and see if she appeared between Mr. Tunnelson's tobacco leaves.

When he saw the two fuzzy Afro balls of his friend's dad-made hairdo, he left the sound of his mama churning the rock salt around with the ice chips to make his birthday ice cream. Chubby legs in cut-off shorts, he took off after her, and the two ran off into the sweaty, fly- and mosquito-filled fun that only six-year-olds can find inside the stifling mornings of a southern July.

In Mr. Tunnelson's urban tobacco field, they ran up and down the long rows making what Sheila called wild jungle noises. Sounds her father let her make, but noise Bennie didn't tolerate in his house, especially when he was napping, noise that might wake in him a whuppin for Rebecca and B.J., as if they were his to whip. He and Sheila's hollering sounds got louder every time they reached the end of a row and let their bodies crash against the chain-link fence of B.J.'s backyard. Fun that made his chest heave with laughter to clear the baby mucus that was still lodged there since his birth.

When Bennie woke, it was too late for him to take B.J. and Rebecca to the beach, but he took B.J. half a mile down across the railroad tracks to the wider fishing current of the Cape Fear River. His goal was to be still and quiet with a pole stuck in the water, to watch the murk stream by and listen to nothing, fishing. It was the only thing other than the brown liquor and the PCP-laced joint that could bring him down and even him out. He had his transistor radio, antenna stuck up, ready to listen to the ball game. He wanted the boy to have some fun but had cordoned off his heart to keep his junior or anybody else from disturbing the only space where he wasn't having to hold and bear and keep back the demons in his head. The raggedy red cooler with its six-pack, ice, and fish bait sat on the bridge and made a home away from home. The only patch of shade was made by a maple that reached for the bridge as if its duty was to make a canopy for him. And on the concrete of the bridge with his welted legs dangling over was his junior.

Bennie gave B.J. a good switch'n before leaving the house, to show him what was coming if he didn't behave, meaning sit quietly and fish. He gave Rebecca the same switch'n before B.J. came in the house: "It's yo damned fault he don't behave. Don't nobody want a woman who cain't make her kids act right."

The switch'n would make Rebecca think twice about looking sideways at another man, while the switch'n let B.J. know his father would buy him a box of Popsicles if he was still, but another switch'n is what either of them would get if they disturbed his peace again. In Bennie's head, he conveyed to his son that these were the times that he and his little brother Lenard enjoyed, time away from Old Deddy to get some peace, but instead Bennie defended his peace and said what he said after the switch'n, "Fish'n is for men to be quiet, not for a bunch of pussy ass complaining," and wished B.J., "Happy birthday, li'l nigga. Let's go."

Before the two of them headed off, Rebecca rubbed peroxide on B.J. where the welts from the whipping started to emerge in the brown sweat of his little legs. B.J., not knowing any better, appreciated his mama's soothing and his deddy's aggressive attention as a treat. Rebecca soothed and cooed because that was the first day that she would see them off and seek a way out of her misery.

On the first day of school, B.J. didn't ask his mother where she had been. When he opened the screen door he ran through the kitchen, where not even her smell of bacon grease and rose water perfume lingered. "Mama!" He ran into their bedroom, but nothing. The house expanded around him as the walls and ceiling of the J.C. Penney had on what had started out to be the best day. The week before, he and Rebecca went down on Hayes Street dressed in their Sunday best to shop for his first day of school. All he could think about was the excitement of dressing like the children who sat behind Buffalo Bob Smith on the *Howdy Doody* show; all Rebecca could think about was regaining a freedom she hadn't known since her teenage years. Rebecca dug through the discount bin to find the black denim pants and turtleneck.

He sat on the floor next to the department store bin making his two plastic G.I. Joes dance and sing, "Betcha goin' fishin' all yo time, baby goin' fishing too. Bet yo life, yo sweet life, I'm gonna catch mo fish than you." He didn't remember learning the song, but it was his favorite. Rebecca's brown stockinged legs, smell of rose water, and muffled voice in the bin were comfort, the same comfort as leaning against Bennie's leg on the fishing bridge or watching her legs move around the kitchen when he played under the table.

From inside the bin she asked, "What you singin, li'l man?"

"I'on't know," then he heard her voice lift out of the bin and talk with someone, "Hey, how you doin?" He felt the absence of Rebecca's legs. He stood up, "Mama?" but her Sunday tan flats worn down at the heel were gone, and so was she. The fluorescent lights came into view, the sound of the overhead piano music. He looked out beyond the bin into the store with all its people that expanded into a universe. He squeezed the plastic war toys in his fists and whined, "Mama," until he felt Rebecca's hand around his arm. "Boy, I was right there talking to a friend. You act like you been left in the jungle or something."

B.J. sat at their kitchen table wearing the turtleneck and black denim pants from the J.C. Penney bin, listening to the house. He kicked his legs and sang "Fishing Blues." He couldn't wait to tell Rebecca about his day at school, how he taught the other kids the song when they sat in the song circle. The sound of his own voice singing helped to keep the house small, helped to conjure the feeling of a whole circle of kids to help swallow the silence.

That was the first time B.J. heard the voice his father heard, telling him to "Run!" up the Yudam-ni Mountain away from the Chinese foot soldiers. It was a gentle voice that sang back, "Bet yo life, yo sweet life, gonna catch more fish than you." He sat there and let the spirit be, swung his feet like they were moving through the playful resistance of creek water. He sang back with his little lips pointed up to the kitchen ceiling, "Any fish bite if ya got good bait," and he waited, but there were upset footsteps on the back stairs and the spirit left him alone.

Rebecca came barreling through the screen door behind him like she had just missed a bus by seconds. "Hey, little man. Woo, sorry I'm a little late. Let's get the groceries put away and dinner on."

She was different. Her hair, which was usually on her head as two woolly cornrows tucked in at the bottom, was straight, her bangs whipped to the side. His tall, thin mama had turned into a tall, thin model.

B.J. stood up on the chair and looked over in the grocery bag, hoping to find a treat. He surveyed the stuff they could never afford to buy—a red slab of steak on white Styrofoam, a dozen eggs, cream for her coffee, and a box of Popsicles for him. Rather than being excited about all those extras, he asked about the regular groceries, "Where's Dad's beer? Where's the pork rinds?" Rebecca turned to look at her son and frowned. He was spoiling her mood, in the way her father spoiled her mood when she was a teenager being questioned: "Where have you been, young lady? I'm not going to ask you again." Only to have her older, more levelheaded sister, Beverly, answer, "I sent her to the store, but they didn't have any Crisco"—a lie to protect Rebecca, who walked back and forth to the corner store hoping to catch the eye of a marine.

The chair beneath B.J. wobbled and threatened to throw him to the floor where he stood unsteady in the gaze of his mother's strange attitude. He jumped down and caught the scent of someone else's sweat on her. A primal irritation caused him to whine and pout with each stomp to the living room, where he plopped his butt down on the floor to punctuate his upset. "I wanna watch *Howdy Doody*!" Rebecca stomped into the living room behind him and clicked the knob on the new TV. His chest indented the way the soft infant bones of his chest indented when he lay in the bed crying for her milk while she argued with Bennie. He couldn't hold back his feeling of being tired and lost from his mother and wailed out loud into the living room.

Rebecca grabbed him by his chubby arm, her perfectly polished nails almost puncturing his skin. She dragged him with her and clicked off the TV. "Shush! You hear me?! You want to watch TV? Then quit that damned cryin!" She stomped back to the kitchen, the heels of her feet thudded in the crawl space beneath them, bringing B.J.'s tears and inhales without exhales. She shoved a cherry Popsicle into his mouth. The paper down around the Popsicle stick caught the sugary treat and snot, which melted together. The muscles of his tongue and circle of his lips suckled the cold sugar and helped him breathe. "Now, sit still for the lessons like the good boys and girls behind Buffalo Bob."

By the time Clarabell the clown came with antics that made him laugh as if the living room was filled with other boys and girls, he forgot his mother was gone when he came home from school.

For the entire school week, B.J. walked home down Colonial Drive with other children, some older, some in first grade like him. They peeled off one by one. He peeled off before the last two siblings who walked all the way to the bottom of the neighborhood, where rusting trailers were camouflaged in weeds. He cupped his hands and peeped past the curled metal of the screen door before he came into the kitchen, wondering if his mother or her as the angry teenage girl was in there. Nobody was home.

He didn't know to pull up a chair and click on the kitchen light so the house didn't take on the dim late fall afternoon shadows. He just scooted the heavy plastic-and-metal kitchen chair over to the fridge, stood on tiptoe, and reached to get a Popsicle out of the back of the freezer, where Rebecca had pushed them past the cushion of growing frost to keep them away from the boy whose baby fat matured with him. He followed the last command she had given him days before and went to the living-room floor to stare at the TV. That was a Friday. Rebecca came home after his program, and their new normal evenings proceeded.

On Saturday morning, he woke to an empty house. Waking up to loneliness had never happened. Their bed was empty, with the covers tangled and smelling like their sweat. He went to the kitchen and felt his brain scramble and settle itself when he scooted his chair to the freezer, got the Popsicle, and stood lost in the kitchen soothing himself until he heard the sweet singing of the spirit coddle him and coax him to find a way out of his loneliness: "It's *Howdy Doody* time. It's *Howdy Doody* time." He went to the living room in the same way that he went to the rug when his teacher sang, "It's time for music. It's time for music." He forgot about the emptiness of the house when to his delight, on Saturday morning just like after school, he saw the smiling freckled face of that puppet that held him in suspended bliss. In living color with the peacock, except their TV showed only black and white and shades of gray.

Buffalo Bob came closer to the screen. He spoke to the boys and girls at home in more slow earnest words than usual: "Hi, boys and girls. Well, kids, this is our 2,343rd *Howdy Doody* show." B.J. stopped sucking the Popsicle and scooted on the butt of his flannel pajamas to get closer to the TV. "And kids, it's also our last *Howdy Doody* show." B.J. understood *last*. At school they learned *first*, *middle*, and *last*. After *last*, there is nothing.

He sat even closer to the TV, closer than he was allowed, and watched the whole extra-long, one-hour episode, savoring it the way he savored the Popsicle that puddled in the paper. He lapped at the syrupy sweet slowly as he watched even the commercials about Honey Wheat Flakes that usually caused him to fidget and whine.

The fan on the windowsill picked up speed, picked up its hum, and lulled him. In that space just before his eyes fluttered shut, he heard the sweet spirit sing him "Fishing Blues."

He waved his hand at the air of the living room that was shifting from cool southern fall morning to stifling hot afternoon. B.J. pouted, "Stop, leave me alone," like any child missing his mother while somebody tried to distract him with play. He wanted things back how they were, even though there had been bruised and welted skin. In his little-boy understanding, his mother was messing up the family, and he didn't want to smell someone else's sweat on her hands, didn't like her new hair and painted nails.

Rebecca came clapping in the door just as the show was ending and B.J. was about to nod off into an afternoon nap of sadness. He cried out loud in the house like an angry child-ghost, and Rebecca ignored him. *Let him cry himself to exhaustion. Let him play with the G.I. Joes in the weedy backyard until he forgets about being upset.* But he didn't forget.

That night, he took an old grocery list. He gripped his pencil and concentrated to write on the back the words he'd learned from his first-grade primer. His mother sat under the single bulb that hung over the kitchen table, smoking one of Bennie's smokes. B.J. sat on the floor in his room and wrote, "Dad, Mom not home when I came from skool. Mom not home today."

"No!" he heard the voice of his singing companion bellow out into the house, but he pretended not to hear and placed the note beneath the quilt under his father's pillow. When he went to peek at her in the kitchen, Rebecca was standing in the gray light just beyond the screen door, talking in "Um-hums," as if someone was reprimanding her. He heard the low quiet tone of Mr. Tunnelson, their tobacco-growing neighbor: "You got to do right for the boy. Leave if you have to, but you know your deddy wouldn't want to see you sneaking around with another man and makin them kind of mistakes." His voice always sounded like the meditative drone of the bees over the tobacco flowers. His own wife had taken up with another man and split their family in two. His daughter, Sheila, was B.J.'s age and able to be with her deddy only part-time.

"Um-hum. Yeah. I know that. Um-hum." Rebecca answered him with her arms folded low, resting on her hip bones, wanting to say, *But you hear how he beats me. What else am I supposed to do except take up with another man?* She wanted to say, *Your wife was a hussy, everybody knows that. I need somebody to take me away from Bennie. This is different.* Instead, she listened to the man who wasn't much older than her but acted like a father to her. Unlike Bennie, he came home from Korea and took up working hard and toeing the line, and she, having known him her whole life, respected him.

"Yes, sir. I understand."

Mr. Tunnelson did not speak, just looked at her, his eyes in shadow from the porch light over the brim of his ball cap. "Then, best sure better make a plan to leave, rather than a plan to stay and do wrong by your child."

When Rebecca came in to sing B.J. good night, "He's got high hopes, he's got high hopes," Bennie still was not home. She lit up one of Bennie's PCP-laced marijuana cigarettes, just enough to take the edge off. A green endorphin light filled the house and calmed her, and then the drone of Mr. Tunnelson's voice resonated in her head. *Better make a plan to leave, rather than a plan to stay and do wrong by your child.*

She went off to run a tub still singing, "He's got high apple-pie-in-the-sky hopes." She let the shame of being seen down below her father's expectations roll out of her eyes in tears that diluted the bathwater. *Where am I supposed to go?*

B.J. was awakened just moments after falling asleep when he heard the tub run full of water, heard his mother sniffing and clearing her throat.

B.J. was awakened the second time by the spirit, "Wake up, wake up," and then he heard his father's footsteps come in the back door muffled, heard the sound of Rebecca's voice rising and falling in pitch trying to explain something, but her words were cut off by the bark of Bennie's baritone voice. In his sleep, B.J. unfolded little notes, pieces of bubble gum wrappers with jokes and riddles. He was fully awakened when she screamed, "Bastard! Get yo hands off me!" and her body hit the wall behind his bed. B.J. ran to their bedroom door in his pj's with tiny cowboys and Indians warring right side up and upside down on the flannel print. He pounded for them to let him in—"Mama! Deddy!"—but they couldn't hear his small voice over their words and the bass drum of their bodies against the walls and floors.

When Rebecca climbed from the floor onto the bed, Bennie stumbled and laughed his way over to her. The sounds in his head were a haze of music and their screaming boy pounding on the door. The hard liquor in Bennie and the laced cigarette in Rebecca pulled their souls just above pain to pleasure. He thrust into her until they both came and fell into a deep sleep all in one last groan. The three of them dead silent—B.J. in the hallway asleep on the floor, his parents exhausted in the bed.

They slept like intoxicated watchmen who did not know that in the collision of sperm and egg they were visited by the one who lay dormant waiting until the day she could enter the flesh. She lodged herself in the walls of Rebecca's womb and proceeded to grow gills that would become the throat through which she'd speak the truth of who they were.

Four months of Sunday mornings passed, enough time for the moon to make its cycle four times around the girl-child who grew into a yam-size little sister with eyes and hands that had already begun to profess inside the sanctuary of Rebecca's body. It was Easter morning, and B.J. and Rebecca did not go to their Baptist church in Fayetteville where Reverend Boller preached the

Word, wiping the sweat and spit from his mouth, every Sunday, where the congregation sang from the hymnal. They went to the Pentecostal church, where the churchgoers wouldn't ask Rebecca about the purple bruise on her cheek and guess about the purple bruises beneath her Easter Sunday dress of purple irises. They would be too enthralled with the work of praising the Lord. It would take all of their attention to churn themselves up to do the holy dance, to speak in tongues, to run up and down the aisles as if on fire. Getting to that place of abandon took some clapping and singing and banging on the piano, the way the right combination of drink and smoke got Bennie to release his worldly woes. They didn't know Rebecca and Bennie and B.J. and wouldn't be focused on the gossip of who done what to whom as they would at the Baptist church of her upbringing.

She dressed B.J. in his white short-sleeved shirt and the black denim pants from the J.C. Penney bin. She used the tightly woven purple hat she'd saved for this Easter to cover her sweated back hair, and off they went to the Pentecostal church. At home Bennie turned up his first beer for that Easter morning—beer first, then hard liquor, then the smoke to even out his high.

"That's the thing," Rebecca told B.J. that morning, her swollen lip making her speech sound as if she held snuff in her cheek. "That's the thing," she pointed at the white-and-red six-pack that obstructed her view of the eggs in the fridge, "that's the thing that took the marine away and left me with this mess."

EIGHT

Fayetteville, North Carolina
1960

A mother knows when something is to be done, when all-that-is calls for action, but sometimes her spirit is too disturbed to look where she must aim. When her lover's transgressions might stand in the way of the return of the divine child, the sound of her unfed heart churns over the sound of tumbling rocks in the river, creating a fork in the road out of someplace familiar and someplace better.

Rebecca could have gone on to the Baptist church that morning, because it didn't much matter anymore; people in the church and in the community around them had learned to steer clear of the Lees and their unstable domestic currents that could suck in whole humans with tornado force. At church and at the A&P people moved on quickly after "Hey, Rebecca. Hey, little B.J.," and they cautioned the nonchurch folk, like Mr. Tunnelson, "I wouldn't go sticking my foot in that pile of cow shit over there."

Bennie had only had the first beer, had not yet smoked the first joint, and was walking over to put the record player's needle down on Chuck Berry's "Johnny B. Goode" when Rebecca and B.J. walked back in the house. That was all wrong; it was before his Sunday ritual of beer, liquor, and smokes could take him to the serenity of the Cape Fear River, where God held him on a bridge with the sulfur smell of brackish water and the gurgle of the current to hold him for the hour-long peak of his high. The two of them were not supposed to be home. The clap of the screen behind them signaled the closing of the trapdoor on their cage, trapping themselves inside with him.

The pain in Bennie's head pounded against the skull plate of his forehead. B.J. came into the living room headed for the TV in hopes of catching Sunday morning cartoons that he rarely got a chance to watch. Bennie passed him and went into the kitchen and slumped down into one of the plastic-and-metal chairs holding his head. Rebecca reported out to Bennie with her puffy lip while she laughed to herself and paced from cabinets to the refrigerator, getting ready to cook.

"The damned Pentecostals, they got to singing 'Oh Mary don't ya weep . . .' and clapping and singin that over and over till they was shoutin and praisin and scared B.J. away. He was hollerin, 'Mama, I want to go home!' When he saw a grown man all put together in a suit sweatin and running up and down the aisles flailing. Child! . . ." She half laughed through her story to calm her own nerves. The story was her preparation to relax Bennie and tell him she was pregnant.

Bennie shifted his head in his hands, ignoring her over the pain. "Then this big ole woman jumped up and down." Each syllable of Rebecca's voice pounded on Bennie's eardrums. "The boy turned his face to my dress and held on crying into my thigh, 'Mama, I want to go home!' You should have heard him."

Bennie yelled to shut her up. "Stop talking! What the hell is wrong with you!"

The spirit in her womb breathed one breath in the silence that followed his outburst. B.J. stood in front of the TV holding the knob but waiting to hear if the scene at his back would turn to chaos. Rebecca stood with a box of instant mashed potatoes in her hand staring down at her husband, whose body language said, *Woman, if you don't fix whatever the hell it is that you are doing to make my head hurt, I'm gonna beat you from here to next Sunday.*

Rebecca saw herself doing like Mr. Tunnelson told her to, get up in the morning, pack her shit, the boy's shit, the baby in her body, and leave while Bennie was at work. But she knew there wasn't anything out there for a Black woman with no education and children. She yelled back at Bennie, at God, "What am I supposed to do?! I cain't go to my church. I cain't go to their church! I cain't leave! I cain't stay in this damned house! What the hell am I supposed to do?! And be damned if I ain't pregnant again!" Her voice grated against the souls in heaven. A high-pitched and guttural screaming that made B.J. run to her and hold on to her legs, while Bennie heard only the high-pitched screaming of the Korean women eight years silent in his head.

Rebecca screamed it again out into the quiet Sunday streets where neighbors could not hear her. They were all at church, except Mr. Tunnelson, who used the early spring Sunday silence to tractor up the soil for his food garden. "What the hell am I supposed to do?! You hear me?" Rebecca turned in circles now as if her body, the kitchen, the house with its roof and walls could not contain her soul. B.J. turned with his mama until she reached down screaming and peeled her son off her legs. "Get off of me!" He tumbled to the back door from the velocity of her hands. And that stopped her. Bennie got up from the table in his sleeveless tee, muscles clinched. Rebecca saw in his eyes the blank soul, like the morning he stared in her eyes, not seeing her, while he squeezed the life out by squeezing her throat, cutting off the flow of her milk to B.J., cutting off blood to her brain until the sun came—"Wake up! Wake up!"—and thawed the opaque Korean mountain frost in his eyes.

She yelled to her bawling child, who was scrambling to his feet, "B.J.! Go get the neighbor!"

B.J. tripped down the three back steps into the backyard. The tobacco in Mr. Tunnelson's field was already taller than him, and the vegetable field was on the other side of his house. As if he was running to catch up with the small gang of neighborhood kids headed for school, he ran out onto Colonial Drive and to the other side of Mr. Tunnelson's house. The man rode high on the blue tractor, plowing the roots back into the soil, with his back to the boy. The clank and clatter of blades on rocks drowned out the little boy yelling and crying, "Mr. Tunnelson! Mr. Tunnelson!" His muffled voice sounded to the neighbor like some strange buzzing, maybe a distant plane. Mr. Tunnelson looked to the sky where he thought he'd find a pilot writing "7Up," advertising soda on a Sunday afternoon with the skywriting stops and sputters. There were no clouds above the town of Fayetteville, with its houses soon to be filled with the smell of fried chicken and corn bread. He turned the steering wheel of the tractor beneath the reach of his arms and elbows and started up the next row.

His eyes under the tattered ball cap tried to make sense out of what he was seeing—the little neighbor boy sitting at the road in church shirt and church pants crying. The little boy in the stark sun with his mouth wide open to say something that could not be heard over the rocks and worms churned up in the blade of the plow.

Before the neighbor could turn the key to silence the engine, he saw behind the boy, in the glare of Sunday afternoon sun, his fellow vet in the sleeveless tee in the middle of Colonial Drive where the new yellow line had been painted. He saw Rebecca was running, screaming for her son with her arms stretched out, a sight that layered memory over memory of Korean women and their children wrongfully separated by his decision to advance in this world by following commands. He could not hear Rebecca over the memories that he blinked hard to extinguish.

B.J. did not budge, did not move his eyes from the image of the neighbor who cut off the engine, whose boots crunched on parched earth as they landed in the soil the way his boots crunched when he jumped off the running board of his Army unit's truck into the snow to advance up Yudam-ni and rescue the pinned and frozen units. Private Joseph Tunnelson ran and yelled, because he would not get to Bennie in the middle of Colonial in time, "Naw, man! Naw, man! Naw!"

Rebecca did not reach B.J. Her purple dress with the irises constricted her movements. The shot was fired, and she collapsed onto the asphalt. Her folding body brought the veil down in Bennie's mind far enough for him to hear Lottie whispering him awake at the pond, "Bennie, Bennie," for him to see Lottie's body crumple to the ground just before the line of trees that led off into the Mississippi woods.

Bennie's voice was the only sound above the quieting ricochet of the shot: "Rebecca!" Bloodcurdling cry for his mother, and for his wife, "Rebecca!" And there was only one way for the mother to slaughter the irrepressible devil that lived inside of him. He stood on the double yellow line with the brown deputy's car approaching in front of him. "Home!" he heard wail from all the souls and bodies around him. Bennie pulled his hand up out of the way of all-that-is, placed himself on the side with all-that-knows. He put his handgun to his head and ceased to be. Rebecca ceased to be, and the divine girl-child spirit was snatched up out of the womb by a distraught force.

NINE

Fayetteville, North Carolina
1960

The divine protector was left behind in the migration. His six-year-old body and soul were numb at the edge of the tobacco field. His body marked: "To be rescued and matured until called to return home where the divine girl-child will sprout from the womb of the malnourished gardens of the South." His soul marked: "Stay."

Lenard walked into Mr. Tunnelson's living room, where the boy sat on the couch refusing to move unless the urge to pee or the urge to eat sent him running to the bathroom or the refrigerator. Lenard's square, clean-shaven jaw appeared. B.J. did not know he had family. He was just a boy living inside the bubble of his silence after his parents had gone mad and left him behind. He didn't know there was a real adult man, who was the little boy Lenard in his father's drunken stories of the good days that quickly turned into a reason for a whipping. Leaning down in the dim light of the neighbor's living room was a man who looked like a stable version of Bennie, and the boy reached his hand out for his uncle.

B.J. was emergency-lifted out of that chaos of his childhood by his next of kin. His eyelids opened a bit more with every mile as the nightmare sound of his mother's voice screaming trailed off behind him.

The long drive was a blur of blooming trees and the consistent sound of the road beneath Lenard's new baby-blue Ford Falcon as he pointed the car northwest, leaving as few footprints as possible on southern soil.

Treetops gave way to the sparseness of Midwest terrain. Three Black-owned gas stations—in Roanoke, Virginia; Lexington, Kentucky; and Mount Vernon, Illinois—were their only pit stops on the 850-mile trek from North Carolina to Missouri. "Always carry a gas can in case there's no Black gas stations," Lenard said in his nervous small talk, and the boy was too young to know the weight of that advice.

In St. Louis, the contrast of good living eclipsed the rest of B.J.'s memories. Lenard signed the deed on a one-story home in the St. Louis suburb of University City. He knew he was doing the right thing to nurture and provide but thought he was following Pastor Johnson's advice to make sure the boy knew what had happened to him; didn't think that by not harping on the past, he was walking his nephew further away from his own soul. "Leave the past in the past," James had taught him. "Leave your brother where he is." Lenard didn't know that meant he would never see Bennie again. And now, the least he could do was shield his nephew from memories that would keep him from getting on with his life the way James got on with a good life; leave the past in the past. Lenard nodded when Pastor Johnson said, "The grief is his to bear. Don't try and make him forget that hell; try to help him walk through it."

Lenard would say at bedtime, "Pray for Rebecca and Bennie." That just became part of the label for "time for bed."

Lenard made breakfast, lunch, and dinner. Talked to the boy gentle and stern: "Wake up, son, time for church." "No, you can have dessert after you eat the pork chops and greens I put on your plate." "Yes, pull the throttle until it starts, but don't put your hand down near the blade." "Do your homework." "When I tell you something, answer, 'Yes, sir.'"

B.J. was eager to please, to belong. In church, he clapped his small hands together, clapping shut the memory of Rebecca and Bennie: "Glory, glory, hallelujah, since I laid my burden down." But there was something in the boy's eyes that reminded all of them of the deep places in themselves that they refused to sit with, like the feeling of walking into a dark bathroom and seeing yourself in the mirror with no eyes, just hollow darkness inside the sockets.

Sister Collier, the young deaconess of the church, leaned down with her breasts about to spill out of her dress and pinched his chubby cheeks—"You just the cutest thing"—affirming that hellish memories are best left in hell.

B.J. had a routine; he insisted every day on coming home from school and plopping down in front of *Romper Room*. Neither he nor his uncle knew why he focused on the show as if it was going to save him from something. Something about the audience of good white girls and boys surrounding Miss Lois soothed him where he sat eating his after-school treat of Nabisco Sugar Honey Grahams. "I'm going to be on *Romper Room*," he told Uncle Lenard, "Will you take me down to KTVI, Uncle?" but Lenard frowned, not understanding the source of his nephew's request. Didn't B.J. know that some things were progress for Blacks, like education, but no self-respecting Black person was trying to sit their Black child as representative in a batch of white children on TV singing "The Itsy Bitsy Spider"? It just wasn't dignified.

Lenard didn't intentionally hide the truth from the boy, but every time B.J. asked his uncle if they could do something that Lenard realized would stir the past, he cut B.J. off from his own memories, just drew the curtain, the way he had done with his own childhood, pulled the curtains closed just enough to save B.J. and give him the childhood he deserved. The two proceeded, proud like father and son, into B.J.'s well-ordered upbringing. But the truth does not know time. It waits for affirmation like a child who has been plopped down in front of the TV until his world returns.

At the end of the seventh-grade school year, Lenard planned a treat for B.J. as reward for his straight As. The boy watched so many episodes of *Wild Kingdom* that a Saturday morning at the zoo with its monkeys, zebras, and seals would be a dream come true.

He wore bright orange-and-beige plaid bell-bottoms and a rainbow-striped T-shirt that accentuated his persistent adolescent lank. He insisted that his outfit matched: "This looks really cool, Uncle." His uncle found these fashion choices ridiculous but didn't want to step on the boy's emerging manhood and everything that lay beneath, any more than the church members did who questioned him, "Son, don't you want to go with solid pants and a striped shirt?"

"No, sir."

That day, the two of them rode to the zoo singing along to Ray Charles's "Busted" on the radio:

My bills are all due and the baby needs shoes and I'm busted
Cotton is down to a quarter a pound, but I'm busted

They were having so much fun because they weren't busted. They rode through Forest Park in Lenard's brand-new navy-blue, white-vinyl-topped Oldsmobile 98. B.J. held the cards he'd collected of animals with the description of their habitats, their predators. He looked out the window with that arrogant look of belonging that every thirteen-year-old boy should have. Lenard looked over at his nephew and smiled proud. The two of them rode with the top down in a car few Black folks in St. Louis could afford. Lenard was the calculating penny-pincher he had always been.

On the light-gray concrete of the path at the zoo, B.J. knelt down with a couple of nickels and turned the knob to purchase two handfuls of duck feed from a dispenser like a gumball machine. They stood in the hot sun watching the tattered-looking birds fetch the pellets, sometimes flapping at each other, breaking the steadiness of the sun on the pond into ripples. The joy in B.J.'s pubescent tenor and soprano giggle was sweet and familiar to Lenard's heart.

Lenard told the boy, "Stay right here. I'm gonna get one more handful." He turned around, turned the dial, and when he turned back, the railing above the pond was blank, without his nephew leaning there. Marble-eyed fish swam and looked up where Lenard involuntarily looked down into the murky pond for his nephew. For a second, he heard the voice of his own mother floating in a sightless dark dream above the heat and humidity, felt the damp hand of his brother Bennie shaking him awake where they slept until dawn at the pond of their Mississippi childhood. *Look up, look up*, he told himself, and he looked into the faces of white strangers. He knew not to show the panic that tightened in his chest or else they'd think he had snatched some woman's purse. And then across the pond on the bridge, he saw first the orange-and-beige plaid pants, then the striped T-shirt and B.J.'s brown face and the halo of his Afro crown.

When Lenard saw B.J. across the pond, good memories poured into the dried-out places of missing and longing. Pulled by a familiar energy between them, he walked to his nephew on the bridge, never taking his eyes off the images that drew him. B.J.'s brown leather platform shoes swung high above the pond water. His shoes were hypnotic pendulums that took him into memories. His chin rested on his hands, which were on the lower railing of the bridge where he sat. The sun made his Afro almost red where the warm current of air made it sway like the fuzz on the cattail reeds in the Cape Fear River of his memories. One tear dried on his cheek in the breeze.

Lenard could almost hear what B.J. heard, the transistor radio playing an Otis Redding song, the last tune before the ball game. He could almost see what B.J. saw in his memories, the red cooler with the fishing bait and beer, while he fished with his father, and Lenard could almost remember the smokeless fires and the bamboo fishing poles in his own memories of fishing by his brother's side on days when almost everything was right. The stares of the white people who passed his nephew brought Lenard back. Embarrassingly, he looked around, bent down for his nephew's elbow: "Come on, let's go."

In the car, the mood was one of separate thoughts. B.J.'s eyes seemed to wander from road to buildings to the sky, until he said in a half-asleep tone, "I miss my deddy." And there was silence. The only connection between them was the sound neither of them acknowledged, Bennie's voice. *Come on, let's go fishing.* Full memories that Lenard pushed down. If he stayed busy grading papers, tending to B.J., mowing, laundry, church, then he would not have to contend with the guilty thoughts: *I should have invited Bennie to prayer meeting, I should have asked around about where he moved to, I should have . . .* Thoughts that stopped if he called his nephew to supper, filled the grocery cart with school snacks, took him to the zoo. But this was another thing, his nephew being the one to call up the guilt, grief, abandonment that Lenard tried to push down through the digits of his stiff spine into the leather seats of his new car. Half memories that agitated B.J. rose to the base of his adolescent skull and stirred a confusing storm of familiar voices and images that he did not connect to his current existence.

The next morning was Easter Sunday. They went to church, and B.J. heard that choir marching out that song with their feet and double clapping, "Oh, Mary, don't you weep." He pressed his tongue to his teeth, trying to soothe himself as if he was sucking on a Popsicle, remembering something of a day of sugary sweetness and tears. He sucked so hard that the last baby tooth that had long refused to budge came out. He looked over at his uncle with his eyes questioning, "What's happening to me?" Lenard looked to him, offered his open handkerchief for the tooth, probed his nephew's eyes, but quickly convinced himself that the boy was fighting his first Holy Ghost takeover.

Later that afternoon, Lenard sat in his office grading papers before they went to the evening barbecue behind Uncle James's tavern. B.J. sat on the raised gold-stitch pattern of the living-room sofa reading a volume of the *World Book Encyclopedia.* He ate through a whole box of cheese crackers, stuffing them like cotton batting into the cracking-open parts of his heart.

The thoughts that itched inside B.J.'s mind grew in volume

like fusion jazz. His eyes paused on a number. He sprung up off the sofa, a tangle of long arms and legs, and ran to his uncle. The open book with gold inlay letters on its green spine threatened to spill out of his hands. "Uncle Lenard, the moon is 238,900 miles from the earth?" He stood unsteadily, as though teetering high above something dangerous.

For seven years, there had been no light in the dark rooms of B.J.'s brain where the good memories and the bad memories of his first six years existed. But those numbers woke and illuminated something from a distant morning. He stood almost as tall as his uncle in Lenard's office door, holding the encyclopedia open, involuntarily whining. B.J. awakened the six-year old who sat dormant in the memory of Buffalo Bill's announcement of the last day. B.J.'s puckered lips salted with too much of the cracker snack, rounded to caress an invisible Popsicle. He stood five foot six and growing but didn't feel any taller than four feet. His platform leather shoes turned to Keds standing in the living room of his childhood: "Show number 2,343."

He stopped and stuttered, asking his mind why this number was illuminated; it shouted itself into the room, "Uncle, 238,900 miles, 238,900?!" Lenard mistook his nephew's out-of-place upset for mathematical frustration. He kept grading papers and responded to B.J. without looking at him or being mindful of the example used for explanation.

"Yeah, B.J. that's a large number, but not impossible to calculate." The boy listened, wanting the ants itching inside his brain to calm. "Think about it this way. The day I picked you up, we drove 850 miles. If we drive to Fayetteville and home again 140 times, we've been to the moon."

The dim lights in B.J.'s memory of his last weekend with his mother and father flickered at the sound of "Fayetteville" in his uncle's voice, so much like Bennie's voice.

He yelled into the space of the house, his voice cracking from tenor to alto. "I want to go home!" In his head, he saw the irises on his mother's dress when he turned his head away from the man in the suit and the big woman at the Pentecostal church running up and down the aisles shouting and raising fear in his soul. "I want to go home!" He saw the irises again, twisting in a smear of blue tractor, orange dirt, cornflower-blue sky. "I want to go home!"

Uncle Lenard stood up in defense of what sounded like a boy turning into a man ready to wage war against the hand that feeds him, not knowing this was the cry of a body being summoned to its soul's dwelling place. Lenard's own covered memories clambered from under rugs and across the floor before he could think of what he was saying to his nephew. "You think you would have been better off *down south*? This is your home!" Lenard was arrested by the tone in his own voice.

When Lenard and B.J. arrived at the barbecue that Easter Sunday evening, it was fifteen years since Lenard had sat at those same picnic tables, being worked beyond his concern for where Bennie was or what he was doing. Lenard was groomed by James to keep his eyes forward, not looking backward at the likes of Bennie. Groomed toward bloodletting the unwanted parts of Mississippi, with Bennie shed in the outflow.

James groomed Lenard to take up the ways of an urban Black man—hard work, church, earn respect and embed yourself in a community that will have your back if you have to beat back anybody who doesn't respect you. So Lenard was unsettled by his nephew, who sat in the car brooding and angry and disturbed in a way that made Lenard feel powerless. "You can't make me go in there," was all the boy would say. His newly angled jaw and eyes were like his father's, gone stone-cold as if his spirit had vacated and left behind his body to carry out the demands of living.

Lenard left the storm of B.J.'s episode locked in the car parked on the busy street outside James's tavern and worked on transforming himself into the tall, well-spoken math teacher as he proceeded down the gangway toward his community of churchgoers, business owners, and those newly migrated from the South.

Handshakes and half hugs brought him into the smell of vinegar and tomato and smoked seasoned ribs, billows of smoke where James's wide shoulders and big laughter stood at the pit barrel grill. Gray suits and pastel-colored Easter egg dresses, a flock that filled the backyard, obliterating the picnic tables where fifteen years ago Lenard and James took their break in the refreshing stark city cold air, their aprons dirty, their hands as sore from carrying crates as they had once been from holding the plow.

"We earned a man's break, so we are taking a man's break," James had said, not looking his teenage brother in the eyes but looking off to the alley that was neater than the other businesses' back alleys on Delmar, with trash cans in a row and a wooden rollback gate for the delivery trucks. The sky above their heads was bluer than Lenard ever remembered seeing. So much of his time as a teenager was spent with his eyes on the mule's ass, the plow blade breaking orange clay, the wide spread of the tobacco leaves, his own hands. Those days, the blue relief of the sky came into view only when he bent his back to squeeze the muscles in a backward arch. If the clouds were in a whisk that reminded him of mist in the morning of the day that lay beneath words, the arching of his back was only for a short breath. "Work!" was Old Deddy's command, but it also kept Lenard whole and protected from the distant, wailing boy-self buried in his chest. Taking a break would likely break the damn wall between Sampson and St. Louis.

James told Lenard, "The church bell, prayer meeting, show up for work every day, be consistent, hold your head up, and take that Mississippi drawl out of your mouth." Between Bennie and Lenard, only one of the two brothers had enough untouched youth left in him to be molded the way Mr. Drake had molded James. But, the last advice wasn't in Lenard's nature: "Earn people's respect, and if a nigga don't respect you, everybody will back you if you need to put yo foot up his ass."

Lenard showed up to the Easter dinner barbecue, showed up to the same picnic tables behind the tavern where James and he had rested for a spell after carrying crates and cleaning out the grease trap, frost steaming from their mouths, their bodies overheated in the bitter St. Louis cold from the hard muscle work that James said was the hard work of men who knew how to direct their lives.

James turned from the grill, spatula in hand. "Where's B.J.?" His voice matched his assured height, heft, light-skinned Black male authority.

"He's in the car, upset," Lenard did not look his brother in the eyes. And James knew part of his lessons had been lost on Lenard, who was apt to get two things confused—the age when a boy needs to be handled with care and the age when a boy needed to grow into a man by being handled by a man's hands that can knock at the door of his common sense and get him to act right.

That was the first day of B.J.'s teenage testing that should have been taken personally, should have counted for more than angst. But his uncle had his own teenage memories to calm, shush, and quiet. B.J. insisted his uncle buy him the sleeveless ribbed white T-shirts he saw on the father in his memories, and Lenard did, then retreated further so as not to allow his memories to be incensed.

B.J. asked if Lenard had any photos of his parents, asked with attitude, and Lenard didn't answer but told him to change his tone. B.J. stopped asking and told Lenard to drive him to his old house in Fayetteville, North Carolina, not in the educated tone Lenard said would make somebody want to listen, but in the tone Bennie used when telling Rebecca to get dinner on the table: "Drive me the fuck home! Don't hide shit from me."

Lenard reacted, untrue to his feelings but true to his strategy for warring with his own emotions: "I'm ignoring you until you can talk to me like you have some sense." Advance and retreat, advance and retreat, until their dynamic became that of the persistent guilty caregiver and the persistent raging child.

Pastor Johnson said it was the rage a boy feels when the truth is hidden from him. James said, "Whup his ass every now and then, and he'll stop acting out." But Lenard was the one who had to live with the angry ghost who wouldn't do anything Lenard said after that day.

TEN

St. Louis, Missouri
1972

By the time he was eighteen, B.J. had ventured far from the life Lenard imagined for him, the life of a righteous boy of the church, choir member, prayer meeting leader. "Nigga, you talk mo shit than Richard fuck'n Nixon" and other responses twisted his education and his angst into fork-tongued comments.

Most nights, Lenard sat up late at his desk, nothing but the orange streetlights of their University City neighborhood lighting his office through the sheer curtains. Low on the record player, Mahalia Jackson sang about the virtues of living right and getting to heaven, her voice silky, almost enough to melt the hard knot in his throat. Almost taking him back to the men of his ancestry who allowed the spirit to enter their bodies and take over in full possession, almost remembering his first day at prayer meeting, holding on to the back of his chair, unprepared for the spirit to press on his pains and joys until they came up in tears. He was in control of his life, appreciating the umbrella of his religion but never allowing himself to be caught in the storm of the spirit.

His slumped shoulders and upright head were like the bookends—copies of *The Thinker* statue—that held the math texts on his shelves in place. He couldn't solve the false equation that his teenage nephew put in front of him that said my pain equals your pains. "You are trying me, son, testing my faith," was all Lenard knew to say, but it was not effective against the smirk on the height of the boy who said, *I see right through you to your weak spots and, yes, I am in pain, and it is your fault.*

The boy's tongue tempted a beat-down so he'd have a reason to fight: "Your faith in what? In who? Say what you mean. See, nigga, you don't know what you talk'n about." Lenard's eyes bulged in confusion half the time, not knowing what to do about that level of disrespect.

Ten o'clock on a school night, everything in University City and in St. Louis was closed. *Being Black and in the streets could get him killed* was all Lenard could think. He found himself wishing he was a drinker or a smoker so he could live through the complications of feeding someone as tall as him, a man by all accounts, except that his mind had not matured. James, on the other hand, did not mince words in the boy's presence: "Look, young blood, don't make me put my foot up yo ass." At church, Pastor Johnson coached Lenard to say something more akin to "Get the car back by ten o'clock, or the consequence is you won't be able to use the car for a month." Pastor coached him, all the while assuming Lenard had done as he advised on the day he went to pick up the boy.

Twelve years ago, James and Lenard sat at a lopsided table in the full yellow light of the windowless tavern on Monday morning after receiving the news from the Fayetteville sheriff, who called the St. Louis police to report to the next of kin that their brother was gone. The news was that he had taken his wife, Rebecca, the woman they had never met, with him. They were told the other news that left the sounds of their heartbeats echoing in their chamber of grief and guilt, that there was a son waiting to be rescued from the whole mess.

James scooted from the table and went into actions without feelings, "Let's go see Pastor Johnson." He pulled the heavy tavern door tight into its swollen frame and turned the key. With the gray spring morning of Delmar Avenue above their heads, they decided to walk the six blocks to the church. The back of the brick two-story structure held the entrance to the basement. The backyard was like that of the houses that surrounded the church—chain-link fences, lawns with picnic tables and a barbecue pit, and an alley at the back creating another entrance to the yard. Pastor Johnson's burgundy Buick sat just inside the big opening of the back fence, and the brothers descended the few steps to the basement door and then into the pastor's office. They entered the cool dampness of the room with brown, paneled walls over cinder blocks. The street-level window that offered the green grass of the yard was a focus for the brothers, who both exhaled in the space where another man could hold everything they had lived, without either of them needing to tell the story or explain.

Pastor Johnson had the same cream-toned skin as James, but where James began to grow more fat, Pastor Johnson had muscle. His gray suit fit tight over his arms; the warmth of his face not encumbered by hair gave him a holy, cleansed look. He walked from behind his desk and embraced each of the men, striking them on the back to reactivate their grief-numbed hearts. After the brothers settled into chairs on one side of the desk with Pastor Johnson on the other side, the ritual of their silence was broken. "What you all have as your cross to bear is going to weigh heavy on your hearts for the rest of your lives. There is nothing that can take that away. You have the task of grieving, which has to happen, and retrieving his son, which has to happen now. You can't wait to go get him, and you can't hold off your own grieving."

Lenard's eyes that had witnessed too much turned into those of the little boy who slept on the pallet while the world around him churned him into loneliness without his say. And he made the pact to nurture, provide, and protect, discarding the pact to use his strength to hold the walls of the truth open. He looked at Pastor Johnson and in a quieted voice said, "I'll go get him tomorrow."

In two more weeks, the goal was high school graduation, though B.J. protested, "I'm not going to college. I'm going to Los Angeles to be on *Soul Train*." The boy could not see that he was pinning himself between rebellion and the mandatory draft, pinning himself between the wisdom of his two uncles and his testosterone-need to be right. Testosterone that didn't have anywhere else to go.

Evenings, he used the back seat of his uncle's car to risk the police finding him with the other Black teenagers who parked their cars behind the planetarium at Forest Park at night. He raised the miniskirts of the girls at school who'd made him promise, "Keep your mouth shut or no more back-seat fucking." At eighteen, he demanded the same thing from life that his father demanded. But unlike his father, for B.J. the thrust of his stiff penis into warm flesh was controlled by the Black girls who needed escape from their middle-class lives, and it brought no relief from his pain.

Lenard forged the boy's signature on the enrollment forms for Forest Park Community College. He had a plan in place for when B.J. came around. Even if B.J. missed the remaining ten days of his senior year of high school, he'd still have a C average. Graduation was imperative, and college fundamental to survival, the only way Lenard could keep the boy from being drafted.

Just as Lenard was nodding off in his office chair, his 98 came swinging into the driveway, stopping short of crashing into the garage door. War's "Slippin' into Darkness" on eight-track blared from the speakers. B.J. stayed in the car, rocking it back and forth on the tires he'd worn bald, respecting the electric funk guitar and drums to finish out before cutting the car off. He unfolded himself out of the driver's side, a tall six feet with his Afro in the orange streetlight.

Running the streets and barely eating had taken away most of the chub. That smart, chunky little boy gone, leaving a lanky *Soul Train* reject. A Michelob forty-ounce swung in his hand as he came around the walk to the front door. Past Lenard's office, B.J. pimp-walked into the small hallway, visible to his uncle. He sang out, "Slippin into darkness, ooo, ooo."

"Where have you been, B.J.?" Stern, measured, proper. Lenard's voice didn't even startle B.J. This was their routine.

"Don't worry about it, man, and don't be wait'n up like I'm some li'l nigga who needs a chaperone."

Lenard got up from his desk, and in Pastor Johnson's fire-and-brimstone tone and his own proper math teacher diction, he asked again. This time he approached B.J. in a manner that made him turn around, wanting to defend himself but a bit too drunk to put his guard up.

"I asked you a question, son! Where have you been!?"

"Don't push up on me, man." B.J.'s voice cracked, and in the crack a little-boy piece of himself escaped. "You not my damn deddy. Get the fuck off me."

"I won't tolerate any more disrespect in my house."

B.J. laughed, more like a yawn and cackle combined with his head thrown back, so much like his father. "Man, you hilarious," and then as if someone stood on a stage and told the most rip-roaring joke, he doubled over in the hallway that led to the bedrooms laughing hyena-style, knocking off the wall the framed photo of Black Jesus.

Lenard was not amused. "What is so funny about being drunk and acting a fool?" It was the same question James had asked their brother Bennie on the day they arrived in St. Louis after catching a bus all the way from Mississippi.

When they entered James's tavern, the sound of the bell, like that on their old cow, brought them out of the darkness of Mississippi and into the light of Lee's Wagon Wheel on Delmar Avenue. Lenard had been the one to reach beyond Sampson, Mississippi, send the telegram to the man he knew was his only other relative. James received word that Old Deddy had been killed and that Bennie had looted the local tavern.

Lenard saw Bennie's liquor-yellowed eyeballs in B.J.'s eyes that watered with drunken laughter. "Stop acting a fool!" Lenard raised his voice, rattled at his own loss of composure. At hearing the word *fool*, B.J. curled into himself in laughter that graduated to hyperventilation: "Man, man. Oh my God!" He could barely catch his breath to get the words out, "You are Fred Sanford, and I'm Lamont." He burst out again and used the walls to get himself to his bedroom, "Good night, Pop."

Lenard barely slept that night, and by morning he had decided to try more of the manhandling James suggested. B.J. had already missed the bus, but Lenard didn't have to be in the classroom teaching and B.J. in his seat learning for another forty-five minutes. Lenard went out into the already hot morning. He nodded at his bourgeois Black neighbors, who piled their children into the car, wearing tie and pressed shirt for the dads and a sweat suit for the moms, soon to go out for their morning walk. The neighbors nodded in response, smiling in a way that said, "Poor man, has to deal with that out-of-control bastard." He started the 98, hoping there would be less of a scene if the car was already running.

He made his tall, gangly nephew an egg-and-bacon sandwich, sat his books and the sandwich in the car. *If timed right, I can drop B.J.'s hungover ass off and still get to the morning faculty meeting before the bell rings for classes.*

He knocked on the hollow bedroom door of B.J.'s room, no reasoning in his voice this time, but matter-of-fact like James: "Get up, son." Lenard waited with his hand wrapped around the knob, heard nothing, and knocked before turning it. He ignored the smell of sweat that seeped through B.J.'s intoxicated pores and out into the curtain-drawn darkness of the room. He went to the wooden sliding doors of the closet. Took a T-shirt and a pair of the bell-bottom jeans off the hanger and threw them on top of the boy. "Come on, ya got ten minutes to get in the car, or else you can get out my house!"

B.J. pulled back the covers to see the man he thought was his Uncle James standing like a light-skinned bear over his bed. But it was mild-mannered Uncle Lenard turned into fed-up Uncle Lenard. "You heard me, son. Get up or get out!"

"Damn man! What you ate your Wheaties or drank a fucking beer this morning?"

Rain had gathered in a puddle just outside the front door, and on the way to the car, two of the ten minutes still remaining, B.J. stepped in a puddle that ruined his platform shoes, "Fuck!" He opened the passenger side door still only half-awake and tucked himself in, though the night before, he had been the man in the driver seat.

Lenard added an ingredient to the manhandling that seemed logical: a lecture. "You are almost a man and have to start behaving as such." They passed the stop sign at the corner and made the left turn out of the neighborhood, "Look, son. You have never felt the sun on your back, a whip on your back, the straps of a plow so chaffed into your shoulders every day that they make callouses on your back. That's what I was doing as a teenager. Your daddy and me barely found our way out . . ." Lenard stopped himself, not wanting to bring up Bennie in his own heart any more than he wanted to bring him up in B.J.'s heart.

What was left of the obedient little boy disappeared at the mention of his father, in the same way that the mention of Fayetteville had caused the thirteen-year-old to tantrum.

"Fuck you," B.J. mumbled.

Lenard gripped the steering wheel, to hold himself in place, and was grateful for the stillness a red stoplight offered but didn't foresee the opportunity it offered for an untethered spirit to flee. Before the light turned green, he heard the sound of the door unlatch. B.J. bolted from the car. He ran across the median toward his own idea of how to save himself. Lenard looked up into the rearview mirror and saw his own eyes but did not see the man-size boy who was gone beneath a morning sky, clouded in car exhaust in the Black suburbs of St. Louis. B.J. ran, ending Lenard's efforts at holding his nephew from the violent dangers of being a Black boy.

The cars in the traffic behind Lenard blew their horns, their occupants Black folks almost late for the jobs they could not afford to lose. As Lenard scanned the rearview, they did not just blow but held their palms on the horns, an urgent alarm of all the spirits in his DNA screaming to wake him from the prospect of what he could not control. Lenard rolled on past the green light, to the high school without his nephew.

A feeling of failure lodged in his chest as he straightened himself into a false demeanor of pride. His briefcase of graded papers in hand, his white shirt and tie, black slacks, black polished shoes were a still life in the sea of young folks in the hallway of the high school. He scanned the hallway of Black teenagers the way he scanned the pond that day at the zoo, thinking B.J. had fallen away from him into the underworld. Lenard's hand gripped the briefcase and hoped to see B.J., but the swarm of brown bodies with Afros and platform shoes paraded in smiles and frowns, some of them looking him in the eyes and seeming to scold him, and none of the eyes included B.J.'s. Lenard opened the faculty lounge door, stomached the feeling of defeat, and faced his mostly white peers who taught at the mostly Black high school.

That was it. B.J. was not home when Lenard came in at 4 p.m. With "Slippin' into Darkness" playing in his head, the boy had made his way back to the house that morning and told himself, "I ain't gonna be treated like no little nigga."

He stood on the scale; Black body being weighed stripped down to white underwear at the same place his father sought false escape, the Marine recruiting office. He was in St. Charles, less than twenty minutes from his home, almost twelve years from *the incident*. He answered the medical officer with the respect he'd long since stopped offering his uncle, "Yes, sir! Yes, sir!"

Lenard sat in the folding chair in the quiet Tuesday evening light of the church basement, waiting for prayer meeting to begin.

He did not think to look for B.J. so close to home. He assumed he'd have to drive south to fetch the boy for the second time. He swallowed his Adam's apple, cleared his throat to discourage tears and discourage his mind from realizing that all the book learning and gentle or tough loving from uncles would not save B.J. from his past or his future.

That night at prayer meeting, the congregation started out in supplication and ended up in the hand rhythms that they did not know had descended through the red blood cells beneath their multihued brown flesh from the Ivory Coast to the church pews. Hand rhythms meant for celebration, never intended for calling the hearts of the living to wake up and stand vigil so that the children would not be captured and dragged into the bush to be transformed into warmongers.

"May the words of my mouth and the meditations of my heart be acceptable in Thy sight," clap, clap, clap of chapped hands, and "Amen." Above the church, two clouds opened up with raindrops the size of Serengeti tears.

ELEVEN

Vietnam
1972

When they are young, their flight patterns are not yet driven by instinct; they are driven by the desire to escape whatever familiar has raised them to fledgling—hallelujahs, backyard barbecue, shotgun barbershops. They head north to go west, east to go south, whatever direction is in opposition to wisdom's plan. With that sort of wayward flight pattern, how does fate unite the halves of the self and direct it home to the seat of creation? How do mothers protect fledgling sons, especially if they fly their body into white men's crossfire? How does she wait on the providence that will right them all when her spirit is dizzied in the clouds of seemingly cyclical winds that cannot perceive the linear movement of his self-guided evolution as protector?

B.J. preferred night watch, because it was easier to sleep in the day than in the dark, when he would be awakened by the urgency of surprise attacks. Nighttime, on watch, in control, was peaceful by comparison. He turned into the vampire in the Bela Lugosi films he had loved to watch at Uncle Lenard's. Daytime sent him into a grateful coma; nighttime was when he had his best powers. He watched the last bit of light fall above the mountain and listened to the distant hills, then dispatched every hour—dash dot dash—with his radio to check on the status of the bush-boy members of Bravo Company who lay with their radios. They listened for whispers, smelled for cigarette smoke of Vietcong soldiers who might be on the approach, and then sent their Morse code static response—dash dot dash dot, "Charlie"—to indicate that all was well.

In the night, B.J. could calculate and recalculate the ambush and see his tactical error; it was the moment he got down on his knees in his bell-bottom pants, his heart beating, angry at Uncle Lenard for thinking he could tell him what to do, and slid his tiny suitcase from under the bed to launch his escape. Two mornings before that day, B.J. sat up in church in a pimp hat, frowned at by the elder women, knowing what he was doing, being disrespectful. From the pulpit, Pastor Johnson looked down on B.J. in the congregation, with Uncle Lenard sitting upright in that majestic way, well groomed, well kept, next to the lanky, weed-smelling teenager: "Two men can't rule in one house. God makes it so. Only one tongue, one set of rules prevails, and man of any species must battle to find the alpha."

"Amen." B.J. was listening. He knew he had to go but didn't want anybody telling him that going would equal college, equal him being the pawn to allay his uncle's fears of Black men fighting for the men who chained them. He didn't know they wanted to save him from the fate of their brother.

B.J. just wanted whatever option meant he was in charge of his destiny, not responsible for theirs. That was the tactical error, running headlong into enemy lines without the right artillery. He couldn't go backward; he could just stay awake, so he didn't have to revisit his mistakes. He wrote Uncle Lenard a letter that night with nothing but the moonlight for his lamp,

Dear Unc,

He started the letter, and felt his body relax, the way it had been relaxed from age six to age eighteen, a state of being loved he had taken for granted.

> You probably already know that I joined the Marines. I'm in Vietnam. I have so much to say, but I don't really know how to straighten my thoughts out. I just want you to know that I am alive. I don't know how I'm alive, but I am. I have lost a friend. I have some things to make right, some sacrifices to make. I want you to know I understand the ways you were trying to make me responsible and make a man out of me. I'll probably die here, but I want you to know that I appreciate you.
>
> Love, your nephew, B.J.

Five months earlier, he lay in the bush with his new buddy, Nick Porteli, who called himself the Italian poet. The two teenagers entertained themselves by poking fun at their differences.

"Man, your accent so thick, I have to learn to translate Bostonian into plain English."

"Man, your hair so kinky, I lost my best pack of smokes in that shit."

Guttural, whole-mouth laughter kept boys from the gravity of being men, ordered to lie in wait and kill.

Ten miles behind them lay the road with the armored personnel vehicles they disembarked from earlier in the night, ahead of them more thick brush that tangled at the bottom of a small hill. Just before dawn, this would be their cover as they approached the hamlet. Above the tiny ridgeline was an open field of one hundred yards and, beyond that, the ditches, the barbed wire, and the bamboo wall that their own platoon had helped erect. Their orders: Lie in wait overnight; in the darkness, before dawn, climb the ridge to the plateau, traverse the open field, cut the barbed wire, and flush out the Vietcong intruders from among the innocent people of the hamlet. The wire cutters were strapped to the gunner's pack and would be the first artillery deployed once they reached the perimeter. They would enter the hamlet just as the gray light of dawn gave them sight to surprise attack the insurgents.

But for now, their job was to lie quiet overnight. Take turns at watch, while others in their platoon took turns sleeping. Silence was key to a morning ambush. B.J. complained, "Man, this shit is worse than sleeping up there in the damned rice field."

"Rice saves lives," Nick joked.

B.J. snickered. Two of their platoon mates rustled and reprimanded, "Shhh."

They both fell silent, the wide expanse of black sky filled with stars like their thirty scattered bodies in the brush. Some Vietnamese bodies also lay in wait, boogeymen in other nearby brush. The lizards, the monkeys, the dragonflies, they were all just specks of eyeball-light in the dark, waiting for the next skirmish between dispensable humans. B.J. let the gravity of fear push down on him until he slept as ordered.

The next morning before dusk, their platoon advanced toward the brush in the dark, beneath the stars. Their commander whistled once, with a morning birdcall, to indicate "Halt." For a moment they stood at the bottom of the hill staring into brush thick and gnarled dark as the sky, wondering how they would cut through without giving themselves away. They did not have the home field advantage, didn't know anything about the vines that, once pulled aside, would tangle above their heads and tighten around their bodies. They didn't know about these droplets of water that hung on every fern tendril soaking their uniforms and gear packs already heavy with the sweat of humidity. Once every fiber of their uniforms was soaked down to the socks in their boots, the harmless lush brush came alive to ensnare them in defense of its people. When they had come across this same brush a month before scouting the area, it was a wall of sprouts, at their ankles.

Nick whispered, "How we gonna cut through this shit without sound or sight?" Their platoon commander whistled twice this time with the morning birds to indicate "Advance," and so they did.

Don't panic, Lee, B.J. told himself as he and the others hunched over and climbed the small hill to kill for the first time, but he and half his platoon got gnarled in the brush and had to wait for the gunner's clippers to cut them out.

Dawn was fast approaching as they all regrouped and crested the hill. They heard the two-whistle birdcalls to advance again. They were not supposed to be able to see the waving of their commander's arm at that stage of the advance, but the gray light before dawn revealed him and the front line and then, ahead of them in the one-hundred-yard expanse before the trenches, from the barbed wire and bamboo walls, the Vietcong's new hamlet recruits sprung like forest nymphs camouflaged in brush. They leaped out of their holes, with rifles and machetes that looked like weapons made from sticks and bamboo. Nick and B.J. and the whole immature platoon froze in a momentary trance of disbelief that questioned, "What is this?"

Then their eyes did what they had been trained to do, lock on the moving targets of human brush and take them down as they advanced. B.J. fired off four shots in quick succession at four bush soldiers who made it past the front line. Between the second he fired and the second they crumpled to hit the ground, the sun peeked into the haze of morning, and he saw their small breasts move beneath sack-like shirts before they fell.

Seconds passed as he slipped down into a memory, he and the neighbor girl Sheila, who appeared at Mr. Tunnelson's house only in the summertime. In the living room, he and Sheila fought over the G.I. Joes, wrestling like puppies. Bennie yelled, "Rebecca, I don't want these wild ass li'l niggers running around my house, send them back outside." Bennie came into the living room with a cigarette dangling from his lips and pulled B.J. up by the back of his shirt. "Nigga, what's your problem. Boys don't hit girls."

In the seconds he was lost in memory, the human brush cut down members of his platoon as if cutting coconuts from trees. His heart pounded, closing off his airway, when the platoon leader signaled to fall back from their advance. With gear and guns clacking in orbit around their bodies, the young men ran now, fast enough to break through the kudzu that they assumed would tangle and take them down. Then, "Hold the line!" their commander shouted, hoping they were in control enough of their fears to listen. They stooped low, audibly breathing, and waited, until nonhuman sounds returned, two birds calling to each other at a high pitch, "Nee, nee, nee." The remaining helmets on the front line popped up every few moments, holding their fists up to tell the platoon to hold the line, conducting their hearts to catch their rhythm when all of their minds had begun to take hold of the horror of true ambush.

B.J. knew from his training not to take his eye away from the scope of the rifle if things got chaotic. Low in the field he turned north, east, south, west, circling and breathing. He stopped on the magnified sight of the fallen bodies of women and girls. His breathing more like wheezing now, but he did not take his eye from the scope until he could see that there were no moving targets.

The unit remained paused long enough that decisions were made in the silent huts where the hiding Vietcong crept out of the back of the hamlet into the unforgiving bush of the mountain.

After an hour of stillness, the platoon's orders were to step over and around the bodies of the women and girls and find their own missing comrades in the bush, reach them quickly so that the injured could be saved and the dead could be wrapped. That's when B.J. looked around, seeing familiar faces beneath tilted helmets, and realized Nick was no longer by his side. B.J. yelled for him and heard the terror in his own tenor voice bounce off the distant mountain that the Vietcong scaled under cover of gnarled kudzu, ferns, and the long lashes of palm leaves.

B.J. mailed the letter to his uncle and requested to be removed from night patrol so that he could do the work of balancing the equation of the boy who left home without a word against the man who couldn't hide on night watch any longer.

Sunday morning, Uncle Lenard sang out in the church in his blue suit, "Change and decay in all around I see—O Thou who changest not, abide with me," and the congregation rocked with the hammer of the piano chords. Some of their sons had come home, with fire in their eyes and with missing limbs; some of the other families had been greeted at their doors by uniformed men who would change the trajectory of their dreams and make everything else in the perimeter of the city, the country, the race riots, all of it, become muted when they were handed the folded flag. "Through cloud and sunshine, Lord, abide with me." Lenard lifted his hands to God, gently, dignified, reminding himself that though his only word from his nephew had been the short letter, faith was what sustained James and himself.

James sat, a deacon now. He wore a suit jacket too tight to close in front, his wavy black hair gone half-gray. They prayed for B.J., the gentle boy, whose judgment, like any teenager's, had twisted and turned down back alleys with broken glass.

Lenard sang, James rocked, and they prayed for the pardon of those Black boys still in Vietnam and the souls of those already taken, "Mercy, God, mercy, enough. Forgive us, Lord, but enough."

They imagined God flying over the rectangles of green rice fields, the bodies of fleeing Vietnamese women and children shifting and phasing under the sun's rays into brown-bodied African children hunted by the foreign invasion, the hunters this time their own brown sons in camouflage, lying in wait to run the innocent off the edge of the earth to the ocean of their holocaust. They prayed, invoking the Divine to rise up out of the fields, out of the bush, up out of the asphalt, the ghetto, rise so high that the revelation of the curve of the earth could absolve the sins of killers, their own boy-children now among them. They imagined their Almighty Father, flying low like a chopper firing a spray of baptismal rain of forgiveness. "Amen," the congregation swayed, hands held above their heads.

Their Almighty Mother harmonized with them, knowing and wanting the same. Her spirit flew over the field, struggled against the current of the choppers that cut the air and cut the spirit's intention to bring B.J. home prematurely from his battle-scarred journey.

Every opportunity, B.J. volunteered to go off into the bush, into the hamlets, front-line scout, where he could do as much good as he could in order to make meaning of Nick's death. A better fate than sitting night watch, waiting for death that was sure to come.

Over the next four months, B.J. knew he must have been breathing, because he saw his hands and feet moving, so he knew he was alive. He and the other six men of the small unit were taken off scout duty and called "The Storm," because all of them were eighteen or nineteen years old and followed orders like zombies following their master's commands. They saw only what they were told to see. They never tilted their heads in doubt if they were told by their commander to kill everything out there breathing, told to increase their Vietnamese body count for the promise of a day of shooting hoops and drinking beer.

The Storm was sent to push against a small band of Vietcong who had escaped into the mountains, pushed out by napalm that took away their cover, and were flush against a small strip of swamp with no place to go but the China Sea. B.J.'s body was a member of The Storm, but his spirit had long since left the war, gone dormant, sitting at the edge of the neighbor's tobacco field.

Out of the brush, out of the mountains, out of the swamp, B.J. and his platoon pushed the Vietcong to the sea. The Storm crouched in the high beach grass that hushed and moved like hair in the wind. The smell of salt was in the air; the sun emanated from the sand and made warmth. It was beautiful, and all of the men, those labeled Vietcong with their backs pushed to the sea and those stateside boys who stood in the warm grass, they all turned into boys playing on a Saturday afternoon.

The enemy stood in the rising tide of waves that barreled into their backs, and their last memory was sun on skin and sand in their black hair on childhood vacations with their Vietnamese families. They remembered this same feeling of their little-boy bodies lifted off their little stubby feet with the push of the salt water, then the pull, and the feeling of their mothers' hands around theirs. The sound of her laughter like an umbrella over the sound of pending death.

B.J. remembered the day he and Rebecca ran away from his father. Made their way all the way to Wilmington Beach, where they sat quiet in the peace of the waves in front of them and the hushing of the dry grass in the dunes behind them. For that moment, he was free. He and Rebecca stood barefoot in the sun-warmed sand, the texture of her hand, the smell of his sweaty body like the smell of wet dog.

Ensign Lee closed his eyes to hear her voice again, and minus the one, The Storm was not strong enough to hold against the Vietcong men who stood knee-deep reaching for the last of their ammunition before agreeing to bury themselves at sea. The water rose to take them where they had been pushed into the high tide. From around their waists and their backs, they reached to each other and plucked the grenades from their own bodies as if they were plucking pawpaw fruit from low-hanging branches when they helped their mothers bring home the harvest. They tossed the unpinned grenades into the air before the last swell snatched them into the deep. Above the six marines, the grenades merged the sky and the sand, planted themselves there before the explosions set off in percussions that did not discriminate between American boys and Vietnamese boys but made flower petals of all of the bodies.

B.J. lay planted in the sand beneath the prayers of his uncles. He came to with the sound of the chopper. Its white star frightened him at first, but he faded in and out of consciousness listening to the "Fishing Blues" spirit, who lulled him to calm.

Then, the medic whispered Uncle Lenard's prayer, "Stay with me, buddy. Stay with me."

TWELVE

St. Louis, Missouri
1973

Older, long-gone spirits pushed and pulled and rocked the mother-spirit with the tides and lulled, "Don't lose faith when waiting on mountains to turn to pebbles, for rain to become rivers, for seeds to become the canopy to cover the crowns of heads, or when waiting for the fertile ground of the girl-child's return. Patience is needed for the reoccurring dream to do its work of awakening the half-dead mind disconnected from the purity of the soul that sits beneath the broad, green-fanned hands of deep-green tobacco leaves. Wait."

So she buried herself in the chests of the anesthetized and waited for memory to take them home.

"Chopsticks?" At the corner, there was a hole-in-the-wall Chinese place. So many Chinese takeouts had emerged in St. Louis while B.J. was in Vietnam. Black folks in the city called all these corner restaurants by the same name, the Chinaman Shop. Behind bulletproof Plexiglas, the owner took the money from under the slot, put the food in the drawer, and pushed it out to their customers. This way of transacting business was all over St. Louis now—the bail bondsman behind the Plexiglas, the liquor store with the Plexiglas, and the VA Hospital where the glass had pockmarks from bullets that attempted to penetrate the barrier between insanity and reality. They all tried to protect themselves from the dis-ease that returned in the bodies of Black sons and fathers who used to be the promise of the city.

The Ford plant threatened to close, because the Black men who returned didn't have the limbs to run the machinery and, if they did, were prone to fatal accidents. They leaped into the demolition equipment. They slipped beneath the saws that cut off their limbs to apologize for the missing limbs of friends lost in what was supposed to be combat.

"Chopsticks!?" The short Chinese merchant yelled the question at B.J. from behind the thick glass. B.J. looked around, self-conscious. *How long was I gone?* He felt agitated in his unwashed jean jacket, T-shirt, jeans. The line that formed behind him out of the door held itself at a distance so as not to smell him or be caught in the wake of what they perceived to be unpredictable insanity that seemed to rear its head all over the city.

B.J. responded, meaning chopsticks but saying "Popsicle sticks," looking in the eyes of the Chinese, not Vietnamese, man but thinking of the head count that would mean a day off to shoot hoops at base camp and a cooler of beer; twelve dead Vietnamese equaled a six-pack, just like when he was a child fishing with Bennie. Twelve fish caught without disturbing his deddy meant a box of Popsicles at the A&P. In his head, he saw the Popsicle sticks licked clean and saved for building a fort for his G.I. Joes. *Eight, nine, ten, eleven, twelve.* "Popsicle sticks," he said again in a tone of confidence, hoping that would break the confusing stare of the Chinese man.

A woman's voice from the line streamed in off MLK Boulevard: "Nigga, do you want some chopsticks or not!?"

B.J. grabbed the paper bag with his shrimp fried rice from the drawer. Knowing something off had come out of his mouth, he fled, walking quickly the six blocks back to Uncle Lenard's house, cursing the sun for making him visible to people who peered at him from their cars, from their porches, peered at him.

B.J. lay on his bed as the sun came into the window. In two more weeks, his old high school would let out for summer, and Uncle Lenard would be home during the day. The sun strained to get through the green blankets B.J. had hung over the windows in an attempt to block out the morning. The radio, tuned to KATZ, played Bob Marley's "I Shot the Sheriff," the volume on low. B.J. felt like the discarded remainder of some broken piece of artillery. He lay there in the place where two years earlier, he had schemed a method for rejecting what had been offered him—a home, a shot at college, which would have deferred the draft, would have kept him away from the whole shitstorm that was Vietnam. He lay there asking why Uncle Lenard didn't stop him, why Uncle Lenard didn't tell him about this post-dead state where all he could see in his dreams were his dead parents tumbling out the door of their bedroom and into his world along with bloody, bruised insurgents. The morning heat made the oils of his skin seep out—not sweat, just oil oozing out like the discomfort of sleeping in the jungle in ribbed sleeveless T-shirt and boxers that stuck to his body.

He lay there clocking Uncle Lenard's morning movements, the clank of the thin metal pan out of the pot cabinet, the faucet running to fill it with water, the suction of the fridge opening for him to fetch his egg, the loaf of bread that had to stay in the fridge so roaches wouldn't come for it, the butter, the cream for his coffee. The symphony of go-to-work sounds played out while B.J. looked at the ceiling, in the same spot where he lay on teenage mornings angry that he forgot to do his homework when he never forgot to do his homework, angry that his math teacher stopped believing in him, started treating him like the weed-smoking bunch who hung out behind the field house during homeroom, angry because that's who he was.

He didn't know he had fallen asleep lying there looking at the spot on the ceiling and listening to Uncle Lenard. He woke himself calling out for his night scout buddy, "Nick! Nick!" and then let out a long howl, not like a cry, not like a song, just a long, alto holler, flat without inflection.

Lenard rapped on the door—"B.J.!?"—and entered slowly. His mind pushed back the thought of opening the door to find his nephew in a puddle of his own blood, or dead from an overdose of pills stolen from some open-windowed bathroom's medicine cabinet in the neighborhood.

His nephew lay there, eyes half-open though he was asleep, lips cracked with dryness, whispering, "Mama, Mama?" in little whimpers as if he was helplessly watching something in his dreams that he could not prevent. Lenard could see it: B.J.'s spirit lifted up out of his heavy odorous body and hovering just above his bed, even though his body lay flailing in the covers.

Lenard could hardly catch his breath, couldn't watch or be part of it anymore, and asked God, "Lord God, help?!" *What did I do wrong?*

His answer came in a memory of the promise he made Pastor Johnson, "I won't try and make B.J. forget." Lenard stood there in the heat of the dark room helpless, watching his nephew writhe, deep in a hell his kin had left him in.

He heard, "Get up!" Lenard went over to the bedside radio alarm clock and turned the staticky dial to the gospel music station.

The choir was in the middle, the rising ether, their voices in harmony, "Nobody told me the road would be easy." Inside his heart he said "hallelujah" for the message, wiped his eyes the way he did the morning that he woke to find Bennie had left him alone to till the soil and bear the whip. Wiped his eyes with the back of his hand and pulled the blankets off the window, turned on the window fan, and stood there for the one minute that remained before he would be late. Lenard prayed, "Father God in heaven, extend your love and safety around B.J. and keep him, heal him, walk with him. Help me to know how to help him. Amen."

B.J. followed his uncle's lead and went to the prayer meeting that evening, which turned into more of a speak-out on pain. He fidgeted in his seat, aware of the heft growing around his body like James's heft. What was being said turned to sounds that agitated his cracked skull.

Sister Collier spoke to him, "Brotha Lee, do you want to share out?"

B.J. felt called away from the hovel in his own mind by her familiar voice.

He mumbled, "I'm not trying to be rude."

"It's okay, rude or not, God knows your heart. Anything on your mind is already in the room. Feel free to speak out, praise God."

He looked around at the other men, like chewed plastic G.I. Joes with missing and twisted pieces. He spoke up, but it wasn't filtered. "Y'all talk about not having no home, no country. We all broken and twisted up and are supposed to praise God? Don't you think that's some mean shit to put a nigga out on the battlefield till he's crazy as hell with missing pieces of his body, then bring him home and say, 'Praise God?'"

Sister Collier looked the same as she did when he was a little boy, a round light-skinned freckled sister, with a red, Afro-like halo around her questioning spirit. She was the only female deaconess and took pride in her efforts to help out returning veterans. Her baby-blue polyester pantsuit shushed with the movement of her arms and thighs. She pulled the jacket closed over her large breasts, covered in a striped polyester T-shirt. "Brotha Lee, we all dying. We all searching, trying to figure it out. The question ain't who has it right—the question is, Are you trying?"

B.J. sat in the dipping plastic of the chair, conscious of his own thighs thicker in the past five months; the tiny circle of churchgoers felt small. He heard her words as saying, *You aren't doing anything to help yourself or anybody else. You don't belong here with your bad attitude.*

Then she said, "Your vision of the world might have changed, Brotha Lee, but God is the same God. You just have your faith challenged. That's what believing in God is. When we are children, we believe because our parents tell us to, and later we believe because finally we grow up and have to grapple with death on our own."

B.J. leaned forward, his jeans clean and dried by his uncle. They constricted when he moved. "Sister Collier, you don't even know me. If God was gonna give me faith, he would have done it when I had to grapple with death as a child." Part slap in the face, part last word, part *Shame on you for not helping me when I was a boy.*

He broke the circle and left Sister Collier and the three young Black vets whose eyes he refused to look in, one with a stumped arm, another with a missing foot, and one who looked as normal on the outside as B.J. did and guilty-eyed because of it. When he got to the door of the vestibule, he turned around and interrupted their bowed-head prayers and yelled it out again to them and to God: "You don't know me!" He was gone, up the steps, out onto the street, resetting the worry that always resided in his family's chest.

Sister Collier called Lenard, "Your nephew interrupted the prayer meet'n yelling and carrying on and walked out. You might wanna go find him."

The alley was snug, an urban tunnel with no streetlights, just the occasional light from a house. It felt safe without being constricting. B.J. walked out the backyard of the church and into that tunnel where he could breathe, put his hands in his pockets, and disappear. He heard a warning in a voice he recognized: "Don't go." And the alley went dark, and he felt thirsty, felt the constriction of where his esophagus went into his stomach, felt his stomach contracting. "Don't go." He walked down the alley toward what felt like relief, like feeling rain just ahead when thirst constricted his mind. He heard in the darkness the congregation of the Baptist church of his childhood singing as one wave, "Yes, my soul says yes." Slow and harmonic, and he wanted to satisfy that thirst. The "Yes," became drawn out and high-pitched and brought with it streetlights, car lights. The "Yes" drew out, blaring, and went off-key as it pierced the shattered parts of his brain on the China Sea beach, "Yeeeeees."

The blaring, off-pitch whirring of car horns screamed at him where he stood in the middle of Goodfellow Boulevard. Not knowing they were calling him to live, he answered them thirsty for death. He stood on the double yellow line with his mouth open to the sky, hoping his spirit would fly out and chase after Bennie's and Rebecca's and the unnamed girl-child's spirit that screamed in long blaring calls of Cadillacs, Ford sedans, broken-down Chevy trucks, Black St. Louis folks steering around him, hollering for him to stay.

"Yo nephew standing in the damn street." James got the call before Lenard.

At the VA Hospital, James stood beside B.J. Held him by the arm as though James was scared his matted-Afro nephew would bolt and run. At fifty-six years old, James's knees were sore all the time from holding up his own body and holding back the grief of his life. The jukebox in his tavern, the circular wiping of the counter, the sound of liquor being poured into glasses were all a safe, productive smoke and mirrors that kept him from feeling what he felt. His life had been lived between the safe cave of the tavern and the safe sunshine of the church pew. Not enough movement. His knees hurt, and he leaned on the counter to hold himself up against the possible emotion of having to hold his nephew in this life. Lenard came to join them, walked through the door of the place that smelled like Band-Aids and pus with upright diligence.

With both of his uncles' eyes on him, B.J. felt his chest tightening where he stood. His head floated, disconnected from his spine. The smell of a fragrant Vietnamese flower dominated his trance where he lay, relying on the guardianship of his fellow scouts to take their watch while he took his turn at the vulnerability of sleep. "Slippin' into Darkness" played in his head, with jazz horns and cymbals whisked with drum brushes like eggs whisked in Rebecca's frying pan. He blinked and steadied himself in Uncle James's grip when the nurse pushed the clipboard of forms through the Plexiglas protection: "You have your ID?"

B.J. didn't look at her but frowned and looked to the floor and pulled his dog tags from under his T-shirt. She turned up her volume as if he was deaf: "Do you have your ID?"—like, "Nigga, do you want some chopsticks or not?!" He recoiled against the suggestion that his mind had slipped and fallen away to some place where sane voices had to yell angry expletives to retrieve responses.

He shouldn't have looked at her. "This ain't fucking ID? What the fuck you want from me?!" The heads and eyes in the waiting room of turquoise plastic chairs straightened. All of these men had been where B.J. stood, had learned to tame themselves and erect walls, even if the walls were made of temporary field medic tarp. Walls between the heat of confusion in their heads and the real world that spoke in rhythm and measured tones.

Lenard stepped up in his trench coat, his hat pinched in his hand. "I'm his uncle, ma'am. I'll help him fill out the forms." He put his briefcase on the counter, unbuckled it, and pulled out the forms he had kept for B.J. since he was six years old: Social Security card and a copy of his birth certificate that Lenard fetched from the Fayetteville courthouse on the day in 1960 when he went to identify the bodies of his dead brother and anonymous sister-in-law-with-child at the county morgue.

Lenard on one side, James's buttocks barely fitting in the seat on the other side of B.J., the two held him in place asking questions from the forms. "What would you say is the main reason you are seeing the doctor today?" B.J. just sat there, leering at the other patients in the waiting room and whispering, "What the fuck are they looking at?" Lenard's knee bounced with his own questions.

B.J. learned to separate the difference between what he felt swirling around in his shrapneled head and what he saw reflected outside in the real world. For the next few visits, he sat in the chair at the VA Hospital, wanting to tell the psychiatrist that the yellow chairs were making him feel agitated. "I was little, I didn't know myself as a man yet. I didn't know Vietnam yet, didn't know Uncle Lenard. I was in Fayetteville, and I stood in the middle of the street on that yellow line. I wasn't thinking, I just did what I knew to do, to go with them. I'm calm when no one is bothering me. I don't get confused. I got confused and was looking for my parents. I wasn't trying to kill myself." He knew not to speak about the voices that spoke to him, just speak about the facts of what happened and leave out the part that meant he might need to be hospitalized, strapped into this life.

"Um-hmm," she said, scribbling on the curled-edged yellow pad. "Have you been back to Fayetteville?" When she asked the question, B.J. just sat there, suspended between the brackish water in his brain and the linear path that words take. He looked around the room at the posters, one of a man who was clearly supposed to be a vet in a wheelchair smoking a joint. The poster read, "Drugs are not the answer." She asked again, "Ensign Lee," insisting on calling him Ensign when he preferred not but hadn't had the clarity to tell her that. "Have you been back to Fayetteville since you were six?"

B.J. managed through the distraction and the new sleepiness that came over him, "No, ma'am."

That night he lumbered into the kitchen after his uncle had already had dinner and gone into his office to read. B.J. made himself a sandwich with cold cuts and stood in the darkness of the kitchen eating it. He considered walking into the shaft of light of Lenard's office to ask about a ride to Fayetteville. The sandwich was all gone, and he drank a whole glass of tap water to calm the nerves that rose into his throat before walking to the office door. Lenard startled at the sight and sound of him.

"Uncle?" And they both remembered the day of "Uncle Lenard, the moon is 238,900 miles from the earth?"

The next morning was Saturday. B.J. did not lie in bed asleep waiting for his uncle to go out to cut the grass before making his way out into the house, and Lenard did not listen at the door of his nephew's bedroom wondering if he should look in. B.J. turned on the shower in their green, marble-paneled bathroom, got the best green bath towel, the shaving cream, and the shaver. Lenard rifled through the clothes in the dryer for a pair of jeans, a T-shirt, underwear to set on the hamper in the bathroom.

The bed remained indented with the impression of B.J.'s cumbersome body. Risen from his own death, the smell of skin, hair remained in the tomb of his bed, while the smell of Dial soap, Old Spice deodorant, and shaving cream smoothed him down to new brown skin. The shower steam pulled the alcohol-diluted saline clean from his pores.

They got on I-40. B.J. sat in the passenger side of Lenard's 98. The speed of images passed in his vision, and B.J. shut his eyes to avoid vertigo. He told himself to breathe the way the psychiatrist put it, "slow and drawn-out breaths," but his heart was beating too loud for him to concentrate. Lenard could hear the muffled pounding. He looked in the rearview at the eighteen-wheeler behind them. He calculated pulling over, told himself not to let his heartbeat match his nephew's heartbeat, as Lenard grew just as anxious at the thought of returning again to the other side of the Mississippi River, traveling east and south to retrieve some memory that might kill him but might save his nephew. Slow down, slow down. He was grateful for the green rectangle that meant he could exit. "No, no, no." B.J. waved Lenard back toward the road. "I'm good. I just want to get there. Let's just go." B.J. sat up, and

Lenard sat up straighter behind the wheel. The shadow of a thin cloud traveled above the car. Their breath and heartbeats slowed to match the thunk of the interstate beneath Lenard's unevenly worn tires.

The psychiatrist suggested they operate out of trust, that B.J. let Lenard know if he felt like he was about to let go of life, and Lenard had to trust, leave his nephew, not as a boy but as a man, to have ritual and closure around his parents' deaths. Lenard would have to trust that B.J. would not, like some last blackbird left in the migration, lift up off the ground and fly out after the others.

The two of them stood on the porch where Virginia creeper and honeysuckle vines clung and pulled at the weathered wood of the abandoned house, covering the windows and trailing overhead through the gutters to consume the house that neighbors would rather not remember as the house of too many murdered. They listened to B.J.'s heart pounding in his chest as sweat stains grew beneath the arms of his plain white T-shirt. Lenard blinked and told himself this is not that porch, as he felt his chest squeeze with grief from the days he was left on the porch of his Mississippi childhood, first by Lottie, then Bennie, then Old Deddy. Lenard broke the silence: "Here, I want you to have this." He handed B.J. the leather Bible Lenard carried with him each day in his briefcase, carried it like a talisman that was going to keep him safe from the sorrows of his own past. He stood there in his white short-sleeved shirt, black slacks, nice shoes, always looking professional—"Though I walk through the valley of the shadow of death, I will fear no evil"—and handed the Bible to B.J.

B.J. reached out for the book, put one hand on top of it, the other hand under it. "I remember we never used the front door, always came in from the backyard. So, I'm gonna say goodbye right here, Unc." They both peered around the side of the house at the hip-high weeds that grew as tall as the tobacco stalks in the field next door.

Lenard spoke softly, "You take that Bible for sure if you're going to cross through those weeds."

They muffled their laughter in a hug, the first lighthearted sound that came from the two of them in years. They patted each other hard, as though beating on tight drumheads to awaken the heart. Lenard held on in revelation that this is how he would have sent the boy off to war had he been given the chance. "Alright!" B.J. said, anxious now to traverse the weeds and stand at the door of his childhood.

He stared at the screen door, still with the curly lightweight metal over mesh, an illusion of some memories that didn't want to surface. He kept his muddy shoes on and entered the small kitchen.

Breathe, he reminded himself, and inhaled, then walked to the small hallway that was now so narrow around his body that he felt caught between the door of Rebecca and Bennie's old bedroom and his own small bedroom. He put his hands on both sides of the walls to keep them from closing in, to steady himself against the dizziness that pulled him toward the splintered hardwood floors of the hallway. *Breathe*—but breathing brought the smell of mold, which itched in his throat.

With his hand still on one wall, he opened the door of Rebecca and Bennie's room and could not brace against the falling that made his arm one with the doorframe, and then his arm chafed in the sand of the beach in Vietnam. His head hit the floor just near the foot of their bed. His head a clapper in the hard bell of his helmet. His head asleep on Rebecca's chest where the two of them hoped the man they both loved would not come back that night out of his mind. B.J.'s mind skipped time, his body's nerves took in all of the sensations that tangled in a net between past and present. The brain freeze of Popsicles eaten too fast pounded in his swollen head. The memory to breathe, to expand and contract, was gone, and he was groveling on the beach trying to get to cover.

In that moment, Lenard sat in the motel watching TV in order to keep his mind off his own southern traumas, which made him look out the motel window every time he heard a car motor. He focused his mind on B.J. and told himself that if his nephew needed him, the motel room phone would sound the alarm. But that was assuming B.J. had the presence of mind to go up to Ethel's Walk-Up on Ramsey Street and use the pay phone. In the house on Colonial Drive, B.J. did not remember his promise. The same pull that drew him from the alley to the double yellow line in the middle of Goodfellow Boulevard muted reality.

B.J. struggled to get off the floor and pull himself up on to his parents' bed. The beige mattress under the weight of his body folded into a cradle in the place where rats had removed batting for nests. He lay there for a while, calmed by the swaddling of the mattress, and breathed and waited for reality to return. The moon rose through the netting of vine in the window that used to frame the rising sun in spring.

Breathing steady now, the swelling in his brain subdued, he sat up, followed the moonlight to where it streamed in to Rebecca's nightstand drawer. He pulled to open it, but the drawer jammed on the paper keepsakes Rebecca had stuffed in to hold them close to where she slept. B.J.'s heart steadied. And he remembered being little and sneaking into their room when he was left alone. He would take something, anything—a few quarters or those packets he didn't understand as a child, a square pack like an Alka-Seltzer package but with something round and squishy beneath the crinkly wrapping. Anything to make him feel close to them.

B.J. reached his grown-man hand into the dark spaces of the nightstand, and his finger hung up on a staple. "Shit." He snatched his hand out, and with it came the black backing of a Polaroid with a half-opened staple that hung in the soiled flesh of his longest finger; the tiniest prick of blood opened him to the image on the flip side. A younger version of his mother, and her sister, Beverly, their wide-open faces. He had seen this picture many times as a boy. His mother's hair was long then, her torso narrow.

Beverly's hair was pulled back, with a yellow hibiscus flower tucked into her press and curl. Their faces phased into the faces of Vietnamese girls who sat in his memory detached from any backdrop. In the photo, in the fuzzy distance, three US flags were frozen in a lazy wave to announce the three men who would soon ride through their neighborhood in the middle of the day, faces covered, guns drawn.

B.J. lifted the photo to his eyes in the moonlight and smelled the rose-water perfume through the smell of mice piss. He noticed his steady breathing; the discoveries difficult, but the pull to remember a surge of current in his body. He lowered the picture back into the drawer. Beneath it, folded in upon themselves in stacks of three and four, were notes that had been chewed on by the mice. He leaned them into the light to see scribbled, disjointed letters in his developing six-year-old handwriting. He smiled, anxious to see his boy-self, and got up off the squeaky bed to get a better look in the moonlight. The first note on top: "Dad, Mom not home when I came from skool."

His blood curdled his mind as he heard Rebecca's voice hollering from inside the room, and he folded to the floor. Had he felt a sensation of memory before, something to warn him, he would have told himself to breathe to ward against the crippling twists of pain, but he was the ghost-child again who was left alone in the house, hollering for his parents.

Sometime in the middle of the night, after the moon had made its way to the bathroom window, the kitchen window, he crawled to Bennie's side of the bed, where he rifled around in his father's nightstand drawer. B.J.'s throat constricted with thirst. Half-conscious of what he was reaching for, his hand landed on the dusty, rectangular dented snuff tin that held a tiny lighter and the rolled and laced joints. The voice in his head sang, "He's got high hopes, he's got high hopes." He was helplessly shaking his head, reaching for Rebecca.

The first long drag on Bennie's stale drug brought an opening in B.J.'s lungs; his organs, caged inside his ribs, unclenched. With every drag, the universe expanded and contracted, and he cried in long unrelenting sobs. The drug did what he could not do on his own, breathe, and breathing returned oxygen, blood flow to the shunted-off memories. He heard an electric guitar inside his head that illuminated the memory of his father in the living room, joyfully dancing to the sounds of Chuck Berry on the tiny hi-fi.

The house gave in to a cloudy dawn light, the electricity still not cut on. Swaying and stumbling, B.J. ran from the encroaching memories. Out the kitchen door to the backyard, out of the fence through the tobacco field, past the neighbor's sleeping tar-shingle house, right into the neighbor's garden of cornstalks, bamboo stakes with tomato vines, okra stalks like small trees with a spread of purple flowers that turned into the bush, then turned into the sun-bleached Sunday morning. He ran right to where his boy soul sat waiting for the return of human touch.

The warmth of the soil beneath his church trousers, the blue sky above the small field next door to their house, the royal blue of Mr. Tunnelson's tractor with the specks of rust visible even from where B.J. sat, six years old, his brain humming, floating when the neighbor could not hear the words that came from his open mouth, and B.J. was inside the scene of his last moments with his mother.

He saw Rebecca was running, screaming for him with her arms stretched out, saw his father aim at her back, and he turned to face the neighbor who cut off the engine, whose boots crunched on parched earth as they landed in the soil. He heard the explosion that made his ears ring just above the yelling that came from Mr. Tunnelson: "Naw, man! Naw, man! Naw!"

And then Bennie's voice was the only sound above the quieting ricochet of the shot. "Rebecca!"—the cry that came from his open mouth was a bloodcurdling cry for Bennie's wife, for his mother Lottie, and for the unidentified girl-child.

B.J. saw his father's boots on the yellow line. He saw his mother's eyes stop, drop down to the ground, and disappear. He looked past the crumpled purple iris dress on the yellow line of asphalt. And caught sight of his father's eye, half-cocked. B.J. saw. He saw his father put his handgun to his head and heard the second shot that made his father's eyes stop and disappear.

For the sake of any child born of his blood, B.J. had done the most valiant deed, gone into the vault of his memory, awakened by the sights and smells of his childhood home, and pulled forth the casualties of his bloodline. Pulled his beautiful Black boy soul back into his Black man body. Memories with their darkness contrasted the light and made sight possible, made love possible, and unobstructed the return of all the truth-tellers. He was witness to his parents' death, and to so many deaths, and that was the truth that lived inside him. Flawed and human, as long as he was able, he would hold open the gates of memory for the girl-child's return.

B.J. was awakened by the flat, round circles of his father's eyes. Then the feel of Bennie's hand on his shoulders where B.J. lay in the space between walking with the dead and the living.

"B.J.!" He heard Bennie calling him through the thick sweetness of morning. "B.J.!" Then he smelled the familiar exhaust from the 98, still running. Lenard's call and Bennie's call the same. He called back, "Yes, sir," his voice hoarse like the six-year-old boy waking for Sunday school. When he sat up, he felt the whole heft of his body and every place it had gone and everything it had been through recollected now by his soul.

That afternoon, they stood over the markers; no one ever afforded headstones. "The one on the left is hers, the one on the right his," the groundskeeper told them, but he didn't remember to tell them which way to face.

"It's okay, it's okay," Lenard kept saying to B.J.'s tearful agitated complaint, "How in the hell am I supposed to know which one is which?"

"It's okay."

Relieved that his nephew had lived through the night, Lenard walked out of the rusted gate of the Black cemetery that sat behind the Baptist church and left his nephew there to be at peace with his parents. B.J. folded his hands into each other in prayer, but that did not feel true for him, so he cupped them, making a bowl, his brown fingers like the cane of a woven basket. Without being coaxed, he had washed and shaved at his uncle's motel. The naps of his Afro made a halo of brown where the sun scorched. He bowed his head and did not answer their call to be prayed over, just inhaled and exhaled, and whispered, "No more."

THIRTEEN

Fayetteville, North Carolina
1974

No hearing the "Fishing Blues" and singing where he left off in the chorus. In and out of touch, she touched down sometimes and found him where he needed to be. She tested the potability of his soul with a gentle whisper of his name, but he, like his father, went to the rushing water to shush the sounds, unable to distinguish between unwanted thoughts and essential visitations. And she was satisfied, because when she touched down and tasted the rain of his soul, she also found that he, unlike his father, had been raised by male hands that rooted and weathered and grew him to nurture, provide, and protect.

He wasn't looking for a mate. He wasn't looking for religion or any addendum to his own belief that shit happens and we just struggle and fight like ants and roaches and fish in the creek, trying not to get hooked, but swimming in a direction that always feels like circles even when we're truly going forward.

The house was his as heir's property, belonging to him because it had belonged to Rebecca's father, who B.J. had never met, then to Rebecca and her sister. Now it was his, after his father, Bennie, killed his mother just before killing himself. It was B.J.'s through bloodshed and bereavement, and be damned if he wasn't going to claim what he owned. Uncle Lenard coaxed, "Why don't you come back to St. Louis, son?"

"No, this is home."

B.J. kept his promise of "No more" to himself by reconditioning the place that held the pain, spackling and painting over the punched holes through which he heard whispers. Every nail hammered was like a whipstitch in his cracked-open skull, bone needles reaching across the fleshy chasm where things like death and the deeds of his own killing hands might spill out. Every meshed and mended wall a keloid mound where the unexplained whispers were plastered shut. "The house is settling," B.J. told himself every time he felt their whispers seep through a seam that appeared at the top of a doorframe or mysteriously in the middle of a wall.

He fetched used paint from the dump, fetched scrap wood from the dump, hauled the shit home on the bus even though people stared at him. Being stared at was something he'd grown accustomed to but could only stand for an hour or two. He had taught himself, *If they are staring, they see me, and I am alive.* They stared, and he remained the quiet man inside the bubble of his own goals to hold himself and his house together, resist the pull toward the sounds and dark thoughts. He found normalcy in the rhythm of plastering shut the holes, eating sardines, crackers, Lay's potato chips washed down with a Coke. He accepted the little basket of cucumbers, tomatoes, and peppers that Mr. Tunnelson left on the back doorstep.

One evening, in his raggedy T-shirt that used to be white but was now speckled with hand-me-down paints, B.J. sat on the back steps, feeling the cool of autumn approaching and listening to the crickets, the cicadas already encased in their shells for their next life. He heard the footsteps, something he would always be able to do after Nam, hear breath and footsteps or bellies slithering through brush. "Hey!" B.J. shouted out to Mr. Tunnelson, so that neither of them would be startled.

"Hey, man, how you been over here?" Mr. Tunnelson was still tall and stout, kept strong by his insistence on farming even the smallest patches of earth on each side of his home. He now had salt in his pepper beard and mustache. His tattered ball cap shielded his eyes, which was best for the two of them in this moment of reunion. They hadn't shared so much as a hello since the days that B.J. sat silent on his couch.

"Why don't you come over and eat a meal at the house? My daughter is visiting from DC."

B.J. was still in the midst of fetching the better memories of his childhood that brought light into the house. Uncle Lenard's and Uncle James's deep voices in the choir behind Sister Collier's: "Through so many trials and toils . . . So many trials and toils." B.J. didn't know anything about what his uncles' hands and backs had endured as young Black men until he had done the work to bring himself back home from the blood on his hands in the jungle, back from the bloodstained walls of his home, back from darkness that threatened to drag him from the innocence of his boyhood into the devil's violent storms. He did not know the difference between the spirits that called him to manifest good and the violent demons that called him to turn his hand upon himself or someone else. So he shut them all out, along with any intruders who knocked on his door to call him out of himself.

At the mention of Mr. Tunnelson's visiting daughter, B.J. remembered Sheila—the girl who wasn't always at Mr. Tunnelson's house but was there often enough that the two of them were playmates. It took being a man, with paint-flecked clothes from rebuilding his own house, for him to remember that Mr. Tunnelson and his wife lived in different places, and Sheila was the first kid he knew whose parents had the sense to know that "till death do you part" wasn't supposed to be taken literally. She lived part-time with her mother in DC and with her father in Fayetteville until her mother was walking to work one morning and collapsed. Brain cancer struck her dead like a drunk driver whose ritual was to take someone with him every time he turned up the bottle to quiet his own pain. At her mother's request, she was buried in a dignified Black cemetery in DC, having paid for her headstone from her hospital bed:

HERE RESTS
LUCY MARIE TUNNELSON 1932–1972
MAY SHE REST IN PEACE

B.J. fiddled with the edge of his T-shirt: "Sure, man. I can come by."

Sheila sat under the lamplight of Mr. Tunnelson's kitchen table. Rebecca had taught B.J. to speak to the neighbors, be polite, but don't go up in folk's kitchens.

"Don't stand out there. Come on in." Mr. Tunnelson belted from where he was washing garden vegetables at the sink and wearing a white butcher's apron. The light drew B.J. into the house with a sound that was in his head, not out loud in the room the way it seemed, a peaceful buzz that spoke to and aligned his nerves, called them into formation.

When she tilted her head and said, "Hey," B.J. noticed her. Her voice was free in her throat, so clear, like a voice that hadn't known battle. Her Afro was so soft that it fell in the middle. He noticed for the first time her sweet caramel-brown skin. She was the womanish rendition of the girl he had never looked fully in the face, just run wild with, seeing her from the side, or the two of them looking out and seeing the clothesline, the tobacco leaves, the kudzu that took over the trees of the creek from the perspective of Tarzan and Jane.

She stood in her father's kitchen, a resurrected good memory that did what good memories can do. The sight of her placed his feet on the ground, the sky above his head, and made him feel home, as if "Hey" was some chant that called newborns to the shore of the living.

That summer, they signed themselves over to each other at the county courthouse and tilled the soil behind their home. Plants had been his enemy, wrapping around his ankles and wrists like shackles that snared him for Vietnamese soldiers. She showed him what she had learned from her father, how to intend what is planted and grown from the soil, mint, marjoram, basil, sage. "Farming was ours before they made us do it for free," she told him. The ones she planted made their ways into teas and soups. She showed him what she had learned growing up with her mother and their Black feminist friends in DC, how to grind the herbs to extract the darkness, got him to sweat more, pee more, and talk to her more about the sin everyone knew of the Fayetteville man who shot his wife and himself. Got him to talk of the little boy who disappeared and came back after Vietnam seemingly unscathed. Those stories, which had been boarded up behind shut lips, had been felt again in the ways that were healing, and then B.J. packed them into boxes, taped up and marked "To the Grave."

"Don't succumb to the isolation, man. Don't let the demon drag you down." Sheila spoke to him from the place where she assumed she had faced her mother's death in real time. She had allowed herself guilt for being on study abroad in Ghana when her mother needed her most, guilt for abandoning her own father. In real time, she had let guilt and grief take their turns until she had made temporary peace with "Here Rests Lucy Marie Tunnelson" and loved herself into knowing that it was not her absence that had brought about her mother's death. Peace that reminded her she had a living parent and that abandonment could be reversed with commitment.

She coached B.J. about his quiet as if the two of them were the same, as if his quiet was what would do him in, rather than realizing that in his mind it was the action that kept him sane. Quiet calmed the anxiety, but to keep the heavy sleep of depression at bay, B.J. had to stay in motion. He took up a daily ritual: measure twelve feet, two inches, build something in the house, a bed for the two of them, bookshelves, the frame of a shed where he could build all night if need be.

Together they saged and brought the house back to life, scrubbed away the sounds of tormented bodies against walls. Sheila said, "We are restoring their voice among the ancestors who sing us out of deep pain." B.J. listened, repeated what Sheila said about his parents being ancestors, though he would never understand how two people could love and hate each other so much that the only songs he could hear of them in his head were sounds that still made the pounding in his chest quicken when he thought about them. *Ancestors? Okay.*

Sunday morning, Sheila melded the ways of her DC mother who always knew that vegetables, fresh-picked fruit, and hand-pounded grain belonged to Black people long before the word *diaspora*. Blended that knowing with the southern ways of her father and made her and B.J. a big breakfast, of tofu eggs, biscuits, and fried apples. Her hair was plaited into pickaninny braids that would later be picked out into her light brown floppy Afro. On her suitcase record player, Stevie Wonder's "You Are the Sunshine of My Life" played. She snuck up behind him where he was working in the yard, hammering to build the new shed: "Oh, what? Did I hear you say something?" She giggled, poking fun at his muteness, and hugged him around his heft. The two of them were the same height, but her body stayed in the frame of teenage thin bones. Under the morning sun, grass and sawdust at their feet, they were a still life of green, gold, and black African-print dashiki against paint-speckled T-shirt and stained jeans.

She kissed his neck where his short Afro almost trailed down his back. "When you come in, I'm trimming that up, baby."

"Yep," he mumbled with a handful of sixpenny nails sticking out of his mouth. The music wafted out the window to the backyard. She gently pulled the nails one by one from between his pouty lips and kissed him. B.J. didn't have much to say, but if she begged, he would sing for her. "Sing to me, baby."

He looked out beyond the shed to make sure her father wasn't coming through the yard to visit the way he did much too often. B.J. cleared the sawdust from his throat and woke the crooning teenage voice: "You are the sunshine of my life." She sang back, "Forever you'll stay in my heart," and Sheila danced, content with the slightness of his personality that beamed through just enough to keep her satisfied with Fayetteville, North Carolina—not DC, not Ghana—as home.

She pulled on B.J.'s arms that once bopped down an imaginary

Soul Train line, and he acquiesced and let himself be awkwardly yanked around to the rhythm. He shyly smiled at her and led her to the bed he had built for the two of them in the room that had been cleansed of the ghost of his parents.

Two months later, Sheila came into the kitchen where B.J. sat at the table. She was glad to catch him before he ran away from her Sunday morning ritual of a big vegetarian breakfast. Clouds brought the sweet smell of rain on faraway dry soil into the kitchen window.

She danced around and laughed, and it was infectious. B.J. giggled back at her, a sound that rarely came up from his gut even though he had no idea what was so funny. She reached for his hand and put it under her dashiki, her hand in control of the foreplay. Her tummy was warm and soft and goosebumpy. The two of them were still chuckling when she sat down on his filthy jeans and said the words that planted her firmly in southern soil, planted B.J. firmly on this side of the living, and announced the third coming of the girl-child who would proclaim all the spaces where the sun blistered over the head as wherever-she-wanted-to-go.

"B.J. This is your baby."

PART THREE

The Spirit

FOURTEEN

Fayetteville, North Carolina
1975

If spirits had booties to shake and hands to raise up in praise and feet to stomp up the dirt floors of huts and sheds and urban fields, they would. Sometimes nothing changes for a long time and then one day, in one moment, quick so you don't miss it, it happens. She finally arrives. She, the unanticipated response to other folks' plan of attack.

On the day the girl-child was born, B.J. leaned over his prized band saw to make the crib mobile. The bulb hung from the ceiling in the fall air, keeping the shed warm, its cord extended into the kitchen window for electricity. He wanted to be alone, but the uncles and his father-in-law had come out of the house the minute his wife, Sheila, started a conversation by pointing out, "These are teas to help when my breast milk comes in."

They sat like a chiefs' council in the backyard in old wooden church folding chairs fetched from the dump. They made a row just inside the opening of the shed. It wasn't easy to find a conversational intersection between Black urban farmer, Black math teacher, Black tavern owner. They landed on B.J., their common denominator.

Uncle James took the lead, "You done got real handy. I was noticing the craftsmanship of all the baseboards in the house."

Aside from calculating measurements, Uncle Lenard knew little about construction, "You can really tell why you get the big contracts on the other side of Ramsey Street."

Everything at the top of the hill on the other side of Ramsey Street was new development. Sometimes the new homeowners accidentally made a wrong turn and ended up on Colonial Drive. They rolled down toward North Street in their BMWs, hoping to find an outlet, only to end up where B.J. spent a lot of his childhood fetching crawdads, at the butt bottom, where the mosquitoes were the size of sparrows.

"Yep," B.J. responded, reaching for the next piece of wood to cut out the elephant. Mr. Tunnelson sipped his beer and sat up after leaning forward, elbows on knees, to get relief from the height of Uncle Lenard and the heft of Uncle James. "Yep, really good supports and spacing on the joists that come off the crossbeam." He pointed up to the top of the shed.

Uncle James added his two cents to have the last word, like the bullfrog who had to make his croak the loudest: "Could use to have been put on a foundation even if it's cinder blocks. Son, did you measure this opening for the standard width and height of premade shed doors?"

B.J. flipped the saw back on, so it wouldn't appear rude that he didn't answer them but would look as though he was rapt in his project. The three of them made a grumble of chaotic sounds as unbearable as the pre-execution pleas of Vietnamese men and the tangled spirits that Bennie had plastered and silenced in the house. Being talked at and watched made B.J.'s heart beat a little harder and his head itch. If he looked at them, he felt the pressure of their expectations for normal words.

Uncle James sat back in partial warmth of the shed, pulled his sweater around the orb of his belly in discomfort at his nephew's silence. He wanted B.J. to speak up and seem less odd to the father-in-law, who might not understand the nuances of his son-in-law's behavior. The wooden folding chair threatened to give beneath James's heft. And he added an awkward response to ward off the residue of death that he felt in the fall air: "You thought about a will, son? You and Sheila need to consider not just ways to get the life you want, but ways to keep from having your property taken away. Life don't give what you're owed, more likely to rob you of what you're owed."

B.J. didn't look at Uncle James when he let the band saw slow to a whir: "No, sir."

And then showed the defiance that was always there but wasn't likely to come out unless agitated. "This isn't Mississippi. Nobody's gonna ride up in a white hood and take the land."

His three male kin fell silent, while the crickets chirped in response to the coming of dusk. The sipping sounds of lips on beer cans, and water for Uncle Lenard, were the only sounds until the clapboards of the house moaned and bulged on the matter. Then the screen door clapped behind Sheila.

"B.J., Deddy, my water broke!"

After hearing Uncle Lenard's tales of Lottie, the Mississippi mother with the black ringlets of hair who got herself lost to avoid the beatings of her husband, and after hearing her father's tales of B.J.'s mother, Rebecca, who just wouldn't leave her husband, Sheila decided to name the onyx-eyed flesh of her flesh Lottie Rebecca Lee. It was her attempt to honor the memories of women whose names were honored only in their son's nightmares. The ornery old Black nurse who was there for B.J.'s birth reversed all that Black feminist intention when she took one look at the child and chanted a curse over her head, "Lord Jesus, if that ain't the blackest little baby born this side of heaven."

B.J. didn't want to think about what all that meant, and all that talk of mothers' pains and who was too dark and who was too light just made him numb, so he just said something neutral and true—"That's a beautiful name for my beautiful baby"—and smiled.

Lenard was too proud to make sounds after Sheila asked, "Will you be her godfather?" Tears rolled down over the tension of his smiling face while the nurse roughly used the bulb syringe to suction the blood and mucus of the womb from the baby's nose. James stood the farthest from them all, one eye squinted. The anesthetized part of his childhood brain almost recognizing in the girl-child the one who came into his life, came into his home, and shone a light on all that was hypocritical in his world. He frowned like an uncertain twelve-year old boy, unimpressed, then fake-smiled when remembering he was the adult, uncle of this being.

Her blue-black eyeballs rolled around the room and landed on each of their silent eyes. With sight from her soul, she saw her youngest brother Lenard, her brother B.J., bereft of her older brother Bennie, who twice barred her path. Before the nurse placed the girl-child's head in one of Sheila's hands and her bottom in the other, the baby's eyes scanned the radius of the room, looking for her first mother and her second mother, whose names adorned her new life, and her eyes rested on Sheila. With her stare, she requested that she be a soul harbored in this life until such time as she could fulfill her purpose. By reaching for her child, Sheila agreed. And the silent bridge of their eyes paralleled the cord that was soon snipped between them, leaving Lottie Rebecca with one ear turned toward this world and one in the spirit plane where her soul had so long awaited entry.

At six years old, Lottie Rebecca Lee called Sheila Mama, but she called her father B.J., and no one questioned that either. In her mind, she couldn't call him what Sheila cooed, "Call your father Deddy." She told people she was older than her father, and they laughed. She told them what somebody called her at school, which she thought was a compliment since it was what they called the smart one in the book of stories that sat on her shelf that B.J. built, two feet high next to her twin bed: "Tar Baby!" The caramel-skinned kids laughed, and she laughed with them, negating their teasing.

"I'm Tar Baby," she laughed from her gut. Sheila pulled Lottie Rebecca's arm, hoping to pick her up and walk away from the women who came over to talk about Black women's issues. She whispered, "Don't tell people you are Tar Baby—you are *my* baby." But Lottie Rebecca bent her body in half so that her butt would be the anchor weight to hold her truths in place.

When Sheila was a child, every new moon her own mother prepared for the book club women. She danced around the house to Bob Marley in T-shirt, hoop earrings, soft Afro, and wrap skirt. Lucy Marie Tunnelson, proud divorcée, cleaned their brownstone apartment for the women who were dark and round, dark and tall, redboned with bushy eyebrows. Sheila remembered her own chin on her mother's muscular shoulders, the smell of body oil and hair oil, patchouli, hemp; she was held in the spaces made by the hum of Black women's voices talking about things that felt serious.

"Our bodies belonged to this earth long before white men and even our men tried to hone us into their sex thangs. This earth knew about you before you knew about you." This was Sheila's Sunday school. And the women laughed and patted her place on the couch fetched off the DC streets when her eight-year-old wisdom sprouted: "We are all of woman, even men, because they came out of a woman's vagina."

Their deep guttural and high-pitched cackling voices made comfort, letting her know she had said a right thing, a wise thing. She was never offended, because unlike the daughter she would eventually give birth to, she knew she was a child among adults. When Lucy Marie Tunnelson was gone, all that comfort disappeared with her. Sheila wanted home. Her mother had said, "Spirituality and community are one and the same with home."

Standing at the sink every morning surrounded by her plants, with her screaming daughter and her silent husband at her back, Sheila couldn't seem to reconcile what was spiritual and what was community into what was home. The women in her Fayetteville neighborhood showed little interest in the things that made Sheila feel community.

For her book club efforts, three women sat in the living room, foreign to the Joan Armatrading tunes that came from the little suitcase record player. The singing made the spirits in the walls want to wake up and slow dance with the little hands of the little being who they should leave be. The singing made the three book club women want to cry into their tea: "If I can feel the rain in my face and the moon in my hair, why can't I feel love." Just enough calling to make the women stay, all the while watching the door and wanting to bolt as if there was something of the grief of spirits thirsty to drink their tears.

The two tall, slender, treelike women from the church lived across Ramsey Street. Sisters who remembered their teen days when Lottie Rebecca's grandmother, Rebecca, played the piano at church and they sang in the choir with Rebecca's sister, Beverly. Sisters who wanted to see if candles and plants and new drywall and music that wasn't the blues could cure a house and cure their thoughts that Fayetteville was all there was. For all those years the house was empty, they, like many others, turned themselves around at the bottom just to check on God's way with things. They nodded in accordance with his wishes that wisteria, kudzu, and scuppernong crawl up and cover the house with all the bad memories.

But the son was back; the daughter of the neighbor who witnessed it all was back. The women wanted to see, because maybe the house being saved meant something new and hopeful for their own lives of working the predictable clerical jobs on the base, of Saturday nights mourning the romance they never let into their lives, of Sunday morning church and their commitment to its baptisms, weddings, and funerals.

Their curiosity brought them across Ramsey to the downhill slope of the restored living room on Colonial Drive, but Sheila had a harder time convincing the third woman, from Sheila's side of Ramsey, to come up from the bottom of Colonial Drive to the book club. Sheila knocked on the loose trailer door of the young widow whose husband had also been a marine, before he died of liver failure. The woman didn't have much to say to Sheila but opened the door because she was lonely peeking out of the blinds, one knee on her musty couch and the cushion of her belly growing between her and the rest of the neighborhood. She had seen Sheila walking up and down Colonial Drive with her white-eyed, deep-spirited Tar Baby on her hip, proud with her long wrap held in her other fist to keep her hem out of the pothole puddles. The woman opened the door because maybe this hippie-looking Black woman knew something, since she walked as if she never had nightmares.

"Hey, come to the book club. We're keeping it low-key, reading Nikki Giovanni poems for the first session."

What the hell kind of name is Nikki Giovanni? Do you smell like incense because you are covering up the smell of weed?

"I'm good," and she didn't look Sheila in the eyes. Didn't say what was said after the door was shut: "I knew that was just a bunch of Africa hippie shit. Ain't nobody need friends enough to go up in the house of all that death." But the woman's attempt to survive her loneliness had her sitting squat in the living room next to the two tall-tree sisters, watching a Black child say what she wasn't going to do and not get a whuppin.

Lottie Rebecca pulled against her mother's arm, almost pulling the two of them to the floor. She looked up at Sheila in reprimand with her teeth gritted, both of their Afros making them look kin to each other and foreign to the three press-and-curl women on the couch. Sheila saw them looking up over the cardamom tea, to see her struggling to use her no-hitting ways to get Lottie Rebecca to mind her: "Shh, baby, don't call yourself Tar Baby." But she had lost control of her book club fantasy. Lottie Rebecca knew what she was trying to say, just didn't know all of the words yet to make Sheila understand. Then the tension released. Lottie Rebecca's "Nooo!" that always came before the embarrassing tantrum resounded in the house, and when Sheila turned the child loose, she heard the front door slam behind the three women.

"Love," Sheila's mother had said, "abides all." But all the women of Fayetteville, even her own child, were challenging the hell out of what she took for granted as a Black woman's peace of mind.

Any time Lottie Rebecca's uncles, her mama, or her grandeddy got started telling her how to be who she was, her little stick arms and small hands professed like an elder, but the squeaky tone that came out of her mouth was like air being slowly released from a balloon: "I'm older than all of you. You don't know me yet!"

They laughed; she put her fists on her hips to scold them, and this made them coo and giggle at her little cocoa-brown, round face, which did not reflect the authority she felt in her head and heart. Those days, Lottie Rebecca Lee tantrummed for hours while distant neighbors hollered down or across Colonial Drive, "Lord Jesus! Whup that child's ass!" Through the curtain of her own high pitch of rage, Lottie Rebecca could hear them and screamed until she fell into a sleep, thinking, *They think they are smarter than me.*

It was Sunday, and morning breakfast was calm for the girl, with the rhythm of Sheila's humming and the ritual of a big breakfast, but by Lottie Rebecca's six-year-old account of things, B.J. should have been at home with her and her mother having tofu scramble and toast and orange juice, all the stuff Grandeddy Tunnelson said was going to turn her into an anemic. "Sheila, you might wanna eat like that, but Lottie Rebecca needs something to make bones and hair out of. What, you trying to starve the girl? Feed her some pork chops or liver every now and then." Lottie Rebecca sat at the table swinging her feet across from Sheila in the smooth pine chairs B.J. made. Her arms were able to reach up and rest on the table also made by her father.

The weekend was a relief from the first week of school. Trying to make friends with the other children proved to be as frustrating as trying to communicate with her family. The day after she got her Tar Baby nickname, she sat at the picnic table in the schoolyard eating the peanut butter crackers she made herself. Smeared peanut butter on each saltine, then placed another saltine on top. She planned to pretend she was B.J. eating saltines and sardines. She felt appropriately independent with the other children, who she thought were all like her because they were all some shade of brown and her height, little hands and feet, a big switch from being in her house with all those ignorant grown folks. She asked the sweet little brown girl with pink ribbons and stiff braids who smelled like cookies and milk, "What do the whisperers say in your house?"

"What?" The girl scooted over with her Wonder Bread peanut butter sandwich hanging from her mouth while she used her hands on the splintered bench to move her more quickly.

"You know, the ones that swirl around your feet at the kitchen table and hum and call your name. Do they whisper names in your house?"

The girl unhooked her legs from under the bench and ran. Her calico dress moved around her body like the shirts that moved on the clothesline in Lottie Rebecca's backyard.

"Wait!" Lottie Rebecca's pinched voice yelled behind her new friend. She knew that once the girl told the teacher, she would be laughed at, and a wide distance would grow between her and the other kids.

She hadn't found words to tell Sheila how the walls of the world outside the house and the walls inside the house had erected themselves around her, leaving a feeling that made her agitated with the thought that people, including her parents, were having one experience of the house, the yard, Colonial Drive, each other, and she was having another. She sat at the kitchen table; the light of the window made pretty shadows of the philodendron vines. Her feet stirred and played with the current of spirits, all of them singing her name, "Lottie Rebecca, Lottie Rebecca," like meddlesome flies that no one else could hear. She grew agitated, wanting B.J. to be there at the table for breakfast, not off fishing. She knew, from the way B.J. shifted his head at the same time that the current of the spirits entered a room in the house, that he heard them too, but he dismissed them, pushed them out of his head as soon as they called his name. He would go to the shed and hammer louder than their whispers—paint, spackle, and caulk to close the cracks that might give them space to speak. And Sheila, if she could hear them, must have mistaken them for the sounds of water running or the rumble of the garbage truck, because she was solid in her movements whenever any disturbance from the nonliving entered her thoughts.

The spirits knew better than to spend so much time disturbing Lottie Rebecca's peace before she had lived in the flesh long enough to move her mind and body to carry out the deeds of all-that-is. But she had stayed so long in the holding of their gaze, cornered in the lit elbow of the womb, rocking in the belly of the ship, at the bottom of the ocean awaiting birth, that they came to her often from the seven generations before. They were playful, celebratory, and sometimes rambunctious, like relatives who coax hands and feet that they no longer possess to dance the dance, drink the drink, testify, and sing, though the one being honored by the ceremony has not come of age.

The spirit energy tangled around her feet faster without B.J. there to pull some of their energy away. Lottie Rebecca's swinging feet, in tiny red high-top Converses, turned to hammers that kicked until she kicked the table to make them leave her alone, kicked it again and again. Sheila recognized the beginning of what might soon turn to bloodcurdling screams that would make the neighbors think she didn't know how to control her own house. She took a deep breath and turned away from the stove, wiped her hands on her dashiki, and walked over to Lottie Rebecca—"Stop it!"—and her daughter closed her eyes, leaving a dark brown wall between them, so that she could concentrate above her mother's distraction, and she got about the business of kicking the energy out of her morning.

Sheila came over to her side of the table and held her arm. "I don't spank, but I will whup your little ass if you don't start acting right!" She had long since made a choice to never spank or cuss, the same promise her own mother had made. But frustration at the separateness of this creature at her table took hold. "Stop it, dammit! Stop!"

Lottie Rebecca's eyes sprung open in reprimand of her mother. "No!" And her voice came screaming out of the hot current of air that trailed out through the back screen door and wrapped around the Sunday morning peace of the neighborhood: "Nooo!"

Sheila looked down at Lottie Rebecca, reasoning away her impulse to silence the voice that did not come through as squeaky cuteness but resonated from someplace deep inside the cage of both of their souls. Lottie Rebecca looked through her mother the way she looked past the eyes and flesh of all her kin in the room on the day she was born, and out of her mouth came the first disturbing thing she would manage to communicate that made sense to her but cast her mother out into a distant landscape that she would spend years trying to traverse back to her daughter. "You stop it, Sheila! They are talking to you too, and you don't say nothing!"

Words from the little mouth of the flesh of her flesh that threatened to shatter Sheila's ungrieved mother-loss. The little being saw the power of the tofu scramble breakfast, teas, and incense and also saw the pain her mother harbored beneath them. Sheila almost forgot who she was talking to when she stood over her child. "What did you say to me, Mtoto? What did you say?"

At the sight of her mother reaching over like a tree threatening to fall, Lottie Rebecca screamed a truth in a voice that was distant and deep and got the attention of Sheila's soul: "Stop acting like you are not afraid of death!" Her little fists were on the sides of her temples to hold her human body in place, to remind her mother of her pact; despite her own limitations, it was Sheila's job to harbor Lottie Rebecca, and her daughter needed that, wanted that, but felt the impending abandonment.

Sheila went running out the back door to her father, her soul reduced beyond her education, beyond what she knew of Swahili songs and Black folktales and wooden toys and all of the right foods to feed a child who is older than her. Lottie Rebecca jumped down off the chair, almost tripping over the energy of the spirits. Her stick-figure legs went running out the front door to the creek, to B.J. who had witnessed death, like her, who had laid rocking in the belly of death.

B.J. was not familiar with the song he heard coming through the humidity and the kudzu, past the static of the cicadas, "Timi timi nyamale, nyamale." It was a song Sheila sang to wake her baby each morning, patting the knobs of her knees calling her to play, but B.J. had long since made his way out of the house each morning before that moment.

He got up off the damp, dark soil of the bank of the creek to peer through to where first he saw only a set of eyes that made him duck and bob his head. He tried to adjust his sight to see if this song in another tongue was from a true being or one of the phantoms of the bad dreams that always caused him to shout in the middle of the night.

When the vines parted, she came into full view, and for a minute he held his chest. The unkempt hairs raised on the back of his neck. He relaxed and sat back down when he saw it was his nightshade, round-cheeked child who stepped out of the bush.

She ran to his lap and whined her complaint, "B.J., Mama act like they not there. I was just kicking them, so they don't hold on to my legs." Then she said what she wanted but no one would abide, "I wanna move. I don't want to hear them no more."

She said just enough that B.J.'s heart stuttered in his chest. He whispered to himself, "Breathe," and held on to her, let her lean her little head on the chest of his soiled, sweaty T-shirt, and they both let out a long sigh the way they always did when the sounds of the spirits calmed down. The throbbing of Lottie Rebecca's temples calmed; the beating of his heart calmed. He didn't need more words from his daughter, didn't want more words. He spoke an apology that he had collected like roots boiled down into a placebo salve for the day he would have to answer her about the voices they both heard. "It's not right my mental stuff passed down through the bloodstream to you. Sometimes, li'l bit, it's good to just put things out of your mind. Singing is good like you do sometimes, or drawing stories like you do, or maybe you can build something, or you can fish with me."

Lottie Rebecca put both of her damp hands in his Afro to hold his skull in place and correct his mind from taking paths to tell lies to himself; the voices were not mental shrapnel or debris, they were visitations whose presence needed to be reckoned with. The Lees didn't go to church. There was the creek and morning sun and the wee bit of cool before stifling heat that grounded B.J. There was the sound of music in the kitchen in the morning, the smell of incense on the windowsill, slithering streams of sweet sandalwood smoke contrasting the downward spiral of philodendron vines over the repaired panes of the kitchen window that grounded Sheila. Lottie Rebecca tilted her head to one side. What was there to answer her need for peace?

"Did they ever use to talk to you?" Her little voice was raspy with exhaustion now. Her lips tried not to burst forth the sounds everybody said they were tired of hearing from her. B.J. heard the voice in the living room when he was a child, singing him the "Fishing Blues" song when his mother, Rebecca, and his father, Bennie, made him the child of their constant warring. He remembered hearing the voice scream a sharp "No!" when he tried to use his six-year-old wisdom to make his parents cease, to pull them into his silence.

He watched sweat roll from his daughter's temples and wanted to apologize for rewriting the truth in order to hide the pain inside his head. It was the only way he knew to protect and love her at the same time. But she was not a child who appreciated security blankets or fairy tales. She squinted her small eyes to look for the parts of him that she needed and he hid from her. She moved her small hands from his skull to the chest of his T-shirt, and when he would not let her see him, she sat back.

The reflecting shapes of sun from the creek made light and broken shadows of leaves on his face in the form of forgotten bodies. They twisted on an invisible breeze, churned in the air around the two of them. She saw the sun rise and set in the brown specks of pigment in her father's eyes and felt the extension bridge that connected the two of them snap when he turned his eyes back to the lapping water.

He unwrapped his arms from her and leaned to where he'd laid his fishing pole on the dark damp earth of the bank. He sniffed and brushed his hand between their two faces as if she was one of the meddlesome memories that needed to be managed in his head. Lottie Rebecca got up off his lap and walked away unnoticed. She looked back at him when she smelled stale cigarette smoke and whiskey held in the humid air. Through the vines she saw a tall, thin Black boogeyman with skin as black as hers sitting next to her father.

Lottie Rebecca ran up the hill on the double yellow line long since faded out on Colonial Drive. Her small feet wrestled inside high-top Converses, fighting against the pain of being in body alone among family, forsaken by her child-body and mind, too underdeveloped to hold the maturity of her soul. Inside her chest, she heaved and cried, "Mama!" for the ones who died with her and the one who did the best she could to keep from crying when her six-year-old screamed unintelligible commands or drew crayon pictures that looked like death coroners' wagons and bloody eyes and hands over mouths.

FIFTEEN

Fayetteville, North Carolina
1983

They want you, Lottie Rebecca, because they can see all the things you are that they are not. They hope that you will carry the burden and change the tides. But they want all of that without having to tolerate your volume, your attitude, the intensity of your intelligence, or any of the other qualities that make it so that the mind, body, and spirit that you are can drag them all from the imprisoned side of the river to the freedom shore.

At night, B.J. watched TV in his chair in the living room that held space for his little-boy self, who once sat crisscross in the same place watching *Howdy Doody*. He was on to *Bonanza* reruns now, while Sheila sat behind him at the smooth-topped table having coffee with her father. "Deddy, I don't know if maybe something is wrong with her." She unfolded a picture and story that she'd placed in her pocket after her visit to the school earlier that day. She slid it across to her father's dry hands. "Deddy, I went up to the school this morning and her teacher handed me this story and didn't say anything. She just gave it to me. Deddy, you know I walked right out of there with it in my bag. I wasn't about to sit in front of her blonde-haired self and let her see the look on my face when I saw what was in that story. There's this, and she also drew something and wrote words that weren't in her homework."

Earlier that evening, Lottie Rebecca sat on the kitchen floor, where she wrote over and over words that weren't on her vocabulary list: *Cape Fear, Cape Coast, suicide, homicide, infanticide.* Sheila glanced down at the floor over her daughter's nighttime hair, half pickaninny braids and half Afro, and turned away as fear caught in her heart, making it fumble to catch its rhythm, making her look at her child for just a moment as someone she didn't recognize, drawing and writing things her daughter could not possibly know.

"Ten more minutes to draw!" she hollered behind herself as she walked down the short hallway, away from the husband who used the television as his meditation and the child who stirred her into confusing memories of not recognizing her own mother, who got so sick she turned into a vestige of herself behind the gaunt face of a dying woman.

Lottie Rebecca clicked her tongue to a pinging in her ear. She had learned to make sounds that blended with the constant crackling, pinging, and surging noises of the spirit sounds that went in and out of the wall sockets. B.J. thought she was following his advice on letting there be something in her head, music, drawing, something other than unwanted voices.

"Okay, ten more minutes," Sheila said again from the room where she sat on the bed with a story to read as if she had some control over the fact that the girl was likely going to take ten more minutes past the ten minutes that she had already been allowed. Lottie Rebecca sang from the depths of an eight-year-old tenor voice, her old squeaky sounds replaced now by a voice that sang an Otis Redding song: "I was born by the river, in a little tent, and just like the river I'm running ever since." Sheila and B.J. loved to hear Lottie Rebecca sing in the background as long as they didn't think too much about the songs she sang, the depth of the voice that came from a body too small to hold such a deep drum.

At the end of the evening, Sheila's decision was always whether or not to speak about what they saw on paper in some attempt to reroute Lottie Rebecca's attention or to leave it be. "Mtoto. What's this?" Sheila bent down to the polished linoleum B.J. had laid over the bloodstained linoleum of the story of his childhood. The dark-chocolate face and cotton-white eyes of her child looked up. "I'm writing down the story, Mama." Lottie Rebecca's voice reached high, as if what she was doing was a given for her and everyone else. Sheila got up and pointed to where Lottie Rebecca had scratched with a toothpick through the brown-crayon stick figures with red eyes.

"Baby." Sheila sat down on the floor with Lottie Rebecca. "But what is it, baby? Can you draw . . ." Sheila took a deep breath before finishing her sentence. She didn't want to tempt a tantrum right at bedtime. "How about some flowers or birds?"

There was silence, as if Lottie Rebecca didn't hear her or as if Sheila's questions were too far down in a canyon to reach the ridge where her daughter walked. "And baby, where did you hear words like this?"

Lottie Rebecca looked up at her mother and spoke her first lie about the source of the words whispered to her: "I heard it on *Barnaby Jones*." Sheila involuntarily let out a chuckle at the poor choice of her daughter's lie.

Lottie Rebecca tightened her lips like a vault, balled up the drawing, and got off the floor in one move. Her arms and legs were thicker now with muscle. She wore her short pants and short-sleeved T-shirt jammies with white clouds that she had long since colored eyes on using one of Sheila's markers. She stomped past Sheila with her masterpiece in one balled-up fist and slammed her bedroom door, with her mother on the other side. There were no screams, and Sheila sat at the table and cried without making sounds.

Mr. Tunnelson took his wire-framed reading glasses from his farming shirt pocket and scanned back and forth with yellow eyeballs to read his granddaughter's third-grade masterpiece, then rubbed the black-and-silver stubble on his chin. His brow furrowed, and he looked away at B.J.'s round crown of hair above the back of his television chair. "Yeah," was all he said. Sheila waited for what more her father would say to help her ground her concerns, but he was busy undoing the memories that his granddaughter's drawings stirred—twining vines that reached across the field between where he sat and where B.J. sat silent, a little boy in his memory hollering unintelligible words.

He swallowed down his growing Adam's apple, held his granddaughter's story in one hand, and looked down at the child's handwriting, which was perfect at eight years old. Each letter sat up with the strength of one of her father's constructions. Lined around the story were drawings of frogs in pencil with their heads hanging off. The first words of the story: *Once upon a time, a man went fishing and killed all the frogs in the pond.*

Mr. Tunnelson's concerned eyes looked back at B.J.'s chair again and across the table at his daughter, who looked tired with an exhaustion he understood; she had only one child and had been parenting for only eight years, but the challenges undid everything she knew about herself. He shrugged away the emerging vertigo memory of B.J. screaming for his mother, who fell to the ground before she could reach him. "I think she is just concerned about him fishing and the frogs dying, that's all."

Sheila put her hands in her dashiki pockets and sat back in the chair unconvinced, and she decided not to bring up the fact that the girl talked to somebody in the house when no one was talking to her, then got upset if Sheila asked her who she was talking to, then went in her room and whispered, answering someone back, "Yes, I'm Lottie Rebecca." Singing and drawing and singing, "Yes, I'm Lottie Rebecca."

The quieted part of Sheila refused to conjure the memories of her own mother getting dizzy, talking to herself, until one day, in her daughter's absence, the cancer cells floated around in her brain, spoke their minds, blocked blood flow to her brain, and took her home with them.

Not everything out of Lottie Rebecca's mouth was spirit-driven. At some point, the mind and body of puberty led, while the demanding spirits around her acquiesced and awaited the day her body would mature and carry out the deeds that spirit-without-flesh cannot manifest.

It was just before her thirteenth birthday. On the back porch sat the largest batch of sun tea ever. The afternoon fall light shone through the glass jug like light through a uterus; the tea bags, floating life-forms, released their brown into the water. High above the porch, Lottie Rebecca sat, legs dangling from the deck of the platform that B.J. had constructed in the mulberry tree. There was a silent pact between Lottie Rebecca and B.J. to do as Sheila requested and stay home, not leave her alone in the house. So father and daughter coexisted in and around the house on their silent accord.

Lottie Rebecca took her ruler and divided the top sheet of

typing paper into three long rows for the graphics she would draw. This time a woman stood by the water. In the next panel of the story, she unwrapped herself to step into the gentle river. The next panel was the blood-mucked water, the crocodile with its eyes closed. Above the river was one cloud, with eyes of the woman who witnessed the scene below.

B.J.'s saw whirred in the shed below, and Sheila climbed the tree ladder with the comb, brush, and bottles of natural oils in her dashiki pocket to interrupt the girl's silence. The story would have to wait. Lottie Rebecca placed it under the wooden box of pens and pencils she kept in the tree to avoid attracting Sheila's questioning, concerned eyes that said, "Is my daughter going to grow up to be an ax murderer?" Lottie Rebecca looked at her mother sideways, wanting for her mother to say something out of place so she could criticize.

Overalls was all Lottie Rebecca would wear those days. They provided a cloak to make smooth the front of her body, no breasts, no pooch to prove there was room inside her for another life. Sheila wanted the calming dark brown of her daughter's comforting stare but had to be grateful with the feel of her inner knees squeezed against Lottie Rebecca's shoulders.

Sheila pulled, parted, touched her daughter's scalp, left hand, right hand, fingers weaving hair like weaving baskets on the weatherworn platform. Without words, she pulled her child's thick mane into well-hoed rows. Sheila needed to leave the silence alone but used it as an opportunity to explain to her captive why the principal wouldn't let her wear overalls. "There are dress codes for junior high. When you come home after school, you can wear whatever you want, but you have to wear a dress, or a nicer pair of pants and a blouse. You can't wear these things. Do you understand me?" Sheila held the braiding with one hand and used the oily pinkie of the other hand to lift up the strap of the faded jean overalls above Lottie Rebecca's blue turtleneck.

The girl wasn't outwardly defiant anymore. The screaming fits of verbal frustration and rage at those who treated her like an incompetent child had calmed. She churned now in manageable storms of careful intellect. In her mind, she constructed a diverse landscape with separate regions—a sweaty tropical forest, a sandy white-sun seaside with the consistent breath of the wind, a cracked rainless plain with dry riverbeds. One for the spirits who frustrated her with their elusiveness but kept her company with their familiar folds of energy, one for the feelings that were older and wiser than the size of her body, and one for the things she needed to say even if no one would listen. She fetched only as necessary from those regions of her emotional landscape and brought words forward mindfully and sometimes mean-spiritedly, when she thought other people might shackle her freedom for expressing as she wished.

Sheila tilted Lottie Rebecca's head to one side, the tannic smell of tea tree oil and dirt smell of patchouli mixed with the smell of the damp wood of the tree's branches. Tilting her daughter's head was a trick to see Lottie Rebecca's eyes, which usually rolled away from her mother's gaze. The sparrows flitted around in the branches above them, chirping to each other about the giant brown mother bird in turtleneck and dashiki and her furry-headed giant baby bird in turtleneck and overalls who had invaded their tree.

In the long pause, Sheila remembered a moment when everything between them was good. Lottie Rebecca's hands still small as the two of them strolled up Hayes Street, the girl a tiny willful extension of her mother's body. Sheila sighed and waited and parted and oiled and braided until her reminiscing tears receded. She held Lottie Rebecca by the shoulders and turned her to face her mother.

"Did you hear me ask you a question?"

"Yes, ma'am."

"Do you have a response, li'l Mtoto?"

"Please don't call me that."

"Chile, do you have a response to what I explained about you not being able to wear these overalls back to school tomorrow?"

"Yes, ma'am."

"Well?!"

Lottie Rebecca went into the desert landscape for limited words to explain to adults the things they were too limited to understand. She let out a sigh of intolerance and explained to her mother, "There are brand-new pairs at the Gap. Red and green, and they are new and suitable for school. The principal said, 'No jeans' not 'No overalls.' It's a compromise, but I am *going* to wear overalls."

The two stared at each other. Sheila's gaze was full-on, and Lottie Rebecca's gaze was of one knowing eye from her tilted head. Sheila gritted her teeth and questioned if any part of her lived in her daughter. Grandeddy Tunnelson said, "She's acting just like you, sweetheart. She just tells people what she is going to do and does it. Or doesn't tell them at all, just does what she wants and sends you the receipt."

At her mother's funeral, Sheila had stood next to her father, with her mother lying beneath their good shoes that had never been worn to church. Sheila did not tell him that she was not planning to stay in Fayetteville with him. Closemouthed, eighteen-year-old

Sheila planned another semester of study abroad in Ghana, to slip away as she had done before and tell her father in a letter that would take two weeks to reach him.

Lottie Rebecca's round, smooth, dark face was a perfect amalgam of her parents, some combination of warring and running in their spirits. She rarely needed discipline but also never responded to her parents in ways they expected. Sheila turned the girl back around. Rather than smacking Lottie Rebecca's tightly braided head, she returned to the feel of the little hand in hers, the size of a small knot of her own flesh. She leaned in. The boards of the tree platform creaked, and she kissed Lottie Rebecca's scalp where the warmth of little-girl smell faded into the smells of young womanhood. She rested her chin there. "Okay, I won't call you li'l Mtoto, but don't you think it is manipulative to say you're still going to wear overalls? Don't you think it's acting like you a grown woman to say you will compromise on something I'm telling you not to do?"

They could argue until moss grew in their shoes and the sun turned itself off. B.J., like the birds above them, sat quiet and waited for it to be over. His workbench in the shed was where he perched his opinion while he sawed, stacked, nailed, and held his tongue in a vise grip, knowing better than to get in their way.

Above the sound of the saw, dusk began, and Lottie Rebecca's voice remained steady and sure of itself. "You didn't tell me I couldn't wear overalls. You asked me if I understood."

"But you are too young to be acting like that. And too old to be acting like you don't know what I mean."

Sheila pushed the girl's head forward, away from the opening from which the child had been born. She gathered the front of her dashiki that shrouded like a housedress over the matching blue turtleneck that she wore to connect with Lottie Rebecca. She descended the ladder down through the crisp evening air as fast as she could step without falling. Lottie Rebecca's voice chased her mother: "Don't take everything so personal. I have an opinion, and that's that!" Sheila slammed the kitchen door behind her.

Cold, leaving the child to decide right from wrong for herself. Bloodred kola nuts, a blue-green winged bird, and steady streams of black-water current were reoccurring images in Lottie Rebecca's reoccurring dreams that night. She heard, "Now that you are gone away from me . . ." and she breathed deep in her sweaty sleep, cornrowed oily head of teenage Black girl on pillow. Then she heard, "You are a woman now. It's time to go home."

Lottie Rebecca slept hard into the preparations her body made for the next day. She woke with the longing to go somewhere, like the instinctual desire to eat and fill the belly or to rise up and sleepwalk to relieve the bladder. The last thing she heard before waking: "When you reach home, I will tell you where I came from."

That day was Lottie Rebecca's thirteenth birthday. The air had cleared overnight. The weather broke toward warmth in its best North Carolina fashion, leaving a Sunday of seventy degrees.

Grandeddy Tunnelson wheeled the barbecue pit over. Sheila set the boom box in the window facing the backyard. Two awkward Black girls, one with a flip hairdo and a butterfly shirt opened at the collar and tucked in, the other the pubescent girl who in first grade ate the Wonder Bread peanut butter sandwich and wore pink hair bows. This day she wore a skirt that came below the knee, a born-again Christian outfit. They were from farther up Colonial Drive, on the other side of Ramsey's new developments. Sheila took the initiative to invite them. Lottie Rebecca ignored them and left them to sit on the end of the picnic table alone while she took her plate of barbecued tempeh, corn, and potato salad and sat next to B.J. with his plate of pork ribs, corn, and potato salad. She felt witnessed, and when she breathed she could smell the mold in the fallen leaves and the sun heating up the damp places in the yard. "Love you," she whispered, leaning her tightly braided head on B.J.'s shoulder as though she was about to take off for some long voyage. She didn't even realize what she had said until she said it. No one in her family ever said, "I love you." They showed it with making each other things, braiding hair, giving advice. B.J. patted his foot in a worn-down old pair of penny loafers on top of her foot to acknowledge what she said without having to say anything back.

When Lottie Rebecca was done eating, she walked over to the window. She wasn't driven by a plan but was driven by her way of doing, then knowing. She turned off the music and climbed on top of the picnic table in front of her parents, her grandfather, the two uncles, and the two awkward Black girls. They all thought she would wish herself happy birthday by breaking into song or something, but with the one wispy cloud, blue sky, and orange and red leaves as backdrop for her new red overalls, hands on her new hips, she proclaimed, "I want somebody to take me to Africa."

The air above the backyard was silent. The family and neighbors who sat beneath her grew uncomfortable with thoughts of UNICEF commercials, of barefoot Africans with flies around their mouths and swollen bellies. The Wonder Bread born-again Christian girl broke the silence, "Who you supposed to be, Moses come down from the mountain?" The tension split with alto, tenor, bass laughter, "Ain't nobody going to Africa?!" the girl in the butterfly shirt added. They all laughed into the tunnel of their fists to keep the food and shame from flying out of their mouths. "Sit down, li'l bit," B.J. said under his breath, the only one not laughing. He looked up at her as if he was attempting to protect them both.

The eyes that hovered in the cloud above rolled with Lottie Rebecca's, dishonored by the kin who misunderstood that their own innate desire to till orange clay was the same desire to sing songs of children's play in the open grassless spaces outside the bush, to fish for their own dinner, the same desire to go home. Above the chain-link fence of the backyard with the young woman in red on the weatherworn picnic table, the spirits evaporated, and Lottie Rebecca wished she could evaporate too, not be left with people who knew her name but didn't know anything about her. Her uterus quaked the way the earth does to shake off unwelcome inhabitants, and down her leg inside her red overalls, blood streamed like crude oil from cracked earth.

She was most betrayed by her mother, who once sought and visited "home," whose laughter was the first to quiet. Sheila was spooked by her own form on the table, standing at the grave of her own mother at eighteen after being called back from Africa because her mother was gone. She vowed to stay in Fayetteville only long enough to bury her and then to leave the country that would never comprehend the opals of wisdom that were her Black womanhood, never understand the sin of the pebbles of cancer inside her mother's brain that took her too early. Sheila was really making an anonymous pact with her heart to disavow grief with the rituals of right home, right self-love. But her covenant to birth the great-granddaughter, the granddaughter, her daughter would challenge that pact. Lottie Rebecca Lee stood on the table making demands from the freedom side of her mother's long-since-locked dungeon doors.

Now Sheila sat down next to her father, closemouthed, not able to see past the disagreements that kept her and Lottie Rebecca separate, not able to see into the pain that explained their connection. She stared at her daughter and wiped away displaced tears of laughter. In that moment, Lottie Rebecca's eyes turned to her mother, to her quiet father, and then inverted and swallowed the sun.

SIXTEEN

Fayetteville, North Carolina
1992

No matter how old or young your soul, you just want peace of mind. If that comes by wanting something done and doing it yourself, so be it. Time will make the portal of age and circumstance for you to parent yourself in place of the shortcomings of those who do the best they can, who wake and go to bed easily knowing they have done for you, watched over you, held the dam against the onslaught of their own childhood pains. You will forget you are beautiful. You will forget the clarity of your patience and your strength. You will become limited, having forgotten who you are before you were the body you walk in. As soon as you are able with steady arms and legs to support yourself, you will take back your finesse and without malicious judgment of your protector, provider, and nurturer, you will do what you came here to do.

Lottie Rebecca sat at the kitchen table. At seventeen, her bare, wide, dark feet were firm on the humid sticky linoleum. Her ears plugged, Tracy Chapman's tenor voice transported her to the landscape in her head where green was so green that it almost blotted itself out to darkness, air so humid that she grew gills to be one with the thick smells of unknown sea creatures.

In her sketchbook, a woman stood in the road, and in each

panel the road took on a new shape and color. In one panel, a sunrise laid out on the ground in front of the figure, like a field of orange and yellow. In another panel, a spread of laundry—T-shirts, overalls, tattered dresses. In another panel, the field was a blaze of fire in front of the woman.

Lottie Rebecca didn't include words in her graphic tales anymore. It was better to leave no room for Sheila's doubt to enter; undecipherable pictures without the words kept her family from questioning her sanity.

B.J. came in the back door from the creek, his smell proceeding him, mud and the musk that was no one else's but his. She loved his smell that replaced the words he never spoke. He stood quiet at his teenage daughter's back. She knew he stood there capable of understanding the circuit between them, capable of seeing the positive inside the negative spaces of the images. But his spine was so riddled with shrapnel and childhood scar tissue that he mistook her darkness for mistakes he'd made that could be reversed only by his absence.

His own seventeenth year put him months away from being a trained assassin, trained easily because his soul had left his body. He loved Lottie Rebecca, but she saw inside the spaces in his head, drew the images, sang the songs that pushed him to the edge of his own sanity by just being who she was. The older she got, the more she became the invisible thing inside his own mind that needed to be avoided.

The older he got, the more B.J. avoided the emotional expectations of home. He climbed the scaffolding of some new home construction across Ramsey Street at dawn or at dusk so that the other men would never witness him, and the house would never call to him. Some days he climbed past street-level eyes to the highest place in the scaffolding all day for new construction downtown. When he was told by a supervisor, "Work a few days on ground crew," or "Go home. You can't clock that many hours," he stopped up the street at the Ethel's Walk-Up and got a barbecue or tripe sandwich to quietly kill a few hours before descending the hill home. No matter what the weather, he ate the whole thing sitting at the picnic table, even if it was so cold he was the only one out there watching the traffic go by on Ramsey.

"Don't you think you can find your way home before dinner some days?" Sheila mixed cooing and complaining and put a plate of fat-free greens, beans, and brown rice in front of him. He sat under the light of the kitchen table mustering up the tolerance to talk with her for the night, but an hour or two at the most was all the interaction he could stand before needing to run and hide.

"I'm gonna try to start making it here earlier."

She stood with her hands on her hips, knowing that was a lie but loving him anyway.

"Leave him be," her father said when she went to his kitchen complaining.

On weekends, B.J. went down to the bottom of Colonial Drive, past the trailers, to the tributary that over the years filled with rushing water that threatened to take the rusted trailers away but brought catfish and trout right out of the river basin. Shrouded in kudzu vines, home to copperheads and cottonmouths. No one else would go down there, not even Lottie Rebecca.

The quiet and the green reminded him of the way he calmed his mind when he was a child, quick escapes without Bennie or Rebecca. Wordless, thick air, nothing but the sound of cicadas chirping to each other, like Morse code that told him everything was going to be okay.

Down at the creek, he peeled back the metal on a can of sardines, placed them on a saltine, sprinkled the bottle of hot sauce that he carried in his pocket over the treat, and was at peace without a whole bunch of pressure to be in the house and listen to Sheila and say something lucid in response.

Quiet, that's the way he loved them, but after eighteen years of quiet, Sheila complained more. She knew that soon Lottie Rebecca, who sat at the table eating tofu scramble with earphones plugged into her handheld cassette player, would disappear out of their home into adulthood and leave Sheila with the quiet love of her life who didn't have conversation as his forte.

Mr. Tunnelson repeated his refrain to his daughter, "Leave him be, he'll work it out." Because he understood something about the thatched roofs, stuccoed walls, and wailing women and children that had to be cordoned off in Black men's minds. Sheila mourned the perpetual disappearance of B.J. and the inevitable disappearance of Lottie Rebecca, who seemed to follow in his introverted footsteps.

On the night before her eighteenth birthday, Lottie Rebecca lay on her bed. She winced at the pain in the small of her back, springs that after eighteen years had lost their obedience of staying uniform to her growth. She listened to the sultriness of Ani DiFranco's voice that Lottie Rebecca felt held the things she'd lost—full-grown defiance and boldness. The music swept away the ignorance of teachers in cinder block classrooms teaching about things even they did not believe. Her cornrows draped over her shoulders and trailed down her back where she lay on the bed.

Outside the window were the green and gold leaves of fall. On her windowsill, a black bird with a beige-and-terracotta belly opened his mouth with fluffed black head feathers to say something that she could not hear, and that's the way she liked it. With earphones she could be in charge, take them off to hear the spirits and write and draw the babbled words and images. She could block out the commands of the sane world that made no sense to her and made her anxious.

At school, her teachers confiscated her cassette player until the end of each day. It was a quiet ritual: She walked tall in cornrows and cargo pants, turtleneck, ears plugged. The principal met her, dark-skinned like her, proper African man who held out his hand and took the cassette player away. At the end of the day, she strode long-legged and quiet to the end of the hall, opened the door to his office smelling of antiseptic that wafted from the nurse's office. The attendance lady placed Lottie Rebecca's disappearance tool on the counter, and she picked it up, having endured another day of the ignorance of her high school environment, where under their breath they still called her Tar Baby. Basketball-playing tall boys as black as her with red gums that illuminated their teeth covered their mouths to snicker at her when she went down the hall.

At home, Sheila tried not to yell but couldn't help it half the time: "Lottie Rebecca!" She hated entering the girl's room and seeing the battleship-gray walls with slightly less gray storm clouds with eyes. It made her feel uncomfortable in the way that the hospital staff in her mother's last days made her uncomfortable and made her reach across the ocean for distance from the masked hospital staff; all she could see were their eyes.

"Lottie Rebecca!"

The girl could hear the tambour of her mother's voice beneath Ani DiFranco's guitar, but she let Sheila be in sync with the fluff-headed bird on the windowsill, mouth open with no sound. Lottie

Rebecca shook her head from side to side, staying in stasis with the music and her drawings and hidden words until bedtime, knowing that in the morning she would confront her parents.

"No more!" is all she knew she would say. If she kept doing what they said, going to school to be tortured every day, she would die. She couldn't do one more day, and after she made up her mind that she wouldn't, there was no going back.

The worst of it had happened a month before, and Lottie Rebecca couldn't tell her family what they wouldn't believe. They were so happy that she complied and accepted an invitation from the two girls up Colonial Drive, who her mother insisted were good friends. Lottie Rebecca followed them around at the football game, back and forth to the concession stand, with breath clouds between them where they whispered something in the dark in front of her. She walked with her hands in her black hoodie pockets, looked at them with one eye like a raven. Her hood covered the eye that didn't trust them. Instincts told her they were talking about her, but Sheila said for her to leave the cassette player and earphones at home, and "Don't assume that if somebody is talking that they are talking about you. You have to speak up and add to the conversation."

Lottie Rebecca calmed the strange thoughts of how the light from the nighttime ball field made the three of them look like actors in a black-and-white movie. She knew everybody liked Coca-Cola, or at least B.J. liked Coca-Cola with his crackers and sardines. Standing behind their perfectly permed heads, with her heart beating, she got her nerve up. "You guys want a cola? . . . I'm buying." She almost said it normally, except that the strange thoughts took her away and she paused on the word *cola* realizing she had heard the word *kola* in her audible dreams. She wondered why the shortened word was *Coke* but the full brand name was Coca-Cola. Why wasn't the shortening *kola*? The girls watched her pause, and Lottie Rebecca continued her whole sentence: "I'm buying."

The Wonder Bread girl said in Valley Girl inflection, "Yeah?!" As if to say, *Of course you are buying*. She was taller than Lottie Rebecca in heels and hoop earrings and a letterman's jacket. The two pushed past, ordered, and took their sodas leaving Lottie Rebecca to pay. The girl who still liked butterfly shirts took the cans in her arms. The Wonder Bread girl popped the tops. While the short ex–football player counted back the remainder of the generous twenty-dollar bill Sheila had given her daughter, the Wonder Bread girl dropped a little square of LSD-blotted paper in the can that was Lottie Rebecca's. When she turned around, she handed it to her, smiling a smile that Lottie Rebecca awkwardly mirrored.

The two girls leaned on each other in the bleachers lit by the ball field that shone on drunk Black and white teenagers, mostly spoiled military kids unless they lived near the bottom. All of them cheered at the game, smoked joints, or leaned in with laughter. Lottie Rebecca drank the laced soda. By the fourth quarter, her eyes glassed over. She told the two girls, "I want to go home," and they sent her away. "Girl, go! Ain't nobody stopping you!"

All of the cars on the parking lot turned to rusted red trucks that created a moonlit perspective point that led to US 401. Lottie Rebecca walked between them, lulled by the drug that drew her like an Icarus bug into the streak of zooming lights. "No!" she heard in the distance behind a washtub and upright piano refrain—"No!"—and in front of her the highway went black with the force of a wind that felt like a palm or hand cupping her whole body.

She woke up in her bedroom with B.J., Sheila, Grandeddy Tunnelson, Uncle Lenard, Uncle James around her in the lamplight. The eyes in the light gray clouds were almost white in the low light. For a moment she remembered seeing her family like this for the first time. She reached for her sheets to cover what felt like newborn nakedness, but she was still in her black hoodie and long-legged dirty black cargo pants. Sheila grabbed her daughter's arm—"Baby?!"—and there was no explaining that she was not suicidal, that the girls had tricked her, that someone had saved her. They just knew that she was lying in the road, no cars going up or down the highway for the moment that the Black state trooper came up the highway and found a teenager, wayward from the game, high out of her mind. He knew the Lee family and brought the girl home with condolences on his lips for the girl they misunderstood as being their only descendant who followed in the mental footsteps of her other grandfather and her own father.

That Monday she went back to school, because Grandeddy Tunnelson said, "She needs consistency. Don't let her wallow in it." But being thrown into the pen of dogs that tried to kill her was the worst possible thing. She avoided them with music in her ears, so if they saw her and snickered she would not hear them. She avoided them by avoiding the halls just after the bell rang, the last one to linger in her seat in every class, pretending to collect her books, tie her shoes. She avoided and sunk further inside herself.

On the eve of her birthday, Lottie Rebecca stayed awake all night. First, she decided to tell her parents that she wasn't lonely.

Anytime she got lonely, she took out her earphones and listened for her own name, listened for the disjointed words *bush, banton.* But they won't want to hear any crazy shit like that.

The last words she had spoken to Sheila were said the day after the football game: "Don't ever make me do that again! I'm not you! If you want friends, go make them and leave me the fuck alone." She didn't speak to her mother again but righteously accepted her mother's nourishment of tofu scramble, the pasta with spinach, garbanzo beans, and nutritional yeast, the bean patties, the fruit. All of which she ate in her room. She brought her dishes out barefoot, long-legged in jogging shorts and tank top in the middle of the night. If B.J. was still watching TV, he let her be. "Good night, B.J.," and he waved up over the back of his chair. If he was there when she came out before running out the door to school, she grabbed the food Sheila left on the counter: "Good morning, B.J."

"Yep," he said in return, not wanting to rile his wife, who waited with patience and gritted teeth with her arms folded for the day her daughter would return her love.

The night was long. *Surely,* Lottie Rebecca thought, *there isn't anything I can say to get them to understand what I have to do.* With a knot in her throat and the light blotting out the darkness, she heard the horn of the boxcar train that blew in the distance at dawn each morning and knew it was time to walk to school. *I'm eighteen.* She reminded herself that she didn't need their permission to do what she needed to do anymore.

Lottie Rebecca walked into her parent's bedroom without the earphones on and proclaimed over their half-asleep heads, "I'm an adult! Y'all can't tell me what to do anymore! I'm going to Africa."

In the last sleeping hour just before waking, everything is known, everything is understood.

Before she entered the room, Sheila had transposed the sound of the train into birdcalls that held a familiar tone. She opened her eyes to say, "Yes."

A month before, Mr. Tunnelson had dropped off a letter to Sheila that arrived in his mailbox with strange postage and red ink. He stood at the curb patting his earth-soiled shirt pocket for his glasses, then decided that something with all that postage on it had to be for Sheila. He handed the mail to her through the open back screen door.

"Thanks, Deddy." Sheila tried not to appear excited when she saw the handwriting.

"You're welcome!" Her father waved while he was already walking toward his house, waved away some distant memory of advice given to a woman who got tired and sought her way out of her marriage through the wrong doors.

From: Kobi, her best friend, male friend from her study abroad program in Ghana.

Dear Ama,

I think of you often. I found your address in some old things. Perhaps one day you will come home for a visit. I have the house still, plenty of room.

I hope this letter finds you.

Love,
Kobi

The letter had been tucked into her jeans pocket, skirt pocket, dashiki pocket, every day for a month until the morning when Lottie Rebecca unknowingly called her mother to the same fate her heart intended.

Sheila took the money she had saved for the first year of college that Lottie Rebecca refused to attend: "I'm not going to college. Keep filling out applications if you want to." She added Lottie Rebecca's eighteenth-birthday present to her eighteenth-Christmas present and flew with Lottie Rebecca to Ghana.

The morning of their departure, they all dreamed, the three of them in the commingled sweat of the house. In Lottie Rebecca's dream, a peacock stood in front of her out of reach on a bridge made of Popsicle sticks and rope. She felt the depth of the dark-green forest below her, knew that elephants walked on the forest floor. She knew that the breeze that fanned the delicate eyes of the open turquoise-and-purple feathers of the bird was created by the movement of the elephant's ears far below her, and in her chest she felt calm, as if the breeze moved through the stream of blood in the arteries that carried life to and away from her heart.

In Sheila's dream, she kept pulling off the road. She could not see them but felt B.J. and Lottie Rebecca in the car with her. There were eggshells by the side of the road and mushrooms growing where she opened the car door and looked down. There was the stale mushroom smell of a body that was not B.J.'s, and then, as in dreams, the scene shifted, and she lay in the partial daylight of some cinder block building, flesh against her flesh. She circled around the border of sleep looking for a way out of the dream. Her hands ran the length of the body that was not B.J.'s, and she felt her body give in to the tightening and untightening between her legs that sent sunlight and adrenaline up through the core of her body. She woke with the covers twisted between her legs and B.J. still deep in his sleep. The weight of his body pressed his hair flat in the back. His heavy body rested into its indented cradle in the mattress. She fell back into sleep—a dream now of a pelican on a distant beach peering at her with its one eye.

Sheila woke to the sound of B.J.'s morning nightmare alarm. His voice yelled unintelligible words. She rested on one elbow in the silver light of dawn and watched him turn his face from left to right as her own thoughts churned. *How will he get along mornings when I'm gone? I can't wait to have time away, feel who I am again outside of Fayetteville, find who I am without B.J. What's it going to be like for him waking up Christmas morning and I'm not here?* Her heart quickened as his tossing and turning mimicked her struggle with guilt and the pull to be free.

The top sheet from their bed twisted around his legs. She inhaled the smell of his body odor, his onion-and-hot-sauce scent and oily sweet liquor in his funk though he never drank after finding his new life. She closed her eyes to bottle up that smell and remember it when she missed him. The small black hairs on his chin bristled with the fear in his nightmare and his pores stood up as little brown bumps. Sheila listened for a while the way she always did to see if anything made sense before waking him. "Baby, wake up! You're dreaming."

"Umm," B.J. yawned and sighed, satisfied, accustomed to her voice leading him out of bad dreams and into the morning. His voice was hoarse, but he was anxious to share the dream that for a change was shareable. "I was dreaming there was a storm, a hurricane, and I was coming down the hill from Ramsey Street, trying to get to the house." He lifted his arms above his head and looked up at the popcorn ceiling. "The wind was blowing out of control.

I was running and only gaining an inch or two, then I was pulling on the door of the house. I knew you and Lottie Rebecca were in here, and that's where I wanted to be. I told myself, 'I'm gonna get this damned door open' even though the wind had me off my feet, and in the air, except my hands were on the knob. I knew I could do it."

He was quiet now and let out a satisfying sigh.

This was the most Sheila remembered B.J. saying in one sitting. She smiled and listened as if watching a movie. "Man, don't stop there, what happened?"

"Oh, that's when you woke me up." He smiled and sat up on his elbows to kiss her with his chapped lips and got out of bed, not lingering even though it was the morning Sheila and Lottie Rebecca would leave him at home and go across the pond to the Motherland.

Sheila stood in the kitchen, rubbing her neck. B.J. sat at the table eating the last of a rib left over in Styrofoam. "I don't want you eating that while I'm gone." She pushed back the thought, *Then maybe I shouldn't go.*

She walked over and opened the freezer so he could see the healthy meals she had prepared for the ten days she'd be away. B.J. licked the sauce from his fingers. "Yeah, I'll eat that for dinner every night, and pack some up for lunch too." Sheila knew better. *He's going to stock the refrigerator with soul food from Ethel's Walk-Up, and Deddy won't be any help, wheeling that damned grill out into the yard.*

Sheila and Lottie Rebecca lifted up off the ground. The tarmac turned to a strip of gray in a patch of wintergreen beneath them. The naps of North Carolina pine trees became the tops of the heads of ancestors who whispered, *swoosh*, as Lottie Rebecca and her mother entered the clouds. Lottie Rebecca's own voice in her chest quieted. She did not know there was a knot that clotted just after birth, a tangle of uncommunicable feelings until it was a flow of energy that hummed with the sound of the plane's engine. The hum took over the whisper of the ancestors' swoosh.

SEVENTEEN

America to Ghana
1993

Love is not to be mistaken for the need to fill holes in hearts. Muscle sinks. When the heart muscle gets weighted down, filled with gravel instead of grain, it sinks that much faster. Good hearts make lots of mistakes. It's your job now. You will have to stop on your way to where you are headed, pick the stones out of the hearts of your guardians. Lay their pasts to rest on the banks and forgive them, so they can help you swim across to the knowing side.

All night, they flew over the ocean where her cousins' cousins' cousins' mouths, hands, sex, and hair follicles were in the waves and were the sediment on the ocean floor.

The girl's legs were so long that they stuck out in the aisle like oars outside of a boat while she slept. When she woke, they were approaching a new shore like a receding hairline—concave at the most wounded places—and then there was an air traffic tower like the one at the Raleigh-Durham Airport, a tall concrete pole with an upside-down octagon on top where white men waved their hands over panels and controlled the sky the way they controlled the sea.

Lottie Rebecca's eyes were wide. In her sleep, she had become her mother's child again, acquiesced into letting the wisdom of her elder lead in this journey that she knew to take, felt called to take long before she knew why.

They stepped out of the airport into the humid sun, smells of burning trash. Lottie Rebecca's eyes took in the sight of more Black people in one place than she had ever seen. Most of them as Tar Baby black as she.

They were the two women, younger and older of the same body, the women whose only sign of a male family member was B.J.'s green Marine duffel bag, which carried their clothes. It was the length of a small body. Sheila lugged it with both hands, certain now that she had done the right thing. The familiarity of the place woke up a part of her that had been dormant for years, but motorbikes, cars, plane engines, voices shouting without restraint put Lottie Rebecca's mind in sync with her father's sealed-off memories of the streets of Saigon. She slowed to feel the sympathetic pull toward him, while her mother quickened her pace to accept the pull of this familiar city. And then, her mother's back was two steps too far away in this sea of brown skin that camouflaged her and hardened the knot of tangled feelings and words in Lottie Rebecca's chest. She wished B.J. had come with them, but he avoided loud, crowded places like the grocery store on Saturdays and refused to ever consider plane travel. Lottie Rebecca fell three paces now behind her mother, who lumbered with the bag toward the street. Felt her mother slipping away into the crowd that was familiar to Sheila yet foreign to Lottie Rebecca.

Sheila hadn't spoken of it, had not taken the letter from her pocket, but the girl felt their different pulls inside the exposed belly button beneath the seam of her cropped black tank top. Lottie Rebecca reached for her mother's arm, but she was too far away to catch. The sound came up through the whole tower of Lottie Rebecca's height, punitive and urgent: "Mama!" The gele-wrapped green, red, gold heads of African women caught in the flow of chaos stopped, tweaked their ears to listen to the call that was the same as those of the children who never made it out of their wombs and to the surface for a first breath. "Mama!" They stopped, then remembered themselves in the griefless movement of their lives and resumed their hustle, realizing the call for mama was not from or for their children.

Sheila had cut her Afro, wrapped her short naps of brown and white in a gele of purple and white, and like the other mothers paused with the alarm of the call, just long enough for Lottie Rebecca to catch hold of her mother's strained arm. "Girl, what is wrong with you!? I'm right here."

At the street, they scanned the movement for the blue Mercedes of the cousin-of-no-blood-kin. Sheila had written to him,

> Dear Kobi,
> My daughter is the age we were when we met. I would love to bring her to experience home.

She made sure to make mention of her husband to quiet the thoughts she projected onto Kobi, who might feel hopeful as he read her letter.

> My husband and I have been listening to this girl say she was going to Africa since she was thirteen years old. Let me know if you can accommodate us.
>
> Peace and love,
> Ama (Sheila)

He was the young, short, cute brown boy from Howard named Alfred Haskel before he and Sheila left the US on study abroad, but named Kobi Ahmad in Ghana. He and Sheila lived in the home of Dr. Ahmad, whose last name Kobi privileged himself to. Dr. Ahmad was the only female African biology professor at the University of Ghana at the time. She lived with her husband in London when she was not teaching and during the semester hosted students in her home in Accra. Wherever she lived, Kobi lived, until she retired and remained in London and he remained in her home in Accra, where he followed in his othermother's shoes as a professor of biology at the University of Ghana. His reply:

> Yes, cousin, I will pick you and your little one up at the airport, and you will stay at the house, and the two of you will be my charge for the ten days you are at home. Perhaps I will be able to convince you to stay longer and celebrate Christmas. My semester is almost complete, and my time will be yours fully at the end of your stay. Look for my dusty old Mercedes, and do not judge its condition. Cars are few and the roads are rough here.
>
> Peace to you too. Love,
>
> Kobi

Sheila could hear the British accent he'd acquired from Dr. Ahmad. She smiled at the emerging memories of her youth—brown skin, white teeth, smell of sun, trips to the coast. She did not let herself question the stir of feelings in her core.

The floors were slab concrete in this house. The walls were gray cinder blocks inside to hold the coolness and painted yellow on the outside to deflect the heat of the sun. Each room had its own screen door with bars, and an outdoor covered courtyard felt like the corridor of an outdoor strip mall. Lottie Rebecca felt as though she was walking through a familiar world that was inside out.

Sheila scolded her daughter for unlatching the wooden doors on the wall of the compound, scolded her for walking over the grate, the only bridge over the rain ditch that separated the tall yellow walls around the yard of the compound from the street. "Don't go outside the compound walls without Kobi," she said.

"I didn't come here to be Kobi's prisoner. I came here to follow the call of something for *myself*." Sheila heard but had learned to ignore proclamations from her teenager that sounded like *I came here to follow the things that you as a lowly human don't understand.*

One morning, Lottie Rebecca sat in the gazebo in the yard, where the yellow walls of the compound reached up around her so high that all she could see of the Africa that called her were the green eyelashes of palm trees. The metal grate that rattled every time Kobi's car rolled over it on entry and exit stuck out like a rusted tongue, mocking her from the big wooden gate that was latched unless Kobi unlatched it. The whole thing seemed ludicrous; the mother who read *Our Bodies, Ourselves* and talked freely about the health of her vagina adhered to rules about a woman's place. Lottie Rebecca watched an arm-size, green-and-gold socket-eyed lizard that came every day over the wall to peer at the new American zoo animal.

She heard a call, like a child crying through the voice of some wild bird, and she did not stay put. Out the gate and down the dirt road that looked more like a dirt alley with the sun beating on the nest of her Afro as she walked. Her tall, African-idol-looking self marched down to where the road ended at the bush. There, she found the gate to a garden, Akosua Buor Garden. This time the call was so loud, it echoed against the green forest wall of the bush that butted up against the end of the neighborhood. She could see above a hedge of bushes a fan of turquoise-and-blue feathers and heard the shaking of them like a handful of Grandeddy Tunnelson's tobacco tied and shook for bugs. Dust covered her toes in sandals, and she walked toward the sound, but before she could enter the little paradise, in the distance, Kobi's squat, dark voice and body yelled, "Mtoto!" In the alley with cinder block walls and deep rain ditches of black oil-slicked water on each side, there was no place to turn or duck to get away from the rule that "a man must be with you at all times."

There were too many things to remember, and after being called back like a goat that had escaped the compound walls, Lottie Rebecca lay on the squeaky springs of her bed in her and Sheila's room. She kept still to feel the breeze from the courtyard at the barred door and the breeze from the barred window.

She lay there feeling her head anxiously half-empty. The unbearable heat coaxed agitation. *Why did I insist on coming to a place where people call my mother Ama? A place where we can't go anywhere without a male escort, where they eat fish stew for breakfast, and they don't eat lunch at all, and dinner is more fish stew with sticky bread called fufu that is more like white, viscous Silly Putty than anything I've ever known as bread? A place where B.J.'s presence in our lives is not acknowledged?*

A breeze never came, never brought the familiar spirit-voices that were all she knew as answers to her thoughts. "I will find you," Lottie Rebecca whispered to the muted spirits that she had never been without and didn't know she missed until they were silent. She lay on the bed that smelled of old leather and sweat, held her pencil over the rough textured paper of her sketchbook, waiting. She had taken for granted the flow from the energy to her hand, but there was no energy coming into the room, no energy going out.

In the heat of the afternoon a rooster crowed, and seven neighborhoods deep other roosters crowed as if they couldn't respect the proper timing of a rooster call at dawn. In the back courtyard, the sound of her mother's voice went from soft to what Lottie Rebecca's young womanhood recognized as sultry; her voice swayed and acquiesced. On the page, Lottie Rebecca drew dots, stars scattered with no pattern, no connection, like separate beings with no sense of themselves or anything else.

She longed for the sound of her mother's footsteps, which only days before had signaled the invasion of her space. She needed some familiar sound like the missing voice of the spirits that called her there only to abandon her. Sheila called from the yard where she was stripping more bamboo for her baskets, "Lottie Rebecca!? You still want your hair braided?" And she was temporarily relieved of the profound loneliness.

Sheila sat on the sofa with Lottie Rebecca's bony shoulders pinched between her knees to make the cornrows. She pushed Lottie Rebecca's head to one side, bowed her head for the end of each braid. Lottie Rebecca allowed the overly tight braiding without complaint, because it helped her to feel something.

The girl wasn't trying to make her head dangle like the weight on the end of a fishing line, but she could barely keep her eyes open or support her own head for the weight of humidity and depression. "Hold your head right, girl, and quit acting like a baby." She didn't answer her mother but let her mother's roughness be an excuse to release the tears that rarely came but would release the pressure of missing her father, of missing the spirits, and missing her mother who had turned into Ama. Tears and snot flowed, and Lottie Rebecca's shoulders jerked where she was held in place by Sheila's knees.

"What is the matter with you, girl?" Lottie Rebecca didn't know how to tell her mother that she had been abandoned by the voices in the room and in her head, left to reunite with her fledgling girl-voice that was more adept at saying what she wanted than this preadult version of herself who had learned, like B.J., that quiet was the best way to deal with a world that preferred alcohol or religion to make the pain go away. If there had been something other than goat milk in the raggedy refrigerator that cut on and off with the surge of electricity, she would have quenched the thirst for a good high that lingered on the back of her tongue.

"I don't know what to do with you. You wanted to come here, and now you are just acting a fool," Sheila said, dismissing Lottie Rebecca's tears and heavy-headedness as teenage angst.

It was the last day of the semester at University of Ghana, and over the sound of the soap opera voices talking in deep concerned Swahili on the TV came the sound of Kobi's car rattling over the grate.

"Ete sen, Ama, Lottie Rebecca," he called as he came into the back door.

Sheila answered, "Ye, ye, ye."

He put his briefcase down on the table the way B.J. put his lunch pail down on their table at home, and he leaned over like a squat tree to try to make eye contact with the swollen-eyed Lottie Rebecca. "You managing okay, Mtoto?" She ignored him for calling to her in a nickname only her mother was allowed to use.

Inside her head she was yelling like her six-year-old self, tantrumming until the kitchen sink rattled and the neighbors stopped whatever they were doing to plug their ears.

He didn't make a big deal out of being slighted, but Lottie Rebecca wished he had. Sheila huffed and nudged Lottie Rebecca's head, and Kobi walked back to the fridge and put in it the closest thing he could find to American soda for his young cousin. He popped the top on one for himself and set one down next to Lottie Rebecca, where it remained ignored on the musty rug.

Kobi broke the awkward moment of Lottie Rebecca's rudeness with unnecessary conversation. "Ahh, the Ghanaians are about to party up for Christmas."

Lottie Rebecca answered through the mucus in her throat, "I want to go home," allowing her untamed younger self to speak. In her head, she said to her mother, *What are you doing? Why can't you hear me? Why can't I hear them? I can't breathe, Mama.*

Sheila felt her daughter's body jerking with tears beneath her. She held the braid in place with one hand. Her body almost remembered to kiss her daughter's forehead, but she couldn't hear the cry of the girl who was so miserable. Sheila turned instead to Kobi, who came and picked up the cold orange soda can as if he was reaching to take food out of a lion's cage.

He tried to speak to what he saw, tears and a mother's punitive pinching knees, but he had no history of the layers of broken, healed, broken, healed places that made up the triangle of Lottie Rebecca, Sheila, and the missing B.J. "I'm sorry, li'l cousin. I'm done with work. Tomorrow. We'll get out and go do something fun." Lottie Rebecca wanted him to shut up and quit acting as if they were true family, but her mind was tired.

He turned up his soda.

Lottie Rebecca inhaled deep, smelling Kobi's cheap cologne in the slipstream of his movements and the same smell above her head on her mother's braiding fingers.

"I miss Deddy!" she whined, though she never called B.J. deddy, coding understood only by Sheila's ears, a distress signal that made her mother involuntarily inhale and swallow guilt for letting some other man soothe that place in her heart.

On the TV that sat in front of them, hyperdramatic Ghanaian soap operas played in Swahili that Sheila could understand, which made Lottie Rebecca feel more alone. She leaned her head back and caught Sheila looking at Kobi and he at her. Kobi saw the girl catch sight of the light beam between him and her mother, and as if reprimanded by her stare, he sat down in one of the mismatched wooden chairs at the table to drink his soda.

Lottie Rebecca spoke into the awkwardness, letting the forgotten climates of separate landscapes merge in her head. Arid, humid, cool winds churned. "Kobi, do you have a mother? I haven't heard you talk about her. There aren't even photos of her here." Sheila nudged the girl's head forward for speaking to what she could not possibly know, that Kobi's mother died during childbirth, that he made other women his mother, each of them flinging him off their hands like unwanted fish guts, until he'd found Dr. Ahmad.

Sheila chastised with a push of Lottie Rebecca's head, and she gathered the hairs on her neck into a too-tight cornrow. Lottie Rebecca's eyes watered from the pain, but she said what would let Kobi and Sheila know that the scent between them was calculable for an eighteen-year-old's mind and body.

"All the mothers are dead." Lottie Rebecca let the free flow of words that she had resisted since she was thirteen have their way, not relenting for the sake of her mother's feelings. "My dad's mother, his grandmother, Mama's mother, and the mothers all the way back to the hut that used to be this living room, they are all dead, but this is my mother, and at home I have a father." She slowed her words, and her head turned to him the way her newborn head turned to everyone in the room on the day she was born, a look that called them all to repent for whatever sins they committed before her arrival. "Where—is—your—Mama?"

Sheila pulled Lottie Rebecca's head to one side to punish the unpunishable truth that came forward in the question. It called forth her own mother into the space where Sheila had sat at eighteen while Lucy Marie Tunnelson lay in a DC hospital and disappeared as martyred leukocytes cleaned the rooms in her Black woman body of every stitch of memory, every bit of sewage from the sea, every wrong thing said into her ears, every dirty thing placed inside the openings of her body. Cleaned, until there was nothing but the cold concrete of tombstone for Sheila to return home to. Sheila shushed her child and scolded, "That's enough! It's too hot and you testing my patience, Lottie Rebecca Lee!"

The girl got to her feet and stood over her mother, who sat on the couch, stood taller than Kobi. Her voice no longer like a screaming toddler or an angst-ridden teenager. Her voice like that of someone tall enough to see the distant curve of the earth and young enough to remember her own voice-as-spirit. She took all of the out-of-place energies in the house and ordered them into obedience. "You are testing *my* patience!"

She stood between Kobi and her mother and pointed first at her mother. "Ama! We didn't come here for this shit." Lottie Rebecca turned and pointed at Kobi next and finding no words to say to his bulging eyes that were startled at the girl's wrath, she turned and stormed down the hall toward their room.

Sheila followed two steps behind her, yelling, "Slam the gate, girl! Lock it, because you don't want me to catch you!" She heard herself and stopped on the other side of the bars that slammed. Sheila's naked feet were cold on the sobering concrete in the house that was too hot for American skin.

Kobi sheepishly took his soda and his mismatched chair and went to sit in the back courtyard to squelch the romantic notion that he and Sheila could be reunited after twenty years of Sheila's marriage to the man she loved. The three of them were held by the quiet tension of the house as night came on.

The moon was long in its sleep, waiting until it was good and ready to rise and illuminate for the mother and daughter the true reason why they had come without the missing person of their flock. To illuminate why they had temporarily flown off course like the tenth generation of birds thrown off migration to land in the place where their spirits used to congregate.

The moonlight came in silver shafts. The lizard sat in the silver light outside the window and moved its one eye over her, and Lottie Rebecca rolled her eyes and wished for curtains for the windows, for her emotions. Without the voices of the spirits, without the umbrella of B.J.'s silence, she could feel her singular contention with living in the flesh. She heard Sheila's voice apologetic with Kobi out in the backyard, "I need to go back."

Lottie Rebecca sat still on the squeaky bed unmoving, wanting to hear them.

"Do you love him?" Kobi whispered.

"Of course I love him. He's my husband. He's my everything. I've been trying so hard not to feel some kind of way with you,

Kobi, but you are so easy." Sheila felt that word *easy*. B.J. was not easy with his quirky need to be alone, the nightmares full of sweating and garbled talk. Sheila had grown so accustomed to what wasn't normal that she didn't know how relieved she'd be away from him. But she missed him, as much as her raging daughter missed him. The three of them were strung together, and the pull of one could send the others cascading.

Kobi put his finger under her chin and made her look at him in the same shaft of moonlight that illuminated the lizard and Lottie Rebecca's blue-black face beyond the bars. Light and shadows shone on their faces and bodies that wanted to be kissed and held. "You know I respect you. I love you too, but I'm not going to do anything to hurt you or that girl in there." Sheila leaned in to kiss him, and Lottie Rebecca leaned into the silence trying not to yell "Oh Lord!" at the cheesy soap opera behavior of her mother.

Kobi put his finger over Sheila's lips. "I'd rather hurt and have you as my cousin than put you in a situation like that. That's your husband at home and your daughter in the other room. It might not be easy, but she did speak the truth." Kobi looked up and his one tear reflected the moonlight like one piece of stardust. "I've been too long looking for my mother, just making a mess, you know?"

Sheila's tears flowed slow, pushed out by the desire she did not let herself admit. She had brought Lottie Rebecca to Ghana to fulfill the girl's dreams and without letting the truth rise to the top of her mind; she had come to find a homeless romantic to hold her homeless romantic side that was always in love with B.J. but felt alone even when they were together. She walked in bare feet across the concrete going cool in the night toward the locked gate of her and her daughter's room.

Lottie Rebecca stood in the dark mirror. The girl saw the pear shape of her own dark face in the foggy speckled image. She liked the dark, liked looking at her own image in the dark. She touched the perfection of the cornrows Sheila made and admitted to herself that they were too tight, made her head hurt when she blinked or shut her mouth. She couldn't even look down without feeling like the tension would split her brain, so she stuck her pinkie finger into the end of one of the braids to bring back the comfort of her Afro. Sheila blew a huff of snot laughter and tears at the unabashedly Lottie Rebecca gesture.

Lottie Rebecca turned around at the sound of the alarm of her mother crying. She undid the dead bolt and reached for Sheila, held her like she was the child and Lottie Rebecca the mother. She stroked her mother's short Afro: "It's gonna be okay, Mama. You know Deddy loves you so much, he just was done to in so many ways that he cain't let himself feel that stuff or anything else sometimes. His love is that kind you got to listen for, Mama. That's all, and if you not quiet with him, it'll float down the river right past you." Sheila's body shook, and Lottie Rebecca didn't know if her mother was laughing or crying now. "Don't go looking for love in that little squat Kobi." And Sheila cried out the shame into her daughter's solid chest, realizing how much she missed B.J., would miss them as a family once Lottie Rebecca found whatever she was looking for all of her life.

As the moon rose higher in the sky, Sheila sat on the bed, sat Lottie Rebecca between her knees, and ran her own pinkie finger along the ends of the braids to undo the binding. She smoothed tea tree oil over the raised bumps where she had braided her daughter's hair too tight and sniffed to keep the snot from streaming down onto her daughter's head. "I'm sorry, Mtoto. I'm sorry.

I have a hard time sometimes too. I don't even know why I came back here."

Lottie Rebecca turned around and looked up at her mother. The specks of moonlight picked up the light in their eyes like cats in the dark bush. "Mama, you came here because I asked you to."

Sheila huffed a half laugh and wiped the snot with the back of her hand. "Do *you* even know why you wanted to come here, Lottie Rebecca Lee?"

It was quiet; the house was quiet. In the distance, the bass of street parties in the dark, the smell of hair oil, the smell of nighttime summertime, burning trash, held things still. And Lottie Rebecca cracked open the door that had been so long slammed in her mother's face. "I think I've been following the voices, Mama. But I don't even hear them." She was quiet, the two of them listening to Accra's night that did not know time between dusk and dawn. "I feel like I ran after something all my life that ran me off a cliff. Maybe I'm crazy." All the braids undone now, Sheila rested her fingers on her daughter's warm scalp.

"You the only one of us not crazy, baby," and that was almost enough said for Lottie Rebecca to be satisfied.

"Mama?"

"Yeah."

"Did you sleep with him?"

"Naw!" Sheila whacked at her daughter's shoulders with the unwrapped head covering and covered her mouth in embarrassment.

"Okay then," Lottie Rebecca said, letting her mother know that answering the question was satisfaction enough to end the conversation.

The two tall, thin women climbed into the crossbar shadows of moonlight in the bed and tossed and turned in fitful thoughts, until they came to rest.

The next morning, the hot morning breeze streamed in over the concrete floors of the house, an ancient form of air conditioning. Mother and daughter sat over the fish stew, while Kobi took his breakfast in the dusty yard as some punitive measure that neither of them needed him to take when things had already been settled. Lottie Rebecca bit her thumbnail and dipped her spoon into the disappointing breakfast. The pendulum came to rest, the air cleared, the two of them talked the way Sheila talked to her own mother before disease and the threat of abandonment muted them. Lottie Rebecca poked her spoon in the fish soup. "It's just like, nothing here is what I expected, and I don't even hear the spirits or anything. Maybe this was a mistake."

Sheila turned her bowl up for the last of the liquid. "Things don't happen by mistake, Mtoto. It's more like we think we are supposed to do something for one reason, but we get taught the hard way that there's a whole other reason for the journey. Kobi is off work now. I'll ask him to give us a ride to a beautiful rain forest I want you to see. We'll make a day of it."

"Mama, can we just drive ourselves?" Lottie Rebecca knew the answer before asking and moved on to say the thing she meant to say. "I think I'm supposed to go to the slave castles."

Sheila swung her legs out from under the table and paused before getting up. "Daughter, I can't hear spirits speaking to me, but I know one thing, it's not someplace anybody our color needs to be revisiting." She might as well have said to her daughter's contrary spirit, "Daughter, let's go."

When they rounded the cobblestone path and walked into the stucco white walls of Cape Coast Castle, tears streamed down Lottie Rebecca's face. When they stood in the courtyard and the guide spoke about the British wife of a slave trader who was so ashamed and dehumanized by the killing and torture of brown people that she killed her own children and herself, Lottie Rebecca cried. When they stood at the wall high above the beach and looked out through the white stucco arches at the innocent brown thin boys boarding the colorful fishing boats for the day, the horizon above them stretching out until blue-gray water merged with blue-gray sky, she cried. The smell of her own salty tears blended with the salt in the humid air.

Sheila trailed two steps behind her daughter, feeling the pull of sorrow from her child, who she thought just liked to learn things the hard way. In the blinding bright white of the walls that loomed around them, Lottie Rebecca stood in her black tank top and let Sheila speak. "Baby, I can't stand to see you crying like this." She barely got the words out before the water welled up and pushed up out of her eyes like a wave induced by the rising moon of her daughter's emotions.

"I can hear them" was all Lottie Rebecca answered, and she walked toward the doors where she had to duck down to descend into the dark, cavernous, dank chambers where blood still lined the stone walls and stone ledges, showed the imprint of bodies that had starved and died, their souls depressing into the rock so that some girl with unusual eyes, unusual ears would see and hear them and call out the way they did.

The guide was far ahead of them with a small group of white Americans and one fair-skinned Black American college student. Where Lottie Rebecca and Sheila stood, a circle of daylight surrounded them, though the dungeon cave was sealed. From Lottie Rebecca's throat in a long drawn-out guttural dirge came "Mama! Mama! Mama!" in a spiritual, cry-like hymn, she sang through the verses, her voice rising and falling and crashing in the waves of the melody. It shook the walls of the cave, shook, until she was spent.

When she opened her eyes, the cave and all of its dwellers, those alive and long since dead, cried, hard droning sobs, the way she had all day.

Outside the cave, the sky whirled and kissed the dark brown crest of Lottie Rebecca's forehead, like the sun that kissed B.J.'s helmet on the China Sea beach one day. The warm grass whispering and the water giggling like boy-children playing on the beach long before they had been betrayed, captured, and told the painful lie that their hearts were malleable enough to commit the same sins that had been committed against them for the promise of a God-granted manhood.

In that moment, she understood the spokes of broken brown that struck out from the irises to the rims of Uncle James's, Uncle Lenard's, Grandeddy Tunnelson's, and B.J.'s eyeballs. And it all made sense, the presence of evil and fear inside her male kin's eyes as they tried to be still and bring home valor instead of the stories of broken bones and cracked skulls that collided with the momentum of their pain. She watched the boys with long, brown, stick-limbed arms and legs laugh and roll heavy nets into the boats for a day of fishing, and she cried. The tide knocked against their legs and the bow of the boat the way it knocked against the shins and thighs of the bodies who were netted and dragged across the ocean, had beauty snuffed out in darkness of the bellies of ships until love could be resurrected by the planting and replanting of a Divine seed.

She looked up at the sun, right into it without it burning her eyes, and she breathed a message to her father: *You don't have to be alone anymore. You don't have to stress no more. I am here.*

PART FOUR

Sankofa Homecoming

EIGHTEEN

Accra, Ghana
1993

A mother can go backward only by loving forward into the space above the soil and beneath the firmament. Walk the earth, lay some to rest, and birth the hands and feet that will dredge the waters for the missing digits in the spine of each generation.

They rode past all of the paramilitary checkpoints near Cape Coast Castle, and they were deep in the bush of indifference, where police didn't care to go because there was nothing to be gained by harassing the villagers, who owned nothing except the right to take the machete to the yellow cocoa pods and sever them from the trees.

Lottie Rebecca stuck her uncovered head out the window. Her Afro moved in the wind. A tall, gangly version of her mother.

"What did the ancestors tell you?" Kobi asked from the front seat. The hot, humid air whispered past his oily skin to answer him. Lottie Rebecca's knowing that day had not come in a string of words. It did not know time but came in the way of a jolt of truth, like skewers through all of the moments of doubt and of voices denied.

"What did they tell you?" Sheila asked, her hand on the sticky duct tape that covered the back seat. She was tempted to inch toward her daughter. "Um-hmm," Lottie Rebecca answered to help her mother be still.

The hot wind on Lottie Rebecca's face turned to a warm breeze, and she saw B.J.'s face in the reflection on her own face in the side-view mirror, a lens that held all of the faces inside of the dungeon, held what she knew of the places B.J. had been and what he had done, from the childhood note with words his father misunderstood to the China Sea beach where B.J. made the ocean into blood. Memories that came out in his screams at night. She understood the width of the palm leaves that were his hands, how silencing his hands with building and fishing was how he tried to keep her from harm. She understood and wanted to let B.J. know that he was safe now. But he was thousands of miles away, and the course of the wind and smell of earth and dung of ancient animals as they entered the rain forest commingled with her thoughts.

She heard on the force of the wind, "Woooooo ahhh!" An open holler, high-pitched like the birdcall she heard days ago. She stuck her whole body out the window, perched her butt on the thickness of the doorframe of the raggedy Mercedes, and called back in a long, bright holler that opened the cartilage between her breasts. A sound like the sun and raindrops in the air, the same water and light that broke away and exposed her body the day she flowed out of Sheila.

The sound called to Sheila too and opened the center of her chest and made her smile without the thoughts about what Black women should and should not do. Lottie Rebecca heard her mother inside the chamber of the car calling back, "Ooo ah, ooo ah." Kobi laughed out loud. Lottie Rebecca pulled her body back into the car to see what needed to be witnessed. She heard and didn't recognize her own voice that gurgled a giggle like water tumbling in the pebbles deep beneath a waterfall. And that was that; the tension that threatened to break mother and daughter receded.

Sheila and Lottie Rebecca playfully rose to stick their bodies out and sit on their separate doorframes as if climbing on to an amusement park ride. In that moment, Lottie Rebecca got to look at her mother without her looking at and minding her child. Eyes closed, Sheila inhaled deep into the closed capillaries of her lungs and remembered the morning her mother found out she was leaving for Ghana.

IV drip, head bandaged from brain surgery. "Six months, get your affairs in order," and her mother did. She made her own burial plans and continued to be a mother, knowing she would not teach her daughter everything she was to learn. Sheila wasn't mature enough to know that her mother could die. In her eighteen-year-old heart, she still thought her mother was responsible for everything she felt, even the fear of being left alone. All Sheila wanted was out from the smell of antiseptic, out from the sight of her mother not looking like her mother. Like an eighteen-year-old wanting a long drag on a blunt, she just wanted to get far away from the intensity of pending grief.

But Lucy Marie Tunnelson knew. She looked at Sheila, who looked away. "Daughter, you'll keep running until you follow in your own footsteps and give birth to the girl-child who you gonna look at and see the same hip bones, same eyes, and you won't be able to run anymore."

The warm wind wiped the tears back on Sheila's tight skin. And Lottie Rebecca saw the Black girl from Fayetteville and DC.

The parking lot of Kakum National Park was like Lottie Rebecca's high school parking lot. All the cars and buses were coated with a layer of orange dust. In the distance sat a park-type office building designed for the comfort of Americans, especially if they were white, a perfect rectangle of red colonial bricks.

Kobi approached the window, said something fast in Swahili to let them know that he had once been a guide and that they didn't need one on the hike up the mountain to the extension bridges. Kobi ducked his head down to the height of the window to pay. Lottie Rebecca looked over at her mother and shared out loud, "That's the same way B.J. ducks down to the window when ordering food at Ethel's Walk-Up. I miss him."

"Yep!"

And in the way that Lottie Rebecca once moved with the fluids of her mother's body, she heard with Sheila the Stevie Wonder love songs from her mother's first days with B.J. and knew that Sheila wished she could have known, without ever leaving home, that she loved B.J. in a way that could subvert Serengeti storms, harness tornadoes, bone-deep love.

Sheila looked sideways at Lottie Rebecca as if witnessed and to the parking lot knowing that if she hadn't promised her daughter that they'd climb the mountain high above the canopy to walk across the bridge in her dreams that she would turn around and have Kobi drive them straight to the airport in the name of love.

NINETEEN

Ghana, Rain Forest
1993

Eyes steady on the road. Well done, faithful to thine own self and to the seven generations before and the seven generations to come. Well done, protector, provider, well done. The river has narrowed for you now, you can cross, wade in, and surrender and come over to the seeing side. Your life has not been in vain. She has risen from the water, flown high above the curve of the meridian, seen the cord between mother and her scattered children. Well done.

"Take Nothing but Photographs," the sign read, the last readable thing before they exited the daylight and walked under the canopy of the dark forest, where the layers and layers of leaves created a dank, green night sky. Lottie Rebecca had already stuck a smooth mahogany wooden seed into her pocket from the cushion-composted floor of the forest. "B.J. is gonna want to feel the wood from this place. Can't get that in a photo."

Beneath the canopy, they were cool, like on the days when Sheila was little and it was so hot in Fayetteville that her father covered the windows with blankets, turned on the window AC unit, and let her and B.J. lie on a pallet on the floor and watch TV until they saw Rebecca or Bennie coming down the street and sent the boy through the tobacco, over the fence, and into his own home.

When they got to the top of the mountain, Kobi, Sheila, and Lottie Rebecca stopped before a small platform of eight wooden steps that led to ropes and planks that floated above the canopy of trees until it reached a second canopy of silk cotton trees, the same trees that enveloped them with their skirts on the forest floor. These trees jutted toward the sky above the mountain and spread their fingers out to anchor the ropes and planks as though playing finger games of cat's cradle with yarn.

The climbers' clothes were heavy from the water in the air and from their own sweat. The platform was much like the one B.J. built for Lottie Rebecca's alone time, except the rope bridge extended out toward the view of hazy mountains. Like a never-ending snaky spine, it swayed and moved to match the movement of the trees that almost touched the clouds. The silk cotton trees that had lived longer than any white man's sins nodded, though there was no wind.

Kobi explained to his two cousins the way the bridge might feel beneath their feet and offered the intellectual facts of the German and the Ghanaian who collaborated to engineer the thing. Behind him, Lottie Rebecca had taken off into the perspective point of the bridge's ropes, imagining B.J. as the engineer, counting the distance in feet with his own steps. Her mother looked up, and the girl was planks away in the distant green. The egret-like form of her body almost floated with the bouncing of the bridge. A trembling song rose in Sheila's chest. She moved past Kobi and started off behind her daughter. At first, not in sync with her movements, their bodies rebounded against each other's steps. Then, despite their emotional distance, their breath and heartbeat caught the same rhythm, the way they did for Lottie Rebecca's feedings when her body was still plump with her mother's blood. Kobi stayed on the platform witnessing the branches of the bridge moving in accord with the waves of mother and daughter.

The air hummed from the bees that could not fly that high. There was a shush of elephants' ears fanning past the leaves beneath them, and Lottie Rebecca saw her crib mobile, inverted in time. She stopped walking, smiled; "I hear them," her voice echoed out over the mountaintops.

She then heard some distant drum, higher than audible sounds, carrying the beat trailing of a rotund drop of sweat down B.J.'s temple. She heard the saw in his shed that was left whirring to match the sounds of the hums above the forest.

B.J.'s chest hit the sawdust floor of the shed, crumbs of wood and particles of sand on the China Sea beach of Vietnam. The healed seam in his skull cracked open and let the memory of being a member of The Storm out where it crawled. Ants picked up the sand particles of memory and marched into his vision over the sawdust. Tears rolled out of his eyes and made putty of the terrain.

B.J. saw himself slipping his palm beneath where his daughter held the rope railings of the bridge in the forest. In his quieting mind, he tried to sing to Lottie Rebecca the song to come and play, "Timi timi nyamale, nyamale" but the song was muted in the sawdust and compost of the forest floor beneath the things he wanted to tell her about the note he put under his father's pillow, about the sight of what he saw himself do in the humidity-fogged scope of the rifle in Vietnam. Sheila's and Lottie Rebecca's hands held on now as the bridge and branches seemed to betray them, threatening to spill them one thousand feet out of the highest canopy like featherless birds.

Mr. Tunnelson sat just yards away from B.J.'s shed, in the house, watching the game, not picking up any sound but the usual whir of the saw. The black ants, Lottie Rebecca, and Sheila came to rest when the drum of B.J.'s heart attacked, then hushed, and his journey was finished.

Lenard counseled from the lesson of pains stuffed over and over and over, "Don't be afraid to have a funeral. We need ritual for our grief. We need to mourn him in real time."

"I'm not an average churchgoing Negro," Sheila sobbed and fussed, then felt sorry for not filtering anger, for being called home from Home again, to her grief.

B.J.'s body was prepared under fluorescent lights. The smell of chemicals replaced the smell of his sweat. The next day, Sheila and Lottie Rebecca stood next to each other, their faces caramel brown and deep, dark cocoa. They were wrapped in dyed African print sent by Kobi. Yellow-and-green adinkra love symbols on fabric that twisted like swaddling around mother and daughter in regal dress. Sunday church clothes for Ghanaian women, their heads wrapped in yellow-green towers that reached to the top of the green tent that sheltered the dug grave. Uncle James came slowly up the lawn into the morning light. In his lumbering walk from the cab Lottie Rebecca could hear the piano music of his church, as if he had brought the spirit of the congregation with him. Uncle Lenard walked tall and proud behind him, both of them in black suits, stout older brother and his younger brother whose plow-pushing muscles had long since softened.

When the hearse arrived, the two uncles and Grandeddy

Tunnelson wore the white funeral gloves and joined the funeral directors as they slid the black lacquered casket purchased by James. Slid it from the back of the black wagon the way the Fayetteville coroner pulled the long drawers out for Lenard to identify the purple tagged toes of his brother and Rebecca, who had broken the heart of the little boy who now lay inside the wood to be set in the earth beside them. Sheila and Lottie Rebecca called out in song.

Kwaheri, kwaheri
mpenzi kwaheri
Goodbye, my love

Lenard, James, and Grandeddy Tunnelson in their deep raspy voices called to B.J. in response and apology, thinking their efforts had not saved him.

Kwaheri, kwaheri
mpenzi kwaheri

And they sang together of one accord.

tutaonana tena,
tukijaliwa
We will see you on the other side, God willing

They repeated until the resonance of their sounds was like the meditative drone of bees that hummed over the fallen fig fruit in the Ghanaian rain forest and over the tobacco flowers in their backyard. The resonance pushed and pulled the valves of their hearts, loosened their tongues, and brought the tears to all of them except Lottie Rebecca. She knew that it was not over.

He was buried past the orange clay, beneath the shifting sediment, beside his parents, but deeper, so that more time would pass before the shifting earth moved his remains far away from his grave marker.

"Can you hear any of them?" Sheila whispered the need for consoling to Lottie Rebecca. The two of them, like colorful parrots, were the last to remain at the grave.

"No, Mama." Lottie Rebecca's eyes looked larger with the colored fabric holding her hair away from her face. "They have all left."

Sheila, her face still wet with tears, asked, "That's a good thing, right? B.J. is resting, and all those spirits are resting, right?"

"No, Mama. They want me to follow them."

PART FIVE

Reckoning

TWENTY

Fayetteville, North Carolina
1994

For whom much is provided, much is expected. Take up your crown, woman, and don't show hesitation in your steps when you walk. What good is it to have instincts if you have to seek advice before following them?

It would soon be a year since B.J. died. Every now and then Mama asked me one of two questions, "Did you hear him?" or "Did you cry, Mtoto?" I answered, "No, Mama," enough times that she finally stopped asking.

If I knew I was going to be dealing with a resurgence of grief and the law that morning, I would have put on the crisp white blouse and adinkra-print purple-and-green skirt, an outfit for getting rid of this doubt and showing courage.

Mama was in the shower, and for the first time in a year, she was singing some old Aretha Franklin song. I rocked with her out in the kitchen in the early morning light that shone through the philodendrons. Every time I felt a surge of missing B.J. or heard discordant notes in my head, I pretended that he was off fishing or up at Ethel's Walk-Up, and that way I didn't have to explain to Mama or Uncle Lenard or even my own head why I hadn't cried. I just didn't feel like he was gone; I knew it wasn't over.

Uncle Lenard called every Sunday after he got out of church. "Don't try to forget him, Goddaughter. Tell me one thing you remember."

"I remember everything, Uncle." And I asked, "You wanna talk to Mama?"

That morning, I felt like it was time. I heard the water go off, and Mama's humming stopped. She called through the thin wall, "B.J., bring me a towel."

I covered my mouth already ten steps ahead to the regret that would activate in the house. "Mama, Deddy is gone." I said the words gentle, the way B.J. would have, and she wailed out into the house half-wrapped in her towel, and I let her fold into my arms the way she did when I witnessed her shame for turning away from Deddy in Ghana.

"We all make mistakes, Mama. It don't make bad things happen though. They are just mistakes." I held her away from me, wrapped the towel and tucked it, and she let me mother her the way her mother might have had she survived. Her spongy Afro soaked my T-shirt shoulder.

She was sitting in the backyard with a cup of tea watching the clouds. I was in the kitchen running mop water to help out, listening to Mary J. in my sixties-throwback, tattered bell-bottoms and a head wrap. I heard footsteps thud on the porch, and for a moment I imagined B.J.'s at the front door, but the footfall was wrong, and no one ever used our front door.

The white sheriff's deputy, like everybody, thought I was older than I was. "A certain comportment," Grandeddy Tunnelson told me. Mama said that the voice I'd spoken with my whole life was one I'd finally grown into. The deputy cleared his throat, paused, held a look of slight remorse when he finally looked me in the eyes.

He wasn't much older than me, a young man with a buzz cut who held his hat in his hand as if he was delivering the news of a son, brother, father killed in some hamlet, so far away that the spirit couldn't sing its way home and deliver the message of goodbye. "Ma'am, we have a court order saying after a year of unpaid taxes the house was purchased at auction. Here is a copy of the eviction that you can go down to the courthouse and view on your own. The house don't belong to y'all by law."

He paused, made an A-frame with his stance. "Ma'am. I'm sorry, but y'all have four weeks to collect your things and be outta here."

The top of my head tingled, and my feet went numb. This was wrong and right. But where was B.J.'s spirit to affirm it? I could feel him. *Deddy, wake up!* I imagined him watching with me as I watched the sheriff's deputy walk down the five rickety steps. I caught my breath and heard myself soothing Mama earlier that morning: "Mama, Deddy is gone."

I shut the heavy front door that none of us used. Dust mites landed on my eyelashes and itched, making me rub my eyes to red. Deddy wasn't gone; like when he was alive, he was present but silent.

The four weeks before eviction were slipping away. Mama and I reentered separate eyes of our grief storms. The two of us went silent in the house in the same way B.J. had been. That's all either of us could give. I held the court order away from Mama and Grandeddy Tunnelson, sure that I was gonna figure something out, but nerves and nightmares kept me from being able to hear. I hadn't heard the spirits, didn't see the images for my drawing. Didn't hear any words. I sat my sketchbook next to my bedside so I could write down whatever answers came in dreams.

That night I slept with the smooth mahogany seed from the rain forest under my pillow. I dreamed I walked across the extension bridge toward him where he stood on the platform in one of the trees. When I reached it, he was gone, and across the expanse of rope and trees he stood on the next platform, just out of reach again. I didn't walk in rhythm this time but ran, knowing the bridge might swing me off and down through the canopy, and I didn't care. His short Afro with the few silver tendrils of gray, his mustache and his beard trimmed the way the funeral director prepared him. He was just out of my reach. He lifted his arms away from his big-bellied T-shirt to draw me to him. Just before I touched him, he disappeared again. My arms and legs felt heavy, and I fell to the planks on the bridge that shifted and made an opening for me to drop through, and I didn't care. I was a bulb of red fig fruit that hung in the trees and that did not resist death as I jettisoned past green leaves toward the floor, anticipating the satisfaction of everything disappearing upon landing. I woke just before my body hit the unswept wooden floor of my bedroom. The covers tangled around my black tank top and clung to and strangled my breasts. "Mama!"

Heavy with sweat, the first light of morning drew me through the hallway to peep in and make sure I didn't wake her. The day before, I heard her talking with Grandeddy Tunnelson about a loan to open an African shop up on Ramsey. She had been worrying herself to death about what to do for money, and I hadn't known she had the tax bill to worry about when the house had been long since paid for by some long-since-dead kin.

Some nights I stayed lying curled up next to her in her room, pretending to watch TV with her until she fell asleep. I listened to her heart beating too fast, heard her heart find a calm rhythm again before sneaking back to my room. Leaving the house she rebuilt with Deddy would kill her.

Through the crack in her door, I saw her body rising and falling. Mama was deep in the stillness of her sleep. A low hum came from the kitchen. The bones in my feet gripped the planks of the wood floor to keep them steady. The morning sun tipped toward amber sunlight that streamed through thick fists of clouds, and I saw him sitting there having his coffee at the old oak table he built.

I stood in the hallway for a while, not wanting to scare him away, and the low-pitched hum and his image slipped out the front door. I stumbled into my boots and followed the scent of his skin and hair, the way he smelled like wine and body odor even though he didn't drink. I followed the smell down to the creek in the early light of morning. Birdcalls and crickets were the only sounds while I walked past the houses where neighbors used to call out, "Sheila, shut that baby up! Whup her ass!"

Past the bottom of the neighborhood's old rusted trailers, I went to find him. His spirit sat on the banks fishing in the creek. His familiar hunch with the fishing pole, and next to him, there was some other male spirit out of phase, a tall, thin, wary presence that turned and looked through me with hollow eyes and said, "I'm taking him." I stumbled back into the tangle of kudzu. Three twists formed in my belly, my chest, and the front of my head. A feeling came over me that first was as familiar as my hand turned small on the indentation of muscle and bone of my father's chest here thirteen rebellions around the sun ago. Some cord between me and my father, between my father and this other spirit, that was eternal and beyond me, just enough beyond me to scare me like the day that my father chose the sun on the fishing waters as his peace over the chaos that was my little head toiling to be here and wanting to be near him. And I felt it, the loneliness of being left to fend for myself.

It sent me running in woman-size rubber boots back up the yellow line on Colonial Drive to get away from the long line of heartbreak and to Mama, who was very much here on earth.

I tiptoed back into the kitchen barefoot as the wind outside the window lashed through the trees with sideways hurricane rain. B.J. was there in the chair. Others around him, then gone, then there with them pulling him. Like static, their images came and went. I ran from chair to sink to counter, trying to tug him back to me, until the wind blew through the window over the sink and my mouth flew open rebuking the spirits, "Stop it! Let him go! Stop it!" and I was on the floor tangling with them where all my life they skirted around my feet. The window above the kitchen sink exploded with the force and suction of the pending hurricane.

Mama's feet thunked on her bedroom floor and in one move she was on the kitchen floor with her arms around the top of my body. "Did something fall on you?!" She was growing frantic, turning my limbs looking for the gash from a pane of glass. I pulled and yanked but couldn't get myself untangled from her to catch him.

"Let me go, Mama. Let me go!"

"Mtoto, what happened?!" She was hollering through tears.

I couldn't breathe. I slapped the floor near the chair where he always sat. "He was here! His spirit was here!" I couldn't stop the siren sound that came from my mouth while Mama held on to hold me in this life. "Deddy!"

She pulled at my shoulders and legs as I tried to get up off the floor. "It's okay, Mtoto!" I scooted on to my knees, reached up to the junk drawer, pulling the whole thing onto the floor, and before it blew away, I handed her the court order. I couldn't catch my breath through the tears that were drowned out by the wind. She took the thing from my hand, couldn't see it in that storm-cloud light. "What is this, girl?!"

"Mama! They are taking the house away."

Tree limbs in the storm knocked against the house like human bodies caught in the wind. All around us, there was knocking on the floor, knuckles, knees, boots, spirits running around the house, parading in and out of the bedrooms, the bathroom, collecting themselves into a stampede. This time, for the first time, Mama heard them too. Her eyes bugged out like she understood what I wanted, to go with B.J., to go with them. She wrapped both legs around me and held me down on the floor, hugging me with the rest of her body the way she did when my tantrums threatened to bring my bookshelf down on my head. I begged, "Mama! Let me go!"

Outside the windows, the clouds thinned and passed over. The sun seared the house with white light. The spirits picked up shoes, dishes, like forgotten things on their way out the door. Then, they tugged at the hairs on my and Mama's heads. We were half dragged, half in the air in their talons, and I tried to make myself weightless. But Mama would not let go, and as if we were heavy prey, they cut their losses, and we hit the floor. The clouds eclipsed the sun, and the spirits banked low to escape the closing fissure, and they were gone, all of them, my deddy among them, like birds migrating south in the wind, leaving me a stray to survive where I had been abandoned.

TWENTY-ONE

St. Louis, Missouri
1994

All the fathers who came before you did not have birthdays with granted wishes. When you lived to see your first score, they gave all their wishes to you.

Mama said she would flip eviction on its head. "We gonna do some traveling, Mtoto. Visit with folks we know, and all of that driving will help us know what's next in life." I heard her, but I knew something different. I knew which direction B.J. had gone and that I had to follow him. My fears of losing Mama and her fear of losing me were the only thing that kept me still.

We packed up the little gray Ford Escort hatchback she bought off a used car lot that Grandeddy used to point out: "That used to be the Texaco station where your other grandeddy worked." I heard him every time he referred to "other grandeddy" but never paid much attention, because I knew from looking in B.J.'s eyes and hearing people in town say that man killed my grandmother and himself that I didn't want any part of me open to that spirit. I didn't hate him; I didn't feel anything for him.

We drove through the hills of West Virginia, which made the engine clatter. Beautiful green mountains, then smokestacks and poverty. Mama said, "Hold your bladder, because we won't be stopping through here." I knew that was right, and when we got to Ohio, I squatted over the toilet in the gas station, pissing, bleeding, and I almost thought I could hear that low hum of B.J.'s spirit between the putrid smell of the bathroom, the rumble of truck engines on the parking lot, and the fear of leaving my mama alone in the car. But my fears of being raped or lynched were more powerful than the residual flight patterns of any spirits.

We exhaled all the way to Uncle Lenard's door, where he stood in a sweater, a white button-up shirt, and a pair of sensible slacks and shoes, like the Black Mister Rogers standing on the concrete-slab ground-level porch of his University City house, waiting. I felt woven back together when he hugged me and Mama at the same time. "Glad you all made it. That's a long drive for certain."

Uncle James rang the doorbell. I was so used to people knocking that it startled me into a little jump, and Mama leaned on me and laughed, "Girl, you look like you still in West Virginia, about to jump out of your skin at the sound of a doorbell."

I laughed, "I know, Mama. I was like, 'What the hell is that?' I didn't know if it was in my head or what!"

I didn't want any cake, but there one sat. I had learned to sit with what I wanted to say before saying it, but not for long. To have feelings and words tangled in my chest, clogged up, was unbearable. Uncle Lenard used a little red gas-station lighter that wasn't cooperating with the slow roll of his thumb over the candles. Uncle James stood up, walrus-size, and said, "I got it." He was the uncle who liked me but looked at me sideways, like he was looking at some wicked part of himself in a mirror. He flicked the thing with his calloused beer-bottle-opening thumb and lit the first of the nineteen.

I spoke up in the dim light of the tiny fire, unable to wait out the rest of the ritual.

"I'm gonna drive from here down to Mississippi."

The other candles did not get lit. The faces of my kin glowed like witches' at a cauldron. "I'm gonna buy a used car with the money B.J. left for me and go down there."

This time, they didn't do what I expected. Uncle James reached over the table and lit the other candles on the round homemade treat. Uncle Lenard bowed his head in prayer when I was supposed to be the one making wishes: "Father God in heaven. Watch over our spirited one. Guide her and protect her. In Jesus's name. Amen." Mama put her arm around my shoulder as if she were trying to hold my body together by squeezing me into her chest.

The night of my birthday celebration, I dreamed I walked past a body of still water and felt drawn by what I thought were eyes. They whispered, "Look." I looked, and there were sun-bleached bones piled in on themselves.

Mama and I stood under the clouds of a fall sky at the auto dealer on the Black west side of St. Louis. I could feel the fog coming off her body, feel her disappearing into grief again. She had never shed her dashiki look of bright colors but had left head wraps and long flowing dresses behind. She looked so strong but still regal in her Jordache jeans and the adinkra-print purple-and-blue top, her mud-print brown-and-beige jacket. I breathed in her earthy smell, holding on to her arm. My unruly hair got in the way of our touch. "Mtoto, get your hair out my face."

We found something to laugh about, though both of us could feel the pull in the center of our chests when the man gave me the keys to the ugly bright-blue Ford sedan. Mama asked every question imaginable—"How old is the battery? When was the last time the oil was changed?"—and made demands. "I'm going to need the record of repairs and the name and phone number of the mechanic."

"Yes, ma'am," the tall thick man who reminded me of a dark-skinned version of Uncle James replied to my mother's big-mama orders.

In the morning, Mama held on to my arm. She leaned her warm, oily, braided head on my shoulder. "Mtoto. Last night I was supposed to be sleeping and realized something. No one ever taught you how to draw or how to write like that. No one taught you that."

"Um-hm," I let out a little giggle at the slow blossoming of her knowing things I spent my whole life trying to help her understand. She tried to clarify, "I mean. You know. I know you are special. You know . . ."

I kissed her hand and smiled her quiet. I knew what she meant, knew the rest of the words.

At Uncle Lenard's, I slept in B.J.'s old bedroom. Made a small stack of things to leave for Mama, including my old sketchbook. The images on one side and on the other all the words that I now understood. "Thanks, Mama," I wrote on the cover, which handed her the keys to the spaces inside me that I had kept locked away from her.

There was a pull from the three of them, as I backed out of Uncle Lenard's driveway, summoned by my father and a chorus of other spirits who I had disappointed in my embodied life with the rituals and being sewn into the "supposed to's" of the living.

TWENTY-TWO

Sampson, Mississippi
1994

Migratory patterns follow food, medicine, and kinship. But they also follow the recollection of what is in accordance with the Divine. And in her presence, the tanglement of spirits who did so much wrong in the flesh let loose and lay down to rest.

I paralleled the Mississippi River, caught like willing driftwood in its current at a gentle pace from St. Louis to Memphis; but from Memphis, Tennessee, to Sampson, Mississippi, the highway was liquefied movement, with a seventy-five-mile-an-hour speed limit. Cars and trucks became a stream of colors that made it appropriately difficult to see the skin tone of the vehicles' inhabitants. I thought this must have been some way to compensate for the wrongfulness of the highway's lynchings of the past. Without apologizing or admitting wrong, it was made legal for everyone to appear to be running.

Tracy Chapman's "Fast Car" played on a cassette, and I laughed out loud at the coincidence of that soundtrack that took me through the last leg of my trip. Her alto voice and guitar acted as messenger for the valerian-drugged spirits who'd forgotten about their call to me because I was so late responding.

The first thing I learned was that in Mississippi, the cicadas continue to call well into the fall, the snakes continue to slither, and when someone says, "Don't take the rocks from the swamp to put in your pocket," you say "Yes, sir," and leave any notions of rebellion for covert maneuvers as opposed to outward gestures with singular fingers.

The library was in a trailer, which was a slight upgrade from the trailers in the bottom of my Fayetteville neighborhood. The air conditioner dripped in early November onto the patch of weeds that tried to reach up and take over the droning coils of the metal box. The old, matted, burgundy carpet inside held years of mildew smell, and I looked like an awkward bird who had landed in the wrong field during her migration.

"May I help you?" was the squawk of the white librarian, who smelled like butter.

By the third day, she said, "Good mo'nin, darlin."

They kept them all, despite the potential for roaches, every yellowed newspaper. Some of the older ones had been painstakingly photographed for microfiche. Those were the ones I wanted. Uncle Lenard said it was 1953 when the men came and took the land, so I started with that date and the name Pritchard, but I found and woke up the ones I didn't know had been calling me when I came across a bill of sale for "Lottie Pritchard age twelve, 1928 traded to Leander Lee age sixty-two for one wagonload of tobacco, the promise to be kept. If these clauses are not met, the ownership of Leander Lee's possessions shall revert to James William Pritchard and his descendants."

I had been named after her, my great-grandmother sold like a cow to my father's father's father.

The clot from birth reformed in my chest, shame blocking the flow of words. I felt myself fall to the forest floor again, bones splintered open slicing blood vessels, a flow of nectar that drew lynched and prostituted spirits into the trailer like ants and wasps coming for the sap of my humiliated tears.

A rectangular blue box of Kleenex came into view. The butter-smelling white woman had taken my hand off the microfiche handle and placed it on the cool cardboard box of tissues.

The next day, she sat at the microfiche with me, scrolling up and down at a speed that made the machine whir toward each document I asked to see. On a pad of yellow legal paper, she jotted down names, dates. The only sounds were the machine's internal fan trying to keep the big box cool at the feverish speed of my focus and my questions, and the sound of the librarian's occasional apologetic cough that helped her choke back tears of white guilt as she peeled it all back with me and discovered the truth.

This white man Pritchard was my great-grandmother Lottie's white father, ex–slave foreman, shady motherfucker, who from the looks of his grim photo would truly sell the skin off his kin to make a buck. He had fallen into ruin twice, once after a 1928 fire that took with it Great-Grandmother Lottie's Black mother and her husband, took his land, scorched the red clay to terracotta. Pritchard fell again in 1953, when poor investments left him with nothing but his two sons and his black Packard, until he came back to make good on the deed of land that was already secured.

I made mental note of the genealogical facts while the librarian wrote the land and deed facts: "142 acres," "369 dollars," "whereas J. W. Pritchard," "whereas his offspring Lottie Pritchard," "whereas Leander Lee," "keep her," "possession of the land." And the clause we both wrote three times before making sense of it, "Now, know ye, that the State of Mississippi, in consideration of the premises in such case made and provided, hath given and granted, and by these presents doth give and grant unto the said *J. W. Pritchard* and to *his* heirs and assigns, the said tract of land above described; to have and to hold the same together with all the rights, privileges, immunities and appurtenances thereunto belonging, unto the said *J. W. Pritchard* and to *his* heirs and assigns forever."

The librarian and I sat quiet. I was spent and empty, like dead covers after the waking have left them in a clump to pursue the day. The librarian and I were sandwiched between the reality of the past that glared in antique writing on cream-colored pages from the day in 1953 when Uncle Lenard last saw his father and the land, and the reality of the present where the white librarian and I sat half-reformed in 1994.

After our revelation, we let the window-unit air conditioner cool the clammy sweat from the journey we'd both taken. She breathed a heft of air. In a drawling, hoarse tone, as if she'd been awakened from a long sleep, she said, "Well, you can go down to the county courthouse, but when I count them all, his white sons, your great-grandmother, him, every heir are missing or dead and buried in they respective graveyards, 'side from you and your Uncle Lenard."

We were caught in the same eddy of spirits, me and Uncle Lenard, both having lost by accounts of contracts, signature "X" markings, and tribal markings that said, take the mother, take the brother, take the father, and may they serve you well.

"I'm going to come down there, Goddaughter, and help you straighten it all out." I spared him, knowing that something about Mississippi made him straighten his spine and raise his head like he was trying to rise up above something that might drown him.

I refused him. "No, no, sir."

"I don't think I'll ever get too used to your new southern politeness." He fell silent on the phone. "You are a lot like your father." I frowned, remembering Deddy's silence, his persistence in measuring his words, his spirit acquiescing, forcing me to chase him the way everyone chased after his words that rarely came, his attention that rarely came.

"Like him, before he went to Nam. Just like him. Did I tell you what happened that day at the zoo? Him all dressed up the way you used to?"

I cut him off to spare us both the colorful stripes and plaids story that was probably camouflage over something much more important for his emotions. "Tell Mama I love her, and that it will be alright."

"I don't think anybody doubts that. We just want you to know you don't have to do this by yourself, and honestly, I'm just proud that we have somebody like you on our team."

Uncle Lenard had already broken into laughter before he finished his sentence—"a little sistah who doesn't play."

"Uncle! You can't say 'doesn't play' after saying 'sistah.'" The circle of the phone's mouthpiece caught our chuckles, the warmth of breath, and I didn't feel alone. "You got to say 'The sistah *don't* play'!"

We quieted into intentional sighs. "Niece, do you remember when I taught you how to play chess?"

"Yes, sir. How could I forget? I sat on your living-room floor, all pissed off that you wouldn't let me watch cartoons, while you ended each game, 'Checkmate,' then told me to fight back." I hummed a laugh, and he did too. "I fought back until by the time I was ten years old, I could beat you just about every time."

"Sure did. That's the same age your father was when he started beating me at chess. If it weren't for Nam, and the mess that happened when he was little, I know he would have been a lot like you." It was silent. I didn't like being baited into traps to make conversation on subjects I'd already closed off.

"Niece?"

"Yes, sir?!"

"You are the unanticipated response to other folks' plan of attack. I'm proud of you."

I felt a shiver in the heat of late fall in the Mississippi air when I heard the little boy in his voice, his first acknowledgment of my way of being beyond what could be factually accounted for in white men's footnotes or my parents' DNA.

"And Uncle, I'm gonna be proud of you once you do me a favor and tell my mother I love her and everything is going to be alright."

He laughed from his gut. "Checkmate."

A black dress in mid-November. It was the only decent-looking thing I had put in my duffel bag, Deddy's duffel bag. Mama said every woman needs a plain black sleeveless dress, and depending on whose gathering she shows up to, she can wrap that in some mud print and be ready for the court of her ancestors or throw on a blazer and be ready for white men's court.

At sunrise, I left the motel, shut the door hard to close the swollen humid wood into the metal doorframe. Breathed in the salt air, sound of morning crickets, to soothe and calm the stirred bees in my stomach. Down the planked metal stairs to the office, where the manager was just raising the blinds to look out onto the parking lot. I saw myself in the reflection of the door: yellow-and-green headdress, black dress, black boots, and yellow-and-green shawl with adinkra tie-dyed symbols. Not quite what Mama schooled me to wear. In the reflection, my brown, inverted pear-shaped head was filled in by the sagging beige flesh of his face before he opened the door.

"Good morning, young lady." The manager walked behind the counter. When I first arrived in Sampson, he didn't have anything to say to me. Just did business straightforward without looking at me each day. Took my cash for the next night's stay, gave me a receipt, and turned back to the TV precariously anchored to the wall like a hospital TV suspended by a brace. We had both softened. Each of those mornings, I hoped the damned TV would slip forward and kill his mean redneck ass, but now he felt familiar.

"Thank you. I really appreciate the room and the stay."

"When you out there, if things ain't right or anybody try to bother you, just come on back here, or give them my name, you hear?"

"Yes, sir."

He waved me on, and I scooched Deddy's old duffel bag up on my shoulder, threw it in the back of my ridiculously bright-blue sedan, and in a cloud of muffler fumes headed out on the last leg of the southward journey.

At seven in the morning, the heat forced me to stick my dark wing out the window to catch the breeze the car made through the humid air. If I had told my mind that I was in Ghana, my eyes would have believed me, the way the dusty roads gave way to asphalt to let me know I was approaching government property. I waited on the wrought-iron bench of the courthouse steps for the 8 a.m. opening. I had planned to spend my whole day there, but word had already circulated around the little town that Pritchard's kin had come to collect what lay in estate. The way of legal matters in Sampson was to give you the facts, hand you the sheets of courthouse papers, and if there was any shooting to be done to make the papers true, that was between you and the challenger to battle out and report back so new papers could be drawn. They just handed me the deed and collected my ten dollars for the transaction.

By the time I reached the road that turned off the Dixie Overland Highway, I imagined myself walking up to the door, seeing the barrel of a rifle, and being shot at through the glass panes in the door. I imagined myself falling to the ground and struggling to get a glimpse of the white faces that peered out. Maybe this was the battle the spirits called me to take up and fall down for. I told myself to stop it.

My heart beat hard, wishing I could undo my choice of African head wrap for breaking the news to white squatters that my uncle and my tar-skinned self were the rightful owners of this land.

When I approached, there was one being on the porch in the distance with the glare of sun as a screen between us. I could see the light skin, loose bluish clothes.

A ring of dust floated up off the ground, then paused just before the face of the being on the porch, and I paused. All the bravado and the knowing that had brought me that far faded where I stood, just before the island of weeds and the two oak trees that were circled in by the driveway.

Like the sound of rain on a tin roof, a high-pitched plucking sound sped up as I walked to the porch. The sternum bones of my chest pulled open.

A low-level hum settled into the bowl of my pelvis and resonated between my hip bones, a sound so low that it could be heard only by taking in the smell of sun-cured, fallen, composted tobacco leaves and remembering the sight of rainwater that had run year after year into the drainage ditches of Accra and settled into the earth and made its way to the unseen pond just west of my body that rose up in the sulfur seraphim-mist just at sunrise.

She stood up on the porch above the ring of dust that blocked my vision, and seeing the sun-tightened skin and long black tendrils of hair, my breath became thinner than the air. I ran toward her. Like Christians who have never seen Christ know him, I knew her.

Up the three steps, the wind was knocked from my chest by her embrace, and I grew gills inside her womb.

Being born was the second most significant moment of my life. Holding on to the flesh of my flesh closed the space between being called and responding.

I pushed back to look her in the eyes. And they were round and so deep that I could see a reflection of orange earth that still floats in the dermis of my spongy feet from the Ghanaian soil. So deep that I saw the body of still water in my dreams, saw the veins in the dragonfly's wings that dipped and fluttered, breaking the stillness of the surface.

An adrenaline surge of knowing raced through my body, to my mind: "I know you." And she placed one hand on the plate of my broad skull to take me away from my logic. She placed a finger on her lips to make me quiet, and I didn't want to look at her now, half-frightened by what I saw.

Through the morning mist that danced on the pond, I saw her eyes looking back at me in 1942, saw the eyes of the boy whose life had murdered my first and second coming, and I would have snatched his life away had I flesh and bone to do so. I remembered my spirit being drawn up out of the pond by the wispy cloud of her soul.

I saw him staring into the pond, the thin-armed boy, my father's father. I saw him dragging her body over dew and blood-splattered grass somehow, with the strength of a brown boy fisherman who drags the wet nets. His small hips and spine pivoted to turn her, and me, the seed inside her womb. Something dark inside me rose, and I saw blood spreading, blotting out the yellow on my great-aunt Beverly's yellow dress, the slack pupils of the Vietnamese girls spreading to the edges of their eyelids with death that I saw through the scope of my Deddy's rifle.

"They are all killers!" I yelled to her from an eternal place of disappointment, having acknowledged them all as innocent boys fishing, but not allowing myself to traverse the space of what I already knew, that light cannot exist alone any more than darkness can exist alone. They were still little boys, even after all they had lived through, but they were also my murderers, and I wanted as far from that porch and everything that was part of my male lineage as I could get.

But she wrapped her arms around me and exhaled, holding me in place. The more I resisted, the more her spirit muted my struggle until the taken-for-granted bravado that I lived with all my life gave way to the weight of my Black woman body with its vulnerable skin that punctures and spills out life. Her breath in my ear: "Nothin that has been done can be undone. You got here for a reason. You have to write all their stories down, all of them, not some of them."

And I fell with her far beneath the stillness before there was ever breath, my whole self inside her womb. I felt our spirits on the wind trying to stop the impact, spirit trying to scoop up our kin, singing to brokenhearted boys, trying to slow bullets, caressing the heads of the half-dead, and crying over the hearts of the evildoers. I spoke back to her from my wounded soul. "I have done enough! They don't deserve anything. I don't owe them anything. Not even my father."

"You haven't even gotten started." She pushed my forehead away as if rebuking the devil from my thoughts. "The efforts were mine! But they were efforts that meant little without the force of a hand to push the pen of the stories that could be heard and read and stop the bullets long before innocence turns to the evil that loads the chamber. You have been given everything. You be still, girl, and know that I am, and They are, and so You are."

I stepped back toward her, wanting to quiet her the way I wanted to quiet my mother when she struggled to make my teenage self understand my blessings. I wrapped my arms around her familiar form, depressed my sweaty finger into the pockmark wound in her back to stop our bleeding, fifty-two years too late. In that moment, I wanted nothing else in life but her comfort, but she shrugged against me as if she'd had enough. "And you are in the flesh. Able to do what no prayers or wishes, no love or courage can accomplish without action."

"I love you," she whispered into the chalky bone of my spinal column, and I smelled the iron-blood dampness inside stones that walled the dark chamber of the slave castles. I smelled the warm breath of my grandfather's liquid tobacco spit. She pushed me back, and I watched her lips part. "I love you," and I opened my mouth, like opening my mouth to be nurtured, and the weight of her body dissipated in my arms. I was alone on the extension bridge breathing, curled into myself, no sounds in the stillness, no breeze of elephants' wings to move the trees.

I felt the distance between me and home, my age, my black skin, my womanhood, and the wholeness of everything that could bring me harm in this world. What good was any of this? Why did I need this burden of knowing any of this? I wanted, like wanting earth in my mouth, wanting water in my lungs, wanting to inhale and never to exhale again. I wanted to go with her again, not to be here alone.

The grumble of some distant tractor tilling an old crop back into the soil made my loneliness audible, and I shook, abandoned on the sand and soil of the porch of my kin.

The distant vibration in my inner ear grew closer. I looked up through the murky pond water of my tears to see the old raggedy blue and white-topped 98 coming up the road, making a cloud of dry earth behind it. I rubbed my eyes with dirty fingers to see the man who was the little boy who slipped through the noose of Mississippi lynchings and dead mothers, who once played in the circle of dirt, hoping someone would remember to come back for him.

We did everything that needed to be done by ourselves. That's how Deddy would have done it. Fix the walls with planks of board fetched from the hardware store, which was the feed and seed and the five-and-dime. In every corner of the house, Uncle Lenard told me a story with his eyelids lifted in a way I had never seen: "Write it down, Niece." There was the morning he was left behind from the dogfight, the morning his mother was gone, the nail where the strap from the satchel used to hang, the hook in the barn where the whip still hangs. He told it all as though he was trying to save his dead brother's soul and his own. I wrote it down even when my body wanted to close all its openings and run from the landscape of all the things done wrong.

We didn't ask for help exhuming our mother's bones from the creek. He told me ten times that it was going to be hard for me, that it was hard for him to know what he knew and face what he remembered of how she was killed and then go get her. I told him of the dream of her eyes and the sun-bleached bones. He cried, his prideful stature saying, "I didn't save her. I didn't save him or your deddy either."

We mourned our dead after fixing the house by eating bowls of pinto beans, and the land apologized by bolting with mustard greens, which we steamed and ate over rice. Before the November rains came, while the pond was shallow enough to wade, it needed to be done. When Mama asked if she could please come and help me, she was already in Jackson calling from a phone in the bus station.

It wasn't sad. The three of us wore black rubber boots, did not wear gloves over our brown hands, waded out into the pond. Uncle Lenard to fetch his mother, Lottie, and brother Bennie, me to fetch B.J. and his mother, Rebecca, and Mama to fetch her mother, Lucy Marie Tunnelson. The bones did not elude our hands and slip into the mud, but came up to meet our grasp, smooth like elephant tusks. There was no grimacing, just the ritual of bending and lifting them up out of the mud and into the November sun before we buried them in the soil that was our land.

TWENTY-THREE

When the Spirit Came

Sampson, Mississippi
2003

It is beautiful here. There is a way that the sticks, stones, slither of snakes, smell of oak brush, the woods and all the mulch on the floor of the forest when it rains, soothe my soul. The way the sun shifts in November and banks in sharp beneath the dripping, dark green of the magnolia leaves that are always velvety on the underside with the red seeds that burst slow and sustained from the rough cut of the seed pods that lacerate my hand every time, and I don't mind.

I am home. I watch the spotted newborn fawns every March that don't know any better than to wobble toward me while their mother stomps her hooves, afterbirth still dripping. Each year I back up onto the porch to show her that I have chosen to be here but will be writing the tears away from the pitch-black midnight and stitching the morning back into the song of the land the way it was long before they crossed our lifelines and flipped the darkness on its head. I back up onto the porch, and some days in winter I run off it into the first snow. And my eyes and ears make love with the hush of everything when the frozen blanket cleanses and a hawk flies over crying about the ease of finding food against a white canvas.

I choose you. I see you. You are of me, and I will be here even when and after the rest of the stories come, even the hard ones.

And I know I am in the eye of the storm, living and writing down the beautiful part while I wait for the hard part, Deddy's part of the story.

It is the hottest day of the year. I am lulled into my ritual of harvesting and selling at the farmers' market the basil and tomatoes Mama taught me to grow, the lime trees and pole beans and corn Grandeddy Tunnelson taught me to grow. I am fidgeting around for a shady place to write, an apple wedged in my mouth the way a horse might carry her treat, my laptop keeping my open hands cool.

I sit on the broken weave of a wicker chair fetched from the dump in the opening of the barn and perch the laptop on my worn overall thighs. I look off to the porch for visuals of the next part I will write.

I have relaxed into the rhythm of living without stirring fear or hope or thoughts of doing anything except what I do. And his spirit sits there unexpectedly on the steps. Gray stubbled beard and gray short Afro. I do not recognize him until I see in his form and the movement of his searching head the same spirit that I saw beside him at the creek at the bottom of Colonial Drive, when I was six years old and needed him to acknowledge the spirits we heard, but he turned away from me. The same spirit that sat beside his spirit on the anniversary morning of his death when I chased him to the creek for guidance on how to keep the house out of the hands of white developers. He and my "other grandeddy" sit merged, waiting. I sit down with my laptop, breathing the way my father taught me to breathe when stressed. I cannot get the story by peering at him from the barn, but I cannot commit myself to him again.

The sun has arched low over the vegetable field and toward the pond. I am still sitting in the open door of the barn after a good cry, full of memories of all the things he did and did not do and all of my adult-daughter dreams that hoped he'd be here in this adult life with me.

I know that if dusk comes and takes the ominous spirit on the porch away, I will have committed the sin—knowing and not doing what can stitch the brokenness back together.

I play with the bits of apple in my teeth rather than go past the merged spirits for my dinner. I sit here listening to the cardinals call, one calling from the oak tree just beyond the barn door, the other off beyond the edge of the tobacco field. I close my eyes and breathe in the smell of cow manure turned moldy earth inside the barn that wakes up the scene of cows behind me. I can feel my grandfather Bennie as that little boy sitting in this spot, his heart not yet lacerated until cut by the whip that cut his father's and his father's father's hearts. The whip that mocks me, tattered leather on the nail above the old cow stalls. The sun peeks red through the slats of the barn wall. Particles float in the light reminding me.

I feel the twist in my gut, my chest, and the front of my head. I whisper to myself and to the junior and senior spirit on the porch, "This is my home now."

But I know that if I don't let them do what they came to do, call to me, and me do what I aim to do, write their stories, that

I will never hear the end of it in the creaking walls and swirl of voices in my kitchen. With my laptop hinged open, and fear making the land tilt beneath my feet, I walk toward the house, where the commingled spirit waits to tell its stories. His eyes open, his scratchy throat opens as he speaks the Word that has for so long been dormant in the dungeon of our throats.

Acknowledgments

I would like to thank my daughter Alex, who like myself and so many other "spiritfilled" Black girls modeled the character of Lottie Rebecca Lee. I would like to thank Tracy Sherrod, my first ever editor and my first editor on this project. She, like my daughter, myself, and so many "spiritfilled" Black women, also modeled the character of Lottie Rebecca Lee. Thank you, Tracy, for always hearing my voice, inside of and outside of the words of my writing. Thank you, Patrik Henry Bass, for taking up the charge of shepherding *Trinity* through its production stages. Thank you to all of the hard-working people at HarperCollins Amistad. It is their passion and commitment to their work that is not often seen, but without their dedication and diligence so many important works of Black literature would never reach their audience. Thank you to my agent, Carol Mann. Thank you to the readers along the way who helped me to shape, prune, and decorate *Trinity*: Alexis, Pauline, Gumbs, Shay Youngblood, and many others who read a chapter or two along the way. Thank you to my fellow Black Creative friends, artist William Paul Thomas and PR genius Candace Patrice Parrish, for adding your brilliance to this project. I am even grateful to the naysayers; they made me tougher in some of the places where I was too yielding, and they made me more yielding in some of the places where I wanted to kick somebody's butt. I am most grateful to my ancestors, who hearken to me constantly in my dreams, and sometimes when I am walking around in the day and being noisy or silent they hearken to me from the trees to remind me that I walk in this physical life filled with Spirit and therefore knowing all I need to know in order to get about the work I came here to do. Finally, thanks Deddy. When I was a little girl, I saw you do so many violent things and my body bore so many of your violent acts. But still I saw you, the little Mississippi boy by the pond fishing for his dinner. Thank you for letting me write your spirit home.